THE LORD AND THE MERMAID
QUEENMAKERS SAGA IV

BY
BERNADETTE ROWLEY

ACKNOWLEDGEMENTS

To Louise Cusack for her inspiration and advice
over the last ten years.

To my street team who are always there to support me.

To my husband, Michael, and my sons for their unending love and
support and for sharing in the disappointments and triumphs
of a writing life.

DEDICATION

Dedicated to my husband, Michael.

TABLE OF CONTENTS

* * *

CHAPTER 1

NIKOLAS Cosara loved the beach after a storm, and last night's had been as fierce as any he'd seen. Nik always walked the beach the morning after tempest, driven to explore the flotsam the waves left behind. He'd carve the driftwood into the likeness of sea creatures. Sometimes he found treasures in the piles of debris.

A dark mound appeared on the beach ahead. As he drew closer, he discerned a tail, like that of the dolphins which frolicked in the bow wave of boats. Pain seared his heart at the thought of the majestic creature beached, never again to laugh at the folly of sailors. Yes, a dolphin's tail, smooth and gray, not a scale to be seen. No more could be spied of the beast as seaweed and driftwood covered the remainder, along with the strands of a scarlet wig, the kind ladies sometimes wore at court.

Nik tugged at the red strands but couldn't remove the wig from the pile. He dragged the seaweed away instead and froze. He had revealed a woman's chest, complete with perfect breasts. Her alabaster skin held a faint green tint, but he couldn't see her face. Frantic, he tossed away debris, seaweed and driftwood and turned her to the weak morning sun. A pulse beat feebly at her throat, but her breath barely moved her chest. He pushed aside the rest of the debris, his heart pounding fit to burst from his body.

A sneaking, murdering mermaid. Fury swept him and he clenched his teeth to hold in the shriek that fought its way from his throat. At last he'd found a small piece of revenge against the sea nymphs; a life for his brother's. He stared at the perfect features: full pale lips, high cheekbones, long reddish lashes, placed in a heart-shaped face that had likely lured dozens of sailors to their deaths. And that bosom! No man could gaze upon it without wanting to touch the luscious curves. Oh yes, this monster had all the tools of the trade, but she'd not kill another man if he had anything to say about it.

Nik pulled the knife from his boot and raised it, ready to deliver a fatal strike. Something stayed his hand. A kernel of sanity urged him to use this being to discover what happened to Jon. Suddenly, he was looking into brilliant sea-green eyes. A keening song sliced through his skull and he stiffened, the knife falling from his hand.

* * *

I have killed him! Merielle's heart faltered as she watched the man topple to the sand. It was the shock of seeing him standing over her, brandishing the knife, knowing he meant to kill her. Helpless on the sand, her only defense had been "the song". She had used it without thought, desperately, instinctively. The humans were right, her people were monsters.

Meri hauled herself out of the rubbish, her head whirling, and fell back as agony lanced through her right shoulder. She clutched it, resting against the driftwood, breathing deeply until the pain began to ebb. Beached and injured! How her mother would sneer at her! She gathered her breath and pushed a pile of driftwood from her hips with her good arm. This time she was able to roll toward her victim. She placed a hand on his chest, felt its gentle rise and fall. *He lived!* But even as she watched, his skin lost color, his breathing slowed. Meri closed her eyes and crooned her healing song, low at first and then louder, but not so strong that he would regain his senses too soon. His mind waves stuttered and returned to a normal rhythm; well, normal for a human. His broad chest heaved and settled into the even breaths of sleep. She sighed. This man would not die at her hands, making a mockery of her life, of her plans.

She studied the human. His skin was tanned a golden brown and his honey-blond hair tangled into long locks and tied in a bunch at the back of his neck. His lips were full and sensual, his nose straight and strong, slightly broad at the nostrils. Neatly trimmed hair lay above and below his mouth. Even the wicked scar that sliced across his left cheekbone enhanced his beauty, made him appear dangerous, even while asleep.

Meri's gaze fell to the man's torso and there she truly lost her breath. His shoulders had a lovely width, swooping into upper arms the size of most men's thighs. A smattering of golden hair peeked from the open neck of his shirt. Her hand still lay on his chest, so she touched his skin. He groaned and turned his head but did not wake. She seized the knife and hid it beneath her.

He had wanted her dead when he saw her amongst the rubbish. That was natural, their peoples ever at war. She had come here to change that in her small way, but had not banked on the storm. At least it might stop her people from pursuit long enough for her to escape. But now Meri was injured, her options limited. She could not linger in the shallows and around the harbor, hoping to tempt a man to take her into his heart. She had not the strength for that, not for weeks yet if she was any judge of an injury. And this man's hatred was too strong for her to believe he would help her.

Meri arranged her long red tresses to cover her breasts and took deep breaths to calm her racing heart. She could manage him if he reacted with violence again. She could. He groaned again and her traitorous heart leapt. Anything could happen. He was a man, wild and uncultured, beautiful and fierce, and he hated her.

And then he opened his eyes, magnificent turquoise orbs that reminded her of the scales on the little reef fish. She could not look away. He stiffened and levered himself up on his elbows. Meri felt the muscles of his stomach just before she pulled her hand away. His gaze raked over her and she was glad she had covered her breasts.

"What do you want?" he asked, his voice deep and low.

"I do not wish to hurt you, sir," Meri said.

He drew in a quick breath. "You speak my language."

She gave a delicate snort. "Of course I do. If you bothered to ask, I could have told you that earlier. Instead you tried to kill me."

"I contemplated it." He looked around and Meri knew he was looking for his knife.

"Is this what you seek?" She held up the wicked blade, the movement sending a stab of agony into her shoulder. Her stomach roiled at the pain, but she tried to hide it. "I'm afraid I shall have to keep it, if only to ensure my safety."

"You've proven you need no knife, Madam," the man said, rubbing his right temple as if it still throbbed.

"Ho! So now I'm madam. Thank you very much."

"Why am I not dead?" He sat up and Meri braced for his lunge.

"Contrary to your opinion, I did not try to kill you, only defend myself." Perhaps she might talk herself out of this?

The man's eyes narrowed. "Very noble of you, but why would you stay your hand?"

She lifted her chin. "I have my reasons. Besides, why need there be war between our peoples?"

"I've good reason to hate your kind," he said. "Even if it wasn't personal, your people are a plague on the oceans."

"I could say the same. You have no right to sail the seas, dropping your waste and stealing our bounty. But I do not want to argue with you. I need your help."

"Ah," he said, "and now we come to the reason I'm still alive." He stood, wincing at the movement.

"Please, sir, listen to me." Meri realized this man could leave her stranded on the beach. Anyone could come along, and she would have to go through all this again.

"I am sorry that my people have harmed you in whatever way," Meri said, "but I am not responsible. I have fled my family and I need your help."

"Why should I believe you're any different to the rest of your race?"

She drew herself up. "I do not lie."

The man studied her as if she was an unsavory but fascinating parasite. Perhaps she had his interest after all.

"What is your name?" he asked.

Meri's heart quickened. *Progress!* "Merielle."

"That's it? Merielle? No other name to go with it?"

"I have other names, but you do not need to know them. What is yours?"

He hesitated but Meri thought he just might be a gentleman. He did not act as other sailors she had known. He had a smooth veneer he could not hide.

"Nikolas Cosara."

She repeated the name, relishing the sound of it on her tongue, enjoying even more the warmth his gaze created in her core. "I like it."

"I'm not helping you."

"I do not think you are the type of man to leave a lady in distress. I am sorry for hurting you, but I brought you back, and now I ask a favor."

He frowned and sat cross-legged before her. Again, his eyes ran along her face, her body. It heated her even more.

"I don't owe you a thing," he said.

She swallowed her nerves, seeking the strength she required to convince him. "I am injured, sir, and I need a place to recover before I resume my journey."

"I tried to kill you. Why do you think I would now aid you?"

Inspiration zapped through her. "I do not think you would have harmed me. And now we have exchanged names, I believe your honor will not allow you to abandon me." She took a deep breath to steady the sickness in her stomach.

Nikolas shook his head. "Who the hell are you? I don't owe you anything." His eyes narrowed as he gazed at her. "If I did help you, what could you offer in return?"

"Is it not enough to help someone who is down on their luck?"

"Perhaps it would be if you were a human woman, but one of the murdering sea people? I don't think so."

Meri gasped at his rudeness. "Perchance you have no honor, after all?" She must rest and soon or she would pass out.

Nikolas stood and Meri couldn't help but cringe at his abrupt movement. Would he now harm her? She prepared "the song" for she would not give her life to this man.

"Perhaps I've forsaken honor," he spat. "Perhaps your people have carved it from my heart."

Meri's spirit quailed in the face of his bitterness. Had she met the only human man who would not help her? "I know not what I can offer in exchange for your aid, Lord Cosara."

Her words seemed to anger him further. "I'm no lord!"

Panic swirled in her gut, making the pain in her shoulder rise until it was a wave that threatened to engulf her. "Please, I will give you whatever I can, only provide sanctuary until I am fit to resume my travels."

Her desperation seemed to calm his anger. The scowl left his face, and a flash of pity gave her hope.

"I'll grant you refuge for tonight, and as for tomorrow, we'll see. I shall return." With that, he strode up the beach, heading for the cliffs.

Meri had to believe he did have honor to spare for her. Oh, she hated being out of her element and out of her depth. What if another came along this windswept beach while Nikolas was away? What if he never came back? Could she shuffle down to the water's edge and limp along the coast to the harbor, convince a dock worker to take her in?

Meri tried to relax, to have faith that her tanned rescuer would return. She lay back in the debris and closed her eyes, listening to the waves and the cries of the sea birds. The throbbing of her shoulder was a constant reminder of her predicament. Her head began to pound. If Nikolas did not return soon, she would have to roll her way to the water to stop her body from drying further. Already the skin of her tail had taken on the texture of desiccated seaweed.

The gentle swish of the waves and the warmth of the sun lulled Meri and she dozed, only to be awoken by a noise she could not identify. She pushed herself up with her good arm. Nikolas was returning to her, leading a large beast whose color was a shade darker than her tail. Meri's heart leapt into a gallop at the sight of the strange creature.

"Stop!" she said, her voice shrill.

Nikolas halted, frowning. "What the devil for, woman?"

"I would not have that beast closer to me."

His frown deepened and then he laughed. "This is Storm," he said. "He's a gentle horse and won't hurt you."

"A 'horse' you say?" Meri struggled to get her tongue around the strange term. "What is his purpose?"

Nikolas appeared to be struggling to hide his amusement. "His purpose is transport. You are to ride him."

"I decline." She eyed the so-called "gentle" Storm. He chose that moment to snort, and Meri jumped.

"How else am I to get you to my cottage?" Nikolas asked.

"You look strong enough to carry me."

"Well, I'm not capable of getting you up that goat track without Storm's help. You'll ride."

"I will not."

He closed the short space between them and reached for her, his face tight.

"One moment!" she said. "My body craves moisture. If you could submerge me in the waves before we leave, I would be grateful."

He huffed a sharp breath. "Already I'm beginning to regret this," he said, as he lifted her from the pile of rubbish.

Meri gritted her teeth. Depending on the gruff man who held her would not be easy. The coiled strength of his muscles wrapped her securely and the rough cloth of his shirt abraded her skin in the most distracting way. But she knew he would rather leave her and walk away.

Despite that, he lowered her gently into the breakers, steadying her against the push of the waves. "Do you need to be further out?" His gaze remained glued to her face, never dropping to her chest, but a small muscle bunched along his jaw.

"This is excellent. You may retreat." Meri lay back in the foamy wash, luxuriating in the feel of the cool, frothy waves. The headache receded and her tail regained its glossy sheen. When her fingertips had wrinkled, she called to Nikolas.

"I have soaked long enough, My Lord." Meri pushed herself into a sitting position and Nikolas approached with Storm. Did he ever smile? She imagined how a smile would light his eyes and enhance his rugged good looks.

He bent and lifted her, taking care not to bump her injured shoulder. "I told you I was no lord," he said, grunting as he settled her body against his chest. "Have you taken on water? I swear you're heavier than when you went in."

Meri's face blazed. "I may be somewhat weightier than before," she said, "but a gentleman would not make comment on the fact."

"Ah, but I told you I was no gentleman." The merest suggestion of a smirk lifted the corners of the sensuous lips that hovered so close to her face, but Meri had no time to admire his mouth as she was hoisted onto the back of the horse.

CHAPTER 2

NIK gazed up at the sea nymph sitting on Storm and ran his tongue across his lips. Merielle's crimson locks had shifted to reveal most of a glorious full breast, complete with dusky nipple and… well…he was just a man after all. The sooner he got her back to the house and into some clothes the sooner he could treat her as he must. Like an enemy; someone whom he would tolerate for as long as he had to. She was too alluring, distracting, and she was scared stiff, if he was any judge.

He kept his arms looped around her hips and closed his eyes to block out the sight of her bare flesh. Her body trembled as though this was the most terrifying thing in the world, instead of just a ride on an ordinary beast. Nik tried to remove his arms, but she held onto him like a lifeline. Like he would save her. Huh!

"Do not let go, please. I am sure I will topple over."

"You'll be fine, Madam."

"Get me down and carry me, Sir!"

Nik gritted his teeth. "I can't carry you up that track. Stop fighting me!"

"There must be another way. I cannot balance up here, and this beast scares me."

He spied a suspicious moistness in her eyes. *Oh Goddess, no! Spare me her tears!*

"Now don't go crying," he said, still trying to distance himself from that luscious breast.

"I am not crying. I *will* not cry over this horse." She sounded like she was trying to convince herself. Her hands clutched his shoulders, her grip almost painful. "Can you not climb up here and keep me steady?"

Nik gazed skywards, praying for strength. But as he prayed to a *goddess*, he figured perhaps he was wasting his prayers. Now a *god* would have been a whole different kettle of fish. A *god* would have been on Nik's side.

"Damn it, yes, I can ride up there with you. If I must."

"You must."

"You'll have to let me go first. Take a good grip on his mane."

Merielle released his shoulders and he guided her hands to the luxuriant silver mane of his horse. Nik vaulted up behind the mermaid, still unable to believe she was real. If anyone saw them, all hell would break loose. Many folk didn't believe in the existence of the sea nymphs, but in coastal areas believers were more common, especially amongst seafaring families.

Nik reached either side of Merielle and grabbed the reins. She turned her upper body toward him, wrapping her arms tight around his waist. When he urged Storm into a walk, she clung even tighter and a faint cry escaped her lips. Storm danced to the side, spooked by the sound.

"Hush now or we'll both end up in a heap," he said, trying to inject a soothing note into his voice. This was no mean feat as the last thing he felt was calm with Merielle perched in his lap, her hip against his groin, the curve of her breast pressing his chest. He swallowed hard, appalled at the sensations her proximity stirred. She was a mermaid, damn it, not a human. Good for nothing except killing sailors. He had to remember that. She wasn't like him *in any way*.

Clinging to the thought, he guided Storm up the cliff path, trying to ignore the soft curves of the being who had wrapped her arms around him as if she'd never let him go. They gained the top of the cliff and crossed the short distance to his cottage. Nik reined Storm in at the front gate.

"We've arrived. You may let go." Her face was still buried in his chest, her breathing shallow and rapid. Her hands clutched his shirt tighter than clams. "Merielle?"

She pushed her face away and gazed up at him. "Promise you will not let me fall?"

He rolled his eyes skyward again. "Do you think I'm going to drop you on your head after all the effort of bringing you up the cliff?"

She unclenched her hands from his back and he slipped off Storm, careful to keep her supported.

* * *

Meri slid off the horse into Nikolas's arms, and he carried her through the door and into his cozy residence. Flames crackled at the end of the room, and a pot emitted aromas that had her stomach grumbling. Before she could make more than a cursory study of her surroundings, Nikolas deposited her in a chair and strode away. She leaned back to see where he went and the chair shifted, trying to pitch her onto the floor. She grabbed the arms, squealing with fright, but the backward motion halted. A chair that rocked! How miraculous! She experimented with a few cautious rocks backward and forward, deciding she liked this very much.

"Are you cold?" Nikolas had re-entered the central room and stood with his hands on his hips, a scowl on his face.

"I am rarely cold, My Lord."

"Hungry? I have a fish and vegetable soup over the fire."

"I am indeed ravenous, and fish would be delightful."

If anything, her host's scowl deepened, but he crossed the room and retrieved bowls from a shelf near the flames, spooning the soup into them. He then scooped her up and transferred her to a cushioned chair so she could eat at the table. The delicious aroma of the fish mingled with more foreign scents. Meri used a slender utensil to scoop an orange blob from the broth. She popped it into her mouth and chewed. It was soft and a little sweet and…she didn't like it at all. She shuddered and spat the foul lump back into her bowl.

"What was that?" she asked. "It was truly ghastly." Her eyes met those of Nikolas across the table, who was wolfing down the soup as though it was to be his last meal.

"Your gratitude overwhelms me, Madam." He grabbed a hunk of soft, fluffy whiteness and dipped it into the bowl then stuffed it into his mouth. "It's not good manners to criticize the meal a host places before you. Even *your* people must know that."

Meri picked around in the bowl and popped a piece of fish and a tiny shrimp in her mouth. She liked the taste. "We do not eat such fare, so how can I know what to do when it is served? The fish and crustacean I can enjoy, even if it is not straight from the ocean." She gobbled up all the seafood and lifted the bowl to drink the broth. When she lowered it again, her host's eyes were upon her. The intensity in them reminded her of the killer whales who chased her in the ocean.

"How is your shoulder?" He had such beautiful eyes when he wasn't gazing at her as if he wished to kill her.

"It throbs," Meri said, rubbing the tender flesh. "Do you have unguents that would help?"

He stood. "Something of the sort." He moved to the shelves and took down two vessels and a bowl. From one jar he removed gray sticks that he snapped into small pieces and dropped into the bowl. With efficient, practiced movements, he ground the material into powder and stirred it into a pot of warm water, along with a generous dollop of a thick amber liquid.

"Drink this," he said, pushing the mixture toward her.

Meri raised the pot to her lips and sipped carefully. It was sweet but left a bitter aftertaste. She drank it all and a wonderful lassitude flowed through her. Her eyes drifted shut but snapped open again as she felt hands on her shoulder.

"What are you doing?" she asked.

"Pull your hair away unless you wish this ointment to get stuck in it."

She followed his order and heard a sudden intake of breath from her host. He stalked away only to return with a white shirt which he thrust at her. "Cover yourself with that while I tend your shoulder; then you can wear it."

Meri draped the shirt over her chest and Nikolas's hands resumed their gentle application of the sticky ointment. Her shoulder, nay her whole body, warmed under his touch, though his attentions were purely medicinal and the pain they produced could only just be borne.

"You've wrenched all the muscles around the shoulder joint. It'll be weeks healing properly, and you'll be unable to use it for at least the next week." His fingers left her skin. "You may dress now."

"I will require help," she said.

He sighed and walked around to stand before her. He took the shirt from her and shook it out before dropping it over her head and helping her pull her arms through the sleeves. It was a garment such as sailors often wore, and rough against her skin. She pulled her hair from its folds and settled the cloth around her. "I do not like the feel of it," she said. "Though loose, it still confines."

"Be that as it may," Nikolas said, "I can't have you lounging about the place topless. It's not proper."

"No one is here to see," she said.

"*I* am here," he said, "and I would rather not have to see so much flesh." He busied himself putting the medicines away and tidying the kitchen.

Meri thought about his words. Was she so ugly to this man that he did not wish to have her flesh exposed to his gaze? Most men she had encountered stared with open admiration at her curves, had seemed not the slightest bit uncomfortable with her nudity. True, she felt a little disquiet at exposing herself to Nikolas in such close confines, but his words caused her to look at her body with more censure than she normally would.

His words interrupted her thoughts. "You should rest." His eyes raked her from head to tail. "You may take my bed."

"Bed? The term is unfamiliar."

"It's where we humans generally rest. Come," he said, scooping her into his arms. "I'll show you." He walked into another room, her weight seeming hardly to matter to him, so powerful were his shoulders, his back, his legs. Meri closed her eyes at the thought of those muscles wrapped around her. What was amiss with her? Nikolas deposited her in the middle of a soft platform covered with blankets.

"This is a bed. It's where I sleep. Place your head here." He patted a small plump cushion and drew a blanket over her tail. "I'll wake you at dusk." With that he left the room, pulling the door closed behind him.

Meri relaxed against softness she had never experienced before, and eventually she slept.

* * *

Nik breathed deeply as he closed the bedroom door. A mermaid in his home, his bed. What was he to do with her? One night. He could deal with one night. But what then? She was clearly incapable of fending for herself for at least a week, perhaps longer. His gut clenched at the thought of sending her out into the world. Who knew he still had it in him to care about another being? He didn't want company, or responsibility. His self-imposed exile suited him well. Another reason the sea nymph grated on his nerves.

Regardless, she was here and would have to be dealt with. He grabbed some wood and headed outside, seating himself on his favorite chair in the sun. His fingers wielded the knife as his mind sorted the latest problem to enter his life. Before long, a form started to appear, a sea creature with a dolphin's tale and woman's torso. Merielle. House guest, enemy, vulnerable, injured and foreign. As if against his will, the form continued to take shape. He had no wish to create her image, but it seemed his mind, his fingers, had another agenda. And he supposed that carving the sea nymph might help sort his thoughts about what to do with her. So he carved, sanded, polished, and pondered.

As the sun began to cross the horizon, Nik beheld his creation and marveled at the beauty in its form; possibly the most stunning work he had yet fashioned. He wasn't a vain man, but he did have the ability to evaluate his art and he judged this, quite simply, as beautiful. He wasn't a stranger to the magic of creation that artists employed, but this was the closest he had ever come to the process of creation guiding his hand, of the subconscious emerging from his fingers to shape his work. Unimaginable joy suffused him and beneath that, a kernel of disquiet. What did it mean?

As he ran his fingers over the shapely curves and smooth lines of his mermaid, Nik acknowledged one thing. Merielle's appearance in his life was no accident. She had been sent to him, or something within him had drawn her. Could she help him find his brother? He couldn't afford to send her back to the sea, at least not yet. He had to be patient, allow her to heal, and wait for the opportunity she would bring.

* * *

Despite the softness of the bed beneath her, Meri slept soundly for some hours, but awoke to a throbbing right shoulder. She sat up in the bed and tossed the blanket from her tail. It still gleamed in the faint light, a sure sign she was still well-hydrated. Nikolas stuck his head into the room and delicious seafood aromas floated in with him.

She took a moment to admire what she could see; golden tanned skin, unruly knotted blond locks that were now free to cascade down his back, piercing eyes - neither green or blue, wide cheek bones with that wicked scar, and a strong square jaw. He was an individual of uncommon attractiveness. Why ever was there not a woman to share his home? And how did he come to be living in this shack on the cliffs when his whole bearing bespoke power and command. Had he fallen on hard times?

"Hungry?" he asked.

"I am ravenous, Nikolas."

"Good," he said, entering the room fully so she could admire the rest of him. He reached for her, snagging her body to his chest and conveying her from the room to the kitchen table. A bowl of steaming food lay before her. This time it teemed with pieces of fish, mussels, crabs and prawns, and strands of seaweed entwined the tasty morsels. There were no horrid lumps of orange or brown to be seen.

Meri gazed at him in surprise. "This is not the same as the earlier repast, Nikolas. I do not see those..." She could not remember the word for the nasty things.

"Vegetables," he said.

"Yes, that is the word I seek."

"You didn't like them, so I cooked without them. I can't promise I'll always do so, but I can't see you discard so much of your meal. You need your strength."

"It will not be your concern after this night."

"I've been giving that some thought."

Meri's heart jumped at his words, but she pulled her sudden joy back under control. *Wait.* "Oh?" Yes, that was calm, controlled, dignified. She must step carefully with this man, for no matter what she hoped to gain, it would not help to anger him.

Nikolas frowned, as if expecting a different response from her. "Yes. I may have been somewhat hasty to suggest tossing you out after a night's rest." His gaze burned and, under it, she became hot. "Your shoulder will be long healing and you might not survive if I were to return you to the sea. Strangely, I don't wish to be responsible for your demise."

"I am hardly defenseless." Too late, she realized that reminding him of the events earlier when she nearly killed him might not help her case.

"You have defenses, yes, but they won't help you swim and dive and climb." He paused as if to judge the effect of his words. "I'd like to offer you refuge until your shoulder is healed."

"Thank you, but are you certain you wish to do this?"

"No. I'm almost certain I'll live to regret taking you in, but equally, I can't abide the thought of you adrift in the ocean or falling prey to some hungry killer whale."

His words made real her situation, the fact that she had taken her first steps on the path away from her family, the ocean, everything she had ever known. Below her was a yawning great ocean rift, the depths of which were impossible to fathom and the contents equally unknown. The realities of the world Nikolas inhabited might be far more frightening than anything she had yet encountered.

"I've upset you." His gaze trapped hers, not warm, not welcoming, and not trusting.

Meri shivered. She could not tell Nikolas she had turned her back on the sea. One such as she simply could not do that, at least not in this form. He would ask more questions, and if he found out what she truly planned he would never trust her, never let down his guard. No, best just to accept his hospitality.

"I thank you for extending your protection beyond the morrow, Nikolas." She returned his gaze, bemused by the turquoise of his eyes. "You are right. I would be vulnerable were I to return to the sea, but I am equally vulnerable in your world. I do not think you realize how much care I will require. And then there is the need for secrecy."

"I receive few visitors here. As for your care, I think I can manage."

At his smirk, her heart quickened. This man would never succumb to her wiles. He hated her, and the only reason he allowed her in his house was…Why would Nikolas agree to keep her underfoot? He said he could not abide the thought of her alone and vulnerable, but that could not be the only reason. His hatred of her people was personal.

"Why are you really helping me?" she asked. "How can you bring yourself to aid one of the *mer* people?"

A small muscle twitched in his jaw and his shoulders tensed. "I don't wish to talk about this."

"Tell me why you hate me."

Nikolas stood and his chair fell over backwards. He tangled his hands in the locks of his hair, pulling them as if he wished to cause himself pain. Meri watched, trying to wrap herself in calm, wondering if he would reveal his torment.

"Your people killed my brother," he said.

CHAPTER 3

NIK'S heart was turned inside out by the admission. Part of him had been stripped away the day news arrived of Jon's disappearance, and the lack of answers since hadn't helped. His little brother, the boy he had all but raised, the family he should have protected, went missing, presumed dead, on a naval mission last month.

He dragged himself back to the present. Merielle was talking, and her quiet voice slid down his spine, making him shiver.

"If you blame my people for your brother's death, then it is even harder to understand why you wish to help me."

"Perhaps it's revenge I seek?" Nik clenched his teeth to bring his anger under control. She was so calm, so unaffected by his announcement of the event that had nearly destroyed him, and still might.

"Perhaps having you under my roof will give me the answers I want?" He laughed, a hint of madness twisting the sound. "What do you think your people would give me to get you back?"

The delicate muscles of her throat clenched tight. *Ha! At last his words penetrated her calm.*

Merielle pushed her bowl away. She took a deep breath then let it all the way out. "As to what my family would give you, I do not know, Nikolas. I have left my family. I never lived up to their expectations and so I suspect they will be glad to see the back of me."

Fury scorched through Nik. That she could give up her family by choice while he had his ripped from his hands—his parents, his brother, all gone. "They'll search for you."

"Perhaps."

"Is that why you need me? To hide you from them?"

She appeared guilty at his words. He smiled but it contained no mirth. This creature would hide everything from him.

"You will *not* use me," he said.

"You would happily use *me*."

"Yes, I would." He began to pace back and forth across the small living area. "You see, the naval captain who brought the news of my brother's disappearance also brought Jon's personal effects, and amongst them was his diary. In the days before he disappeared, my brother wrote of his love for a mermaid. He described her ethereal beauty and divine voice. He said he'd do anything to make her happy." He glared at Merielle. "Does that sound familiar? It's how you people work, isn't it?"

Merielle raised her beautiful head. She was as regal as a queen; would certainly give his cousin a run for her money. "It could be true."

"Could be true!" Nik roared. "It's in Jon's diary. Do you think he was writing fairy tales?" He leaned his face close to hers. "My brother wasn't susceptible to wild fantasies. If he says there was a mermaid who sang to him, then there was. And then he disappeared, presumed dead."

"I am sorry."

"Sorry won't bring my brother back. Sorry won't give me the answers I seek." He pulled himself back from the brink and drew a long, shuddering breath. "I don't know if you can help me discover what happened to Jon, but it can't hurt to keep you around."

"And so, we come to the real reason you have allowed me to stay," she said.

"No, I'll not have you think I'm solely motivated by self-interest."

"Why would you care what I thought?" Merielle's green gaze bored into him. She could be disconcertingly direct at times.

The words stopped Nik in his tracks. He shouldn't care what this creature thought of his motives…and he didn't. He opened his mouth to reply but she spoke first.

"Stop."

Her voice was curiously commanding, not that he would allow her to rule him. No, never that.

"Why can we not keep this arrangement simple?" she asked. "I need refuge, you must discover the truth about your brother, perhaps find him. We can never be friends, but perhaps we can help each other until our paths diverge again."

"I want to know what I'm getting myself into here. You said you had left your family. What does that mean?"

"You do not want to hear about my family, Nikolas. Suffice to say I do not fit in there and never have. I am a disappointment to them and have chosen to make my own way in the world. Unfortunately, the storm interfered with my plans. But I see how important it is for you to find your brother. Perhaps if I read his diary it would provide some clues?"

Nik drew a long breath. How was he to have this creature in his house for weeks on end, reminding him of his loss, of his war with her people? And he still understood so little of her purpose. "Perhaps. For now, we must prepare for rest." He stood, ready to lift her into his arms.

"Wait. I thank you for your bed this afternoon, but I would be more comfortable sleeping in the rocking chair. If you place it in front of the fireplace, I shall be most content."

Nik could hardly believe his ears. "You'd prefer to spend the entire night in a chair?"

She nodded. "Most certainly. I never sleep but a few hours at night and not on anything as soft as your bed. I shall be happy in the rocking chair."

He raised his hands in defeat. "Fine. I won't argue. I couldn't think of where I was to sleep tonight." He pulled the chair closer to the fire and placed the quilt his mother had made over it to block the chill. Then he gently lifted the mermaid from the kitchen chair into the rocker.

"Lovely, Nikolas. Thank you." She settled into the chair, her green gaze falling upon the flames in the fireplace.

Nik tidied the kitchen, bid Merielle a good night and retired to his bedroom.

* * *

The cottage was silent except for the gentle crackling of the fire, but Meri was in turmoil. Stupidly, she had never imagined that leaving her watery home and finding her way in an alien land would be so confronting. She had never questioned her ability to forge a new path, it had simply been a matter of making the decision to leave and getting on with it. She had not anticipated the storm, or her injury, or the fury of the first human she encountered. Why could she not have found a calm and gentle man whom she could have mesmerized; twisted around her finger until he was besotted with her?

She drew deep breaths to calm the storm within. All was not lost, even though her situation appeared hopeless. Her shoulder would heal, eventually, and then she would have the choice of returning to the sea or resuming her journey to find love. Her heart fluttered at the thought of love in her life; something she had never imagined sharing with another being. Her people did not recognize or value love. Families in Meri's world were simply a mode of raising young and indoctrinating them in the ways of the sea nymphs. There was no love, not even warmth. Families were about ultimate control.

Meri had never fit in. As far back as she could remember she had been puzzled by those around her. So, she had played with the dolphins and whales, and explored her underwater home until she was old enough to be drawn into the world of her adult sisters. All mermaids were endowed with physical beauty, but they had to learn songs to lure their human victims into their traps. The soul of the victim would then be reincarnated into a male sea nymph, restoring the balance in the ocean. Man could not be allowed to plunder the seas without giving something back. That was the legend; what Meri was supposed to believe. But the thought of using her beauty and voice to lure men to their death made her gut twist with revulsion.

And so, she had dragged her tail whenever she was asked to practice her arts. Now, at twenty-one summers old, she should have already made her first kill. Meri was a failure. Perhaps she was one of those lost human souls, reincarnated into a mermaid but missing the crucial instincts of murder and cruelty. She yearned to belong, to be happy. Legend had it that if a man was to fall in love with her, she would shed her tail and become a flesh and blood woman. Accordingly, she had learned the song that would accomplish the feat, when and if she found the right man.

But could she dwell here? Already the food repulsed her, and that horse terrified her. The garments were restrictive and sleeping for half the day seemed ludicrous. It was puzzling beyond belief how the humans lived. And the most frightening fact of all? They lived a mere seventy years if they were fortunate, while her people enjoyed life spans four times as long. *Four times!*

She leaned back in the rocking chair and closed her eyes. There were many uncertainties on this path she had ventured upon. Only time would tell if she had made the right decision.

* * *

Nik couldn't sleep. No matter what distraction he employed, his thoughts churned through the events of the day and dwelt on the disturbing creature who shared his house. That she harbored secrets was certain. That she held the key to discovering what had happened to Jon was possible. That he was stuck with her until she healed was inescapable fact.

His bed smelled of her. It reminded him of his years at sea, tugging at his memory. Seaweed, salt air, ocean creatures - the part of him he had cut off and denied - now stirred, but he ruthlessly stomped on it. The ocean was no longer part of his life. It had taken more from him than he could afford to give, and he'd been right to turn his back and seek a different path.

Except one couldn't turn from everything one had ever known and expect the way forward to be laid out for them. In his case, the future was uncertain, still clouded with the search for Jon, and by the tragedy that had made him reject the ocean in the first place. And yet here he was, living perched on a cliff overlooking the waves, its sound in his ears, morning, noon and night; its produce on his table. And now a sea nymph in his home. If he truly had turned his back on that life, what was he doing here?

Nik was forced to acknowledge he was in limbo - unable to move forward but looking behind every day. Nothing was clear except absolute discontent. It made him toss and turn, pound the pillow and finally, give up on sleep.

The first faint rays of the sun lit the main room of the cabin when he crept from his bedroom. Merielle dozed by the fire, though by the feel of the air, the fire had long been dead. He shivered, his gaze roving over the exquisite features of his house guest. She held something in her hand; it was his mermaid carving of yesterday. Remembering the muse that had guided his fingers in the carving, Nik experienced another spike of unease. Merielle brought chaos to his life, feelings he didn't understand, rage that wasn't normally part of his soul. He wondered again if he'd been right to offer her refuge.

* * *

When Nik trudged back into the cottage an hour later, a cheery blaze greeted him. Merielle was seated at the kitchen table, the shirt tied snug at her waist, her dolphin's tail arranged under the table. A pot of water boiled over the flames. He stopped abruptly in the center of his living room.

"What the hell have you been doing?" he asked.

"Good morning, Nikolas. I have set the fire and boiled the water. How should we break our fast?"

He let out a huff of breath. "How did you do all that?"

"I rolled out of the chair and from there it was simple enough to accomplish the tasks. There were coals left to restart the fire and water to fill the pot."

He continued toward the fireplace and placed the logs he carried on the wood stack. "You'll hurt your shoulder rolling around like that. I'm—"

"You do not want me here any longer than I have to be—"

"That wasn't what I was going to say," he snapped.

"Still, you do not."

Nik clenched his teeth to suppress a sharp retort and waited for his temper to settle before replying. "I was going to say I'm happy to wait on you while you heal. I'd be a dunce to think you could help with chores while you stay here."

"But I can, Nikolas. I will not sit here like some queen and be waited on. Please, give me chores."

He studied her. She appeared earnest enough. If he were in her place, he wouldn't want to be a burden either. "Fine, we'll come up with a list of chores you can do, but I don't want you rolling around the floor."

Merielle's smile stole his breath. It was the first real smile he'd seen from her and transformed her from beautiful to stunning. *Remember what she represents, you dolt!* He shook off the daze and busied himself with breakfast. In no time, he'd made a pot of tea and had left over seafood stew warming on the fire for Merielle. He'd have yesterday's bread and cheese.

He made her a cup of fragrant tea and cut a small slice of bread and cheese for her to try.

"Thank you," she said, popping a portion into her mouth.

Nik watched as she chewed. A myriad of expressions flitted across her face.

"Well?" It would be easier if she'd eat some of the things he enjoyed.

"Mm," she said, taking a sip of hot tea. "Yes, I could eat that, but the tea must be chilled."

Nik relaxed against the back of the chair. "Good, that makes meals easier."

She laughed. "Meals do not have to be difficult, Nikolas. I eat raw ocean creatures. But do not worry. I can go for several days without feeding and suffer no ill."

He tried to ignore the tightening in his gut at her words. She was alien in so many ways. "You're healing, so it's best if you eat well. How's your shoulder today?"

"It aches."

"You should've said something. I'll grind some powder into your tea, and after breakfast I'll rub in more salve."

"Thank you."

Nik took the stew off the fire and ladled some into a bowl, then ground the pain medication and added it to Merielle's tea. They ate in silence, Nik trying to keep his thoughts on what must be done that day.

He cleared his throat. "How do you make your…um…ablutions?"

Color suffused her cheeks. "I bathe. The effect of water on my tail allows an exchange of waste products from my body into the water. If I partake once a day, all will be well."

"Seawater or fresh?"

"Either will suffice. You are kind to ask."

Her polite answers annoyed him for some reason. "You don't have to be so proper with me, you know. I won't suddenly change my mind."

"I do not wish to be a burden."

"Regardless, you will be, no matter what you wish."

She finished her stew and pushed the plate away, sipping on the tea, a frown on her face. "How are we ever to make this work?"

He stood abruptly and stalked to the bench to fetch the salve. "We'll make it work because we must." He stood behind her and tried to expose her shoulder, but the material was pulled too tight. "If you could loosen the shirt, please?"

The fingers that undid the top button and loosened the waist tie trembled. Nik knew he didn't scare Merielle, so why the tremors? Was it the thought of his hands on her skin that unsettled her? Goddess, it unsettled *him*, but had to be done.

He massaged the salve into the bruised tissue of Merielle's shoulder and eventually felt her relax. He relaxed too, enjoying the feel of her skin, just like any woman's. But as his mind relaxed, it wandered to thoughts of Merielle's exquisite neck, arched to allow him access, the corner of her rosebud mouth and the flutter of long red lashes against her cheek. He fantasized about his lips against all those tantalizing places and that was just for starters. Once he had conquered those frontiers, his hands would drift… *Hold it, man. Stop right there! She's your guest, and she's a lying mermaid. You can't bed her!* He swallowed down a surge of regret and pulled the shirt back over her shoulder.

"There you go," he said, his voice croaky. "It feels better today, less swollen."

She blinked several times as if coming out of a trance. "Thank you, that was nice, Nikolas. You have a gentle touch. Perhaps there is something of the healer within?"

"Father was a healer and wished me to follow in his footsteps." Nik flashed her a grim smile. "I disappointed him."

"Why?"

"I had a young man's desire to see something of the world and enlisted in the King's Navy. I worked my way up until I was one step from the pinnacle. Every time I went to sea, it broke my mother's heart. She thought I'd perish on one of my voyages. Father worried too, but I was too arrogant to consider them. I was following *my* dreams. One day I came back, and they were gone. Dead. Father had succumbed to an infection and mother followed. I often wonder if it might've been different if I had been there, been able to nurse my father so he might have saved my mother."

"You must not blame yourself."

He hated the compassion in her eyes. He didn't deserve it. "I ran away from my responsibility."

"That is wrong, and you must know it. Your parents were proud of you. They understood your desire to blaze a trail. I am sure they would not have wanted you to make yourself unhappy by turning your back on the sea. They would not want you torturing yourself now, either."

"You knew my parents well, did you?"

She pursed her lips. "Do not be difficult! Of course, I did not know them, but I know you and…"

"And what? I'm supposed to believe a *mermaid* when she says my parents would have been proud, would not have blamed me? You don't even know what a human family is like. Are your parents proud of you?"

Merielle looked away. She took a deep breath. "No. They are not. I have always disappointed them. Ever since I can remember."

"Just as I thought."

"Perhaps we are not so different after all?"

"Stop right there! This conversation is over." Nik fetched a tub and water for Merielle to do the dishes and stalked out of the cottage. He needed some air.

* * *

Meri's thoughts dwelled on the conversation as she washed the breakfast dishes. What a disaster! She had only been trying to help him see that blaming himself for his parents' deaths was silly. Of course, she was no expert on human families, but she could see the inherent kindness Nikolas possessed; a kindness that broke through even when he dealt with her, someone he considered his mortal enemy. And that compassion must have come from his parents. She knew in her heart they had understood their son's drive to find his own path. She longed to hear more of his years at sea; to understand the experiences that had molded him.

The dishes clean, her gaze fell upon the mermaid carving she had found yesterday. It was exquisite, the carving so expertly done it seemed alive. Had she been the subject? She snorted at her silliness. Of course, she had been the inspiration for this, this...work of art. Meri was pretty certain Nikolas did not know any other mermaids. He had the hands of an artist, a healer, that spoke of a different nature than would normally be expected in a man of the sea. A man of the sea might be an adventurer, a romantic, but not sensitive, artistic and caring, as Nikolas appeared to her. His complexities confused her. Perhaps he would reveal more of himself over the coming weeks, but would it mean she might be drawn to expose her secrets too?

CHAPTER 4

THE long hard ride along the cliffs to Wildecoast was just what Nik needed to clear the disquiet Merielle had placed in his heart. She challenged him on so many levels that he honestly didn't know if he could endure the days it would take for her shoulder to heal. Days of caring for her, arguing with her and facing the gut-wrenching knowledge that her people had taken his brother from him. He prayed Jon would understand his consorting with the sea nymph in order to learn more of his disappearance. He had no wish to be disloyal to his younger sibling. Family was important, even if he had no immediate family left.

Which brought him to the purpose of this trip. He'd not been anywhere near the city of Wildecoast, the King's seat, for six months or more. Even then, it was only to collect vital supplies he hadn't been able to scrounge from the sea, or from the travelers who occasionally stopped at his cottage. Nik sighed. He'd give anything not to be visiting the castle this day. His cousin would only ply him with endless questions, especially when she learned what he had to ask of her.

His cousin was queen of the kingdom, mother of the people, feisty and beloved by all who met her. Including Nik. But she could be a thorn in his side, and he knew she'd hound him on the subject which had been her favorite for the last year.

As he neared the city gate, Nik wondered if he should've dressed for the occasion. His fawn tunic and black breeches were presentable enough but could hardly be deemed suitable for calling on the queen. No matter. She'd always accepted his call in the past and today would be no different. Besides, he demanded the world accept him as he was.

Airs and graces were one of the problems with society nowadays. No one was as they appeared, all hiding their true selves under a cloak of falsehood. Or hiding themselves away from society altogether, like him.

He dismounted Storm at the entrance to the city and was greeted by the guard sergeant.

"Ho, Lord Cosara!" He gave a short bow. "To what do we owe the honor of this visit to our fair city?"

Nik grinned at the rotund sergeant with whom he had enjoyed an ale or two over the years. "Ho, Grif. How's the family?"

Grif sobered immediately. "Wife and brats are well, Nikolas, but my old mam died last month. It was two days before I found her. I should have been there, but she was always so tough. I thought she'd live forever."

Nik placed his hand on Grif's shoulder. "I'm sorry, man, that's a hard loss to bear. Promise you'll let me know if I can help."

The burden of sadness on Grif's features seemed to lift a little. "Thank you, Nikolas. I will. We don't see enough of you nowadays. How do you fare?"

"Getting by. I keep my own company. As to this visit, I wish to speak with my cousin."

Grif's face fell. "A hard day to do that. She has guests, and a funeral to attend."

"I only need a few minutes. Send word to Her Majesty and I'll continue on to the castle."

"Right you are." Grif sent a corporal off with quick-fired instructions. "Stop by on your way out and we'll share an ale."

"I will, my friend." Nik shook hands with Grif and passed through the gate, his spirits lifted by the encounter. He made his way through the milling market crowds to the castle. The steward met him at the gates and Storm was led away by a groom.

"Greetings, Lord Cosara," the steward said, sweeping a bow and fixing Nik with a beady eye.

Nik nodded. "I wish to have a quick word with Queen Adriana."

"This is most irregular, Sir. The queen doesn't normally see visitors without notice, even family members."

"Regardless, Master Adler, you have asked the question of Her Majesty. What was her reply?"

The steward frowned and pursed his lips. Nik disliked men like Adler, puffed up with self-importance and always getting in the way. "The queen will see you, Lord Cosara. Briefly. She's a very busy woman, especially today with—"

"I know," Nik said, "visitors and a funeral to attend."

Master Adler looked even more affronted, if that were possible. "Perhaps next time you would make an appointment with Her Majesty?"

"Perhaps," Nik said. "Now if you don't mind, I'd like to see my cousin."

Master Adler let out a huff, motioning for Nik to follow him as he hurried through the front entry of the royal palace. He was left in a small ante room to cool his heels for half an hour, before being ushered upstairs to the queen's audience chamber. He paced back and forth across the silver and gold carpet, then poured a glass of rich red wine and made himself sit and drink it. Time ticked by as he battled a burning desire to return to his cottage.

Finally, the chamber door opened, and Queen Adriana swept in, dark wavy hair swirling against the deep crimson of her gown. He climbed leisurely to his feet and made a bow that was barely deep enough.

Adriana laughed, her deep blue eyes sparkling. "Niki, you never change." She kissed each of his cheeks and embraced him. He returned the hug. "I am so glad you have decided to grace us with your presence."

"It's good to see you, Your Majesty."

"Humph. Stop that, or I will wonder what you want of me."

"In fact, I do want something, but nothing that's not in your power to grant."

Adriana's eyes gleamed. "You have come to take me up on my offer." She clapped her hands like a small child. "Admiral Nikolas Cosara! It has a wonderful ring, has it not?"

He stepped forward and grasped her hands. "Cousin, I haven't come to accept your generous proposal."

She pulled her hands from his and glared at him. "Niki, when will you stop being stubborn and take the role you were born for?"

"That's your opinion. I have other ideas."

"Like hiding yourself away from the world, wallowing in self-pity? It was not your fault, Niki, none of it."

"I'm not wallowing."

"Oh? What would you call it? Your life is in limbo. I hate to see you waste time in grief and guilt. Life is too short!"

"Enough, Adriana!" Nik turned his back on her and stalked to the window, gripping the sill and staring out over the courtyard. A stunning brunette stood beside a man, his blond locks tied at the nape of his neck. Sadness cloaked the couple, and something else, something more intimate. "Are they your guests, down below?"

Adriana came up behind him and peered past his shoulder. "The Lady Benae Branasar, my soon to be sister-in-law, and the squire, Ramón Zorba."

"Ah, yes, now I recognize him. He has changed."

"He has indeed."

Nik turned at the tone of Adriana's voice. Her gaze was that of a hungry shark. "I know that look," he said.

She had the grace to blush. "I am just looking, cousin. The squire has wonderful…assets. Lady Benae has noticed."

"I'm not interested in palace gossip," he snapped. If he didn't pull Adriana up right here and now, her scandalous thoughts would run away with her. "Is the lady betrothed to the king's brother, Jiseve?"

"Exactly so, Niki, and there is something afoot between those two. You mark my words." She fell silent, a frown on her face. "There will be trouble before long, I think."

Nik drew a deep breath. At least Adriana had been diverted from the subject of his return to the navy. "Now to the reason for my visit," he said, smiling. "Besides paying my respects to you, of course."

Adriana raised her beautifully shaped brows.

"I wondered if you had any old gowns I could borrow?" he asked.

Her eyes popped. "Of all the requests I had anticipated, that was not one, dear cousin. Why the gowns?"

"Must you know?"

"I must."

Nik turned away. What to tell her? "I have a house guest. She has fallen upon hard times and lost most of her clothes. I've agreed she can stay with me for a week or so, but she can't continue to wear my shirts."

"Oh, Niki! Who is she?"

Adriana's attention was now fully fixed upon him. He swallowed down the groan that rose in his throat.

"It is high time you had female company," she said. "Why, if I didn't know better, I would swear you preferred men."

"Believe me, Adriana, I don't."

"Well, you won't find a woman while you're stuck on a cliff, miles from civilization."

"It seems I did find one though, dear cousin." He smirked at the frustration on her face.

"So, this is serious?"

"No, simply an act of kindness until she recovers her former position."

"Which is?"

"I thought you had a funeral to attend?"

Adriana checked the time. "Blast! I must get ready." She threw her arms around Nik and hugged him just as they did when they were children. "You are lucky I am short on time or I would not let you go until I had the full truth of the matter."

"Farewell, cousin," he said, bowing deeply.

"Farewell, Niki. I will send my maid with my old garments packed for travel. If you wait here, she will not be long." She studied him as he fidgeted under her gaze. "Please think on what I said. All of it."

He nodded and she swept from the room.

* * *

After a quick ale with Grif, Nik left for his cottage, the bag of clothes slung across his back. He had to admit the visit to Wildecoast had been good for him. He was reminded of his love for his cousin, and it had been good to talk to Grif. Perhaps he'd been wrong to cut himself off so completely from society.

But as he galloped along the cliff trail, the chill wind in his face, waves crashing below him, he couldn't be sorry he'd chosen to seek refuge in this wild, isolated place. His heart lifted despite the knowledge that he was returning to Merielle - house guest, mermaid, enemy.

He reached the cottage and released Storm into the paddock beside the stable, so he could cool down. When he entered the cottage it was cozy, and Merielle sat singing in the rocking chair. Her voice swirled around him, enticing him to listen, to float away to a place where no ill could befall him. He shook his head.

"I'm back," he said, loud enough to be heard over her singing.

She turned, her glorious green eyes capturing the late afternoon sun, her hair blazing like fire. Merielle was wild, beautiful and untamed. What was she doing here in his living room?

"Welcome back," she said. "You have been gone a long time. I was beginning to worry."

"There's no need for concern," he snapped, dropping the bag onto the floor in front of her. "I brought clothes for you. Dresses."

"Oh!" She frowned. "Why?"

"You must be properly covered. What if someone should drop by?"

"You said this place was isolated."

"Regardless, I can't have anyone seeing your tail. I thought a dress would cover you more fully."

He ran his eyes over her tail. It was plump and gleamed as though recently washed. She looked clean, fresh, enticing. He swallowed as his manhood stirred. *Idiot!* He shook his head, trying to dislodge the unwelcome excitement. Nothing could ever come of it. He really had been out on these cliffs too long.

"Are you well, Nikolas?" Merielle had tied the shirt below her breasts so a goodly amount of cleavage was exposed. He swallowed again, reminding himself they were enemies.

"Yes, just tired. Please try the dresses on. I'm going to fetch supper." He strode from the cottage, intent on putting as much distance between himself and Merielle as possible.

CHAPTER 5

MERI held up a pale green gown. She could not believe the beauty of the dress, could never have imagined wearing anything like it. Of course not! Mermaids did not wear clothes. Under the pale green dress there was a deep purple one, and beneath that, another in turquoise. There was also a simple white garment; perhaps something human women slept in? There was even a comb in the bag, and a mirror. Someone kind had packed this. *Nikolas?*

The gowns were not of the kind simple peasant women wore; Meri was sure about that. She imagined she would need assistance to do up the many tiny buttons on two of the gowns. The third, the turquoise, laced up the front. She would wear it first and surprise Nikolas on his return. Tonight, they would dine as lord and lady. She paused at the thought. Best she got such silly fancies out of her mind right now! Nikolas felt little short of hate for her, and only tolerated her because he thought she could help him find his brother. Yes, he was kind and a gentleman, but he was not the answer to her problems.

Meri was dressed in the turquoise gown by the time Nikolas returned with his catch. Her shoulder ached from the strain of pulling the garment over her head and doing it up. She had combed her hair as best she could and was pleased with the picture that greeted her in the mirror. Perhaps she could become accustomed to this life on land?

Nikolas took two steps into the cottage and froze, his hands full of lobsters, fish and squid. His mouth dropped open as his gaze scorched her up and down.

"Nikolas?" she said when he continued to stare. She suppressed a giggle at the sight of him standing there, the sea creatures dripping water all over the floor.

He cleared his throat. "Yes, um, well…" He looked right and left and then back at her.

"What is amiss?" Meri shifted so she could place the mirror on a low table before her. Pain shot through her shoulder and into her neck and she cried out. Nikolas dropped his bundles and hurried forward.

"Is it your shoulder?" he asked. "I'll mix some medicine." He dripped all over the floor as if he had come directly from a swim. Then she thought of the lobsters and realized he would have had to dive into crevices to get them.

"You must wash and change first, Nikolas. My shoulder can wait."

His gaze ran over her again.

"Do you like the gown?" Meri's face heated at having to ask the question. She was unaccustomed to fishing for compliments.

"It's very nice," he said.

"Nice!" She had never heard such tepid approval in all her life. The gown was exquisite and perfectly accentuated her coloring. She looked like a princess, if she did say so herself. "Is that all you can say after the grief I went through to get it on? Nice?"

He stepped back, frowning. "You look like a queen, Merielle. It suits you perfectly. If I was less than ebullient with praise, it's because I was shocked you looked so…"

"Human?"

"Yes, if you wish."

"Well, I do not…" What did she wish? Had they not decided on the terms they would associate under? He giving her refuge, and she trying to help him find Jon. There was no room for her to expect anything else from him. She was being silly. "Never mind. I am just tired and sore."

Nikolas frowned. "I'll mix your medicine and then wash and prepare supper."

* * *

Nik hurried from the cottage before Merielle caught sight of the bulge in his pants. Mind you, she might not have known what it signified anyway. Things were likely different with *mer* men. He shook the disturbing thought from his head and stripped the clothes from his body. Buckets of water stood in the sun on the western side of the cottage. He doused himself with most of one bucket then soaped himself and his hair, rinsing with the second bucket. The cool water cooled the desire that had gripped his body at the sight of his house guest clad in a queen's gown.

If Merielle were able to appear at court, she would be the talk of the kingdom. She was simply the most beautiful thing Nik had ever laid eyes upon, and it had taken seeing her in a royal gown to fully realize it. He stood, allowing the water to drip from his body, shivering as a cold breeze swirled across his skin. When had life become so complicated?

* * *

Meri's eyes drifted closed as the long, callused fingers of her host massaged the sore tissues of her shoulder. The medicine she had taken and the warmth of the cabin relaxed her, but her stomach grumbled. It had been difficult not to throw herself on the floor and consume those fresh squid, but Nikolas would have looked at her with distaste, and she could not bear that. Squid was her favorite, and to cook it would reduce the flavor. Perhaps she could convince him to slice some fresh for her. Yes, perhaps he would not object to that.

In the meantime, lulled by the warmth spreading through her body, Meri slipped into a daydream. Her mind wandered to the possibilities of a life on land - wedding a human man, never having to feel she was not enough, ever again. She could start over, once she had convinced someone to fall in love with her.

Nikolas had shown her mother's words were untrue. Humans were not monsters, but caring beings who would share their house with an enemy if required. What else in her childhood lessons had been false? She thought fleetingly of her four sisters, now isolated from her. Would they miss her? She longed to meld her voice with theirs once again, wished she could race them across the reef and dive with them into the undersea caverns, where all manner of wondrous creatures lived.

"What are you thinking, Merielle?" Nikolas's deep voice brought her back to reality.

She sighed. "That I miss my sisters."

"It was your choice to leave, was it not?"

"Indeed."

"You can return if you so choose." He wiped her shoulder with a towel and helped her cover up. "When you're well."

"Of course, if I choose." Meri stared up at her host.

"You never did say why you fled your family."

"No. I don't think you would understand."

"Perhaps not."

Could she reveal the truth behind her troubles with her family? Discussing their expectations of her, and how she had failed to live up to them, would only remind Nikolas of the involvement of the *mer* people in his brother's disappearance. No, she best be vague.

"I have never 'fit' into my family. I cannot explain it any better than that. You know how it is when parents have expectations of their children? I just never measured up. In the end, I had to leave or go mad."

He nodded. "I know that feeling."

She held her tongue. Nikolas did not know how it had been for her, or only in the mildest sense. Let him think her experience was as bland as conflicting career aspirations. In a way, that had been the case, except most mothers don't expect their children to murder for a living.

She smiled at him. "Shall we dine, Nikolas?"

* * *

Nik allowed himself to pretend he was sharing table with a normal human woman; one so beautiful she took his breath away. Her hair glowed in the light of the fire and candles, the turquoise gown a stunning backdrop for her coloring. The greenish tint of her skin was only evident in sunlight, and for that Nik was glad.

He had chopped some of the squid fresh. She ate it first, seeming to relish the firm, white flesh. Nik forced back a shudder and turned his attention to his seafood stew and bread.

They spoke of their one common love - the sea; relating tales of ocean creatures, and storms, and their favorite places. Nik almost forgot he hated everything Merielle stood for. Almost. But soon the meal was over, and it was time to get down to business.

He cleared his throat and pulled the journal from his pocket. It was a small leather-bound tome, still quite new. For a moment he closed his eyes, his hands gripping the cover. *Please forgive me, Jon.* He opened his eyes again and looked at Merielle, slowly handing it to her.

Her eyes grew wide. "Jon's diary?" she breathed.

Nik nodded, unable to speak.

She opened the front cover and thumbed through the pages until she came to the last entries. She read aloud.

Tonight I've had a wondrous experience. As I stood watch, a magical sound reached my ears. It was part song and part sound of the ocean, high pitched, like a whale's keening. I searched for the origin of the song and finally saw a figure in the waves - a maiden with luxurious hair, the moon lighting her exquisite features. A woman more beautiful than any I've ever seen.

Merielle looked up, and Nik swallowed the lump in his throat, struggling to hear the account of the end of Jon's days.

She continued.

At first, I was frightened for her, thinking she had fallen off some ship, and I called out. Her song halted and she smiled, so I knew she couldn't be distressed. We looked at each other for long moments before she dived beneath the waves, revealing a tail such as the dolphins have. I gripped the rail, hoping to spy her again, but the waves were quiet. She didn't return.

Merielle fell silent, and Nik knew she was reading the entry for the next day.

"Your brother could not get this mermaid out of his head. She appeared to him again the very next night. Then there is nothing." She looked up at Nik.

He cleared his throat to ease the tightness in his chest. "Jon disappeared the night where there is no entry. He was on watch, and when the next sailor came to relieve him, he found the watch deserted. The captain brought me Jon's personal effects when they returned to shore. This is the only evidence to suggest what might have become of him."

"I am truly sorry."

Nik's jaw tightened until he thought his teeth would break. "Can you tell me anything about Jon's disappearance?"

"Did the captain reveal where he sailed?"

"Jon disappeared between the southern tip of Pirate's reef and the great ocean trench. Do you know them?" He gripped the edge of the table, willing Merielle to tell him all she knew.

"That is a large area, Nikolas. Can you not narrow the search zone?"

Nik pushed up from the table and stalked away. "Jon vanished on watch and no one saw him go. He went on duty at the southern tip of the reef and was discovered missing near the trench. It could've been anywhere in that area."

She drew in a deep breath. "Then I do not think I can help."

* * *

Meri closed her eyes, trying to block out the pain on Nikolas's face. She so wanted to bring him to his brother. He needed that more than anything. The territory he mentioned was large and included the hunting grounds of her family, but she could not tell him that. *She could not!* It might destroy the frail friendship beginning to build between them. Besides, Jon may had fallen prey to another mermaid, unrelated to her.

"I am sorry, Nikolas. It does sound as if Jon was lured into the sea by one of my people, and if that occurred, there is little chance he is alive. He would have met his end in the hope that his soul might be reincarnated as one of the *mer* men, in repayment for his sins."

She flinched as Nikolas turned to face her. "Sins?" he roared.

Meri clapped her hands over her ears, heart pounding in her chest, mouth dry with fear.

He began to pace back and forth across the room, his fists clenching and unclenching at his sides. "My brother was an innocent. He did nothing to harm your people. He did nothing but seek adventure at sea, and for that he is dead!"

"Please, Nikolas," Meri said, desperate for him to stop roaring, "it is not my fault. You are scaring me."

Nikolas halted, staring at her, his eyes ablaze with fury. "Jon is dead, and I hold you responsible. I should never have taken you in, I should've left you on the beach to die. It's what you deserve."

Meri had no idea how to deal with this man. She had never seen rage like this. One false move and she feared he would dump her back on the beach.

"You are a good man. You would not leave me to fend for myself. And the charges you make are untrue. I cannot take responsibility for all the sins of my people."

"So, you call them sins!"

She squirmed, uncomfortable judging her race, even after fleeing their principles. "I find it difficult to reconcile the death of a man as payment for the evils of mankind. I don't believe we should be the judge of humans. I don't agree with human sacrifices for the survival of my people."

Nikolas stared at her. "Who are you, really?"

Meri gaped. "What do you mean?"

"Well, you just denounced your race's beliefs, *your* beliefs, but you're sure as hell not human. What *are* you?"

She lifted her chin, stung by the scorn in his voice. This was heading into areas she had no wish to discuss. "I have no desire to fight with you, Nikolas. You have endured much and I am only trying to help."

"Well help, dammit! Take me to your people, let me speak to them."

Meri shook her head, her heart aching at the distress in his words. "I will not go back. I cannot. I have made my choice and must abide by it. I am sorry, but I will not go back for anyone."

"Then you're out of this cottage as soon as you can fend for yourself." His eyes blazed at her.

"I am sorry," she whispered.

CHAPTER 6

MERI was still awake, and she suspected Nikolas was too. She could hear him tossing and turning. The fire had burned low and she did not have the energy to place more wood upon it.

Reading the diary had moved her. She was seeing first-hand the impact of the *mer* people's hatred of humanity. How many other families had mourned the loss of their young men? It was always the same. Lure the sailor, seduce him over one or two nights, then sing the song that would have him jumping ship into the arms of death.

Her sisters attacked every ship that entered their waters, and Meri herself had practiced her seduction skills on plenty of sailors, including youths like Jon. But she had never killed anyone, much to her mother's disgust.

She had made the correct decision in leaving her watery home. She would never be happy there, and one could not live with honor by denying one's very self. Nikolas asked too much. Meri had broken away from her family's clutches and she would not willingly return to them, even to help him. But had she destroyed her chance at happiness?

This afternoon Meri had thought she detected interest from Nikolas, and they had chatted over dinner like friends. She had begun to imagine he might come to love her if managed carefully. He was so considerate and had gone against his beliefs to help her. His fingers on her skin…She shivered as desire squirmed in her belly.

And now he wanted her out of his home. He realized she could not lead him to Jon. How could she overcome his fury and make him love her? Was it even possible after the events of this evening?

Meri had made a decision by the time Nikolas emerged from his bedroom the next morning. She had to woo her host, and to do that, she must make him understand, get him to empathize with her.

She forced herself to meet his eyes as he entered the kitchen. They were still stormy. He paused, staring at her, and she stared back.

"I've not changed my mind if that's what you're wondering," he said.

Oh, this is going to be difficult. "I did not expect it. I am sorry. I would help you if I could."

"Words! Empty words. All your actions are self-serving. You've fled your people, causing endless heartache for your family. No matter what you say, they'll miss you." He ticked off the point on one finger then raised another. "You keep secrets." He raised a third finger. "You accept my care but refuse to help me find my brother."

"It is not as you say." Meri swallowed her distress and tried to calm her voice. "You cannot have any concept of my family, of my people. I did not want to discuss this with you for I believed it would only alienate you. But I cannot have you think so poorly of me."

He remained silent, his face closed, eyes a stormy green rather than turquoise.

Meri took a deep breath. "From the moment a mermaid is born she is destined for a life of seduction and murder. It was not so difficult when I was small. I frolicked in the sea and learned about its creatures - what was dangerous, which were allies, what I could eat and that which I could not. I played with the dolphins and learned to avoid the sharks and other killers. Later I learned how to fight these threats if I could not avoid them.

"As I neared my thirteenth summer my training in seduction began. I learned the songs, the dances and hand gestures. I watched others, including my older sisters, seduce and murder sailors. And it disturbed me. The more I saw, the less I understood."

She could see, by Nikolas's expression, her story was not working. His face had grown stony hard, his eyes like sharp chips of green granite.

"This life was all I knew, but always I felt something else waiting for me. Never could I understand my sisters, or my mother, and they grew increasingly frustrated with my lack of interest in killing. I could never comprehend how it was right to taint everything that is beautiful in the ocean with death. My society explained that we were correcting the balance, taking an eye for an eye, and procreating our people, but I never understood."

Nikolas had folded his arms across his chest in the gesture humans used when they were uncomfortable.

"I was convinced there was another life for me, and so I fled to avoid the mantle I otherwise must take up - the mantle of deception and death. I will not kill another." Her voice dropped to a whisper. "You must believe me...I cannot go back." All the horror she might face if she returned hung in the air between them. Meri looked down at the mermaid carving she held, and despite its beauty she had to restrain herself from flinging it across the room. She had left that life behind and nothing would entreat her to return. Her gaze met his. "I am sorry. I will not go back."

Nikolas stepped forward and finally Meri saw empathy. She had reached him!

"Someone who has fled their own family can't possibly imagine what it would mean to me to find Jon, alive or dead."

Meri recoiled from his judgement. She must have been mistaken, for all she saw now was disgust.

"I must think." He turned and stalked to the door. "Don't expect me back before midday." The door slammed behind him.

She closed her eyes, concentrating on her breathing. Gradually her fluttering heart slowed, and calm returned. Nikolas was more a wild creature than she was. When confronted, he ran instead of standing and facing her. Did she really want a life with a man such as that?

* * *

Nik flew across the water, wind in his face, the sea spray clinging to him. As he battled the sea and the wind in his small boat, he felt free for a while. But it didn't last. How could he forget he shared a home with a monster? For Merielle was exactly that. No matter that she was beautiful, even regal in the queen's gown, she wasn't human. She enjoyed raw seafood and slept sitting in a chair, and a dozen other strange things he was yet to discover. He didn't want to learn any more about her, and yet she was strangely compelling.

Was it her loveliness? Nik didn't like to think that was all that mattered to him. He liked to believe the women in his life attracted him on a deeper level, answered some need within. There had not been many, what with going to sea and then isolating himself out here for the past year. Increasingly though, he found himself wanting to touch her. He ached to find out how her lips would feel against his. The times when he tended her injured shoulder were torture and delight.

A pang of guilt tore at him. He had fled without ensuring she had broken her fast and wasn't in pain. It went against everything he believed to have her in his home, and yet he did care about her. Perhaps that was part of the rage he felt when she declined to help him, to take him to her community. She disappointed him.

Nik shook his head and corrected the trim of the sail as a heavy gust threatened to capsize the small boat. He couldn't help feeling Merielle had been sent to him by the Goddess, even though he no longer knew if he believed. If that was the case, it must have to do with Jon. But how, if she refused to take him to her people? Was there another purpose for Merielle in his life? It seemed unlikely, for nothing could ever come of their liaison.

He located the small reef off the coast and dropped the sail and the anchor. Perhaps having to concentrate while he dived for lobster would force her from his mind for a time. It was the most disturbing thing about his guest. Since her arrival he had thought less and less of Jon and of his other losses, and more and more of the bewitching, crimson-haired mermaid. His heart was just a shade lighter, and he had started to believe his parents might have been a little proud of him if they had been alive, that they might not have disapproved as much as he thought. Perhaps after so many long dark years, grief was starting to lose its hold on him. Or was it simply that he had less room for grief?

* * *

Meri had breakfasted, washed and was sipping a cup of tepid tea when she heard a horse approaching. She froze. It would not be Nikolas; he was at sea. She might be able to pretend no one was home and the visitor would go away. She smoothed her skirt and ensured her tail was tucked away under the voluminous folds of the turquoise satin. Her hand shook as she brought the cup to her lips.

Footsteps approached and she jumped as a knock boomed on the wooden door. Her teacup wobbled as she replaced it in its saucer.

"Nikolas, are you there?" A strong male voice struck Meri and she shivered.

"It's Kain, Niko." Another booming knock rattled the door. She was unable to move, her thoughts frozen by the fear of discovery - of what this man might do if he found her, let alone discerned her true nature.

The door swung open and he stood in silhouette against the glare outside. Meri had the impression of lean strength and darkness. She could only imagine how she appeared, seated at the table, her heart thudding so loudly she imagined he must hear it.

"Oh," he said, his dark brows furrowed. "I seek Nikolas."

Meri drew together her scattered wits and took a deep breath. "He is not here."

"That I see, Madam." He stepped forward, and she was able to see his features. His hair was short, almost black, with a sprinkling of gray at the temple. Dark eyes assessed her from a lean, tanned face, and his bearing spoke of a man used to command. The way he stared at her made her imagine he could see right into her heart.

"I am General Kain Jazara of the King's Army." He made a short bow. "Who might you be?" Despite the bow, there was nothing friendly in his tone. *Another hostile man!*

"My name is Merielle. I have fallen on hard times and Nikolas has allowed me to stay with him until I am fit to continue my journey."

"So, you're passing through? Where do you come from?"

"I suppose you could argue my origins are your business, considering you are no doubt responsible for law and order in these parts. But I do not agree, Sir."

"General, Madam. And I only ask as Niko's friend. I wouldn't want anyone taking advantage of him."

Meri didn't know how to respond to that. She was glad Nikolas had someone to call friend, someone who would look after his interests. "Nikolas is a kind man. He took pity on me, and I was in no position to decline his hospitality."

The general's brows shot up. His dark gaze hovered over her body and Meri had the impression he missed nothing. She prayed her tail was well concealed.

"So I hear," he said finally. "Niko borrowed clothes from his cousin. They suit you very well."

She inclined her head. "Thank you, General." A sudden question occurred to her. "Who is this cousin? Will she not require such fine gowns be returned before long?"

Jazara laughed. "The queen won't even miss the clothes, Lady Merielle."

Meri gasped. *Nikolas's cousin was the queen?* "Is it true? His cousin is the queen herself?"

"Indeed. Queen Adriana Zialni. They're very fond of each other." His eyes narrowed. "Niko hasn't confided in you then?"

Meri shook her head, trying to get her thoughts around Nikolas and his royal cousin.

"What else can you tell me of Nikolas, General? Fetch yourself a cup and join me for tea. I would serve you myself only I have an injury."

Jazara strode forward and plucked a cup from the shelf in the kitchen. He seated himself across the table from her and poured a cup of fragrant breakfast tea. He also cut himself a slab of bread and buttered it, spooning the sweet honey Meri had grown to love. He did take liberties!

"I'm sorry to hear of your injury," he said. "Has Niko been able to help?"

She shifted in her chair. At least he was unlikely to see her tail when it was shielded by the table. "He has been most obliging. Nikolas has some healing gift, from his father, I think."

Jazara got a far-off look in his eye. "Niko's papa was a wonderful man, a truly selfless individual. Unfortunately, he became ill and died."

"Nikolas told me he was at sea when his parents succumbed to the fever," Meri said. "He blames himself."

Jazara snorted. "He's hard on himself, that one. Any fool could see it wasn't his fault."

"Is that why he stays out here, alone?"

He frowned at her. "If you're just a passing guest as you say, you don't need to know all of Niko's secrets."

"So, he does have secrets? I know of his brother's disappearance. Are there other mysteries Nikolas keeps?"

Jazara stared at her.

Meri had to understand all of Nikolas if she was to aid him. "I think he needs help."

Jazara gulped the last of his tea and got to his feet, staring down at her. "He's fine just as he is, Lady Merielle. Don't go poking your nose into his past, Niko won't like it." He bowed and walked to the doorway. "Farewell, My Lady." The door closed behind him.

Now it was not just Nikolas who knew of her existence, but Jazara and whomever he decided to tell. She might no longer be safe here. What if the queen came to enquire about her cousin? Meri thought it unlikely. She was almost sure a queen would not travel into the countryside on a whim.

* * *

Nik was leaning against the shoulder of Kain's dashing black charger as his friend emerged from the cottage. He was in no mood to deal with Kain's inevitable questions.

"Ho, Nikolas," Kain said, enveloping Nik's outstretched hand in his and pulling him into a brief bear hug. "I've the pleasure of your company, after all. I'm glad I didn't return to Wildecoast without seeing you."

Nik tensed, waiting for the questioning to begin. His boyhood friend had ever been one for inquisition. Small wonder he had entered the army. He looked whipcord fit too, his body honed by hours in the saddle and practicing the sword.

"It's good to see you, Kain. I'd have stopped in yesterday, but I didn't have time."

"I heard you shared an ale with Grif and visited your cousin."

"It's good to know the gossipmongers haven't been slacking off."

Kain's smile vanished. "I'm not here to make you feel guilt for not visiting me, Niko. I wouldn't have been free, what with the funeral to oversee. Damned Brightcastle nobles and their demands, they've kept me away from my duties for too long. Ramón Zorba and the Prince's betrothed, Lady Benae Branasar, left this morning with their escort. One hundred men! And I can't afford them now, with dark elves raiding our forests."

"Wait up! Our forests? Wildecoast forests?"

"The very ones. Zorba and the lady were ambushed on the way to the keep, and all were killed but those two, including the lady's maid. They traveled on to Wildecoast alone, and I was forced to retrieve the maid's body for a 'proper burial'. Best part of a week lost, but at least I was able to confirm the involvement of the elves."

"I had not heard any of this, besides the funeral."

"Perhaps you've been too preoccupied?"

"You met Merielle?"

Kain nodded, casting him a knowing look. "Easy on the eye, isn't she? No wonder you've kept her all to yourself."

"She's injured, man. I'm not going to drag her miles on horseback."

"I might've let slip a few details about you."

Nik stiffened. "Like what?"

"Like the identity of the cousin from whom you borrowed the clothes."

"Thanks a lot! I can handle this on my own."

"Handle what? As far as I can see, you're just helping a stranger. No need for anything to be 'handled' - unless you're getting in deeper than you should?"

Nik closed his eyes, holding in the harsh words that pushed their way to the fore. He opened them again and stared at his friend. Kain was only trying to look out for him.

"I'm fine. What else did you tell her?"

"Nothing, but she's curious. She thinks you have secrets. You haven't told her the real reason you exiled yourself, have you?"

"None of her business, man. None of yours either, for that matter."

"Look, Niko, things happen, sometimes for no reason. You can't live your life looking back. I'm sure the queen has told you this more than once. You're an incredible leader, and with dark elves gathering, the kingdom needs you more than ever. I'd feel a lot better if I knew you had my back. The sooner you pull on that admiral's uniform the better."

He shook his head. "I'd only be a liability."

"Then sort yourself out! Do whatever it takes, because you're wasting your life." He nudged Nik out of the way, mounted his charger, and galloped off without a backward glance.

Nik entered the cottage and crossed to the fire, two lobsters in his hands. He deliberately avoided Merielle's gaze.

"You saw your friend?" she asked.

He concentrated on dispatching the lobsters and slicing them longways. "I'm sorry he disturbed you."

"The general is a very protective man. You are lucky to call him friend."

Nik stopped his chopping and met her gaze. "Just come right out and ask, Merielle. Let's not dance around this."

Her chin rose and she managed to look down her nose at him, even though he still loomed over her. "Dance around what? Could it be you are talking about our confrontation of this morning when you ran away? Or would it be the fact you are a lord and your cousin is the queen? Or perhaps my fears of discovery, now that General Jazara has paid us a visit?"

He stared at her. How dare she censure him? She was just about the most infuriating being he had ever had the misfortune to meet. "I don't know what to say to that."

"*You* don't know what to say?"

"I can't reassure you more visitors won't follow. Kain will probably have us watched. He takes security very seriously."

"And your safety even more seriously."

He nodded. "I didn't run away."

"What would you call it?"

She folded her arms under her breasts and Nik swallowed hard.

"Ah, thinking space."

"I suppose I should become accustomed to you storming out. Why will you not stand and fight?"

"Believe me, when the situation arises, I'm only too happy to fight."

"Then why not with me?"

"You shouldn't mean enough to me...but I find myself...ah, Goddess!"

He wiped his hands on a cloth and came to sit beside her. She stared at him as if she expected him to take her neck in his hands.

"I don't owe you anything, Merielle. You shouldn't expect it."

"I am sorry I cannot help with your search. The need to find your brother is burning you up." She reached out and grabbed his hand in hers. "I hope you understand why I cannot go back. I do not know what they will do if they find me, but I would rather them kill me than force me to kill."

He felt as though a knife had plunged into his heart. "Can they do that?"

She nodded. "They would call one of our magicians to entrance me, and once I had killed a number of times my mermaid nature would take over. I do not want that. It is not who I am. Please do not force me back to them, Nikolas."

Ah Goddess, she's crying. Nik reached out his free hand to wipe her tears away. "I won't do that, Merielle. But don't you see? I'm caught in the middle between finding Jon and considering your feelings. I sailed out today, and do you know what I worried about? You, and the fact I hadn't fed you or treated your shoulder."

She gave a sad smile. "I am not an invalid, Nikolas. I managed very well."

"So you did, but you see my dilemma. I've given you refuge, but I'm incapable of acting the host. I also find the enmity I once held for you is difficult to maintain. I don't wish to betray Jon. I don't know how to be any more."

"Nikolas," Merielle said, his name a gentle sigh on her lips, 'tell me why you are out here alone."

His head snapped up. She had touched on a deep and festering wound. "It's where I like to live."

"But why?"

"I seek solitude since I lost Jon."

"You lived here before Jon disappeared."

Nik pushed up from the table, his chair falling over backward. "Leave me be, woman!"

He fetched the ointment and Merielle undid the front of her dress. When she pulled the gown off her injured right shoulder, the breath caught in Nik's throat. Her skin glowed soft and ripe over the curve of her breast. His anger from moments ago vanished as his fingers itched to caress that which had been revealed. He pulled his attention back to the spectacular bruises that adorned her shoulder. Merielle sucked in a breath as he began to work the ointment into the damaged tissue.

He lost himself in the motion of his fingers against her flesh, working on the hard knots where the bruising was worst. They were becoming smaller, but still she moaned when he became too vigorous. Her head was tilted to one side, exposing the curve of her neck where a fast pulse beat. Skin, pulse, soft pliant curves, all nudged their way into his awareness. He leaned closer to catch a hint of her fragrance. She chose that moment to turn her head and their lips came perilously close.

Merielle's eyes were wide green pools but it was her mouth Nik focused on. Just a brush of lips would be enough for him to judge if the delights her mouth promised were real. One kiss wouldn't hurt. They could go no further than touching anyway. The temptation was too great, and he slipped further under her spell.

Lips touched lips, and Nik groaned as he sank into her lush softness. He fumbled for the towel to wipe his hands of the ointment before laying his palms alongside her jaw, his fingers reaching into the luxury of her hair. She sighed, gripping the bunched muscles of his right arm as if she held onto him for support.

Nik tentatively sought to enter her mouth and her lips parted before his on another sigh. He had her under his command now, if only they could do what his body yearned to. The cold splash of reality made him pause in his exploration of her mouth. This could go nowhere. He pulled back and she whimpered. They stared at one another.

"I do not wish to stop, Nikolas."

He was mesmerized by the delicate movements of her throat as she swallowed. "I don't either, but what's the point. We can't take this to the usual conclusion."

She frowned. "I am sorry, but that was the first time I have been kissed. I do not understand what normally happens."

He tried not to seem surprised. *What the Goddess am I supposed to tell her?* He thought back to the first time he'd discussed the sexual act with Jon. "Kissing is part of intimate relations between a human man and woman."

Her eyes widened.

"Next is more touching," he went on, "usually of bare skin."

"Yes, I liked the touching."

He swallowed again. "When the man is sufficiently aroused…" He reached for Merielle's hand and placed it on the bulge in his breeches. Her eyes widened. "…as I am now, he pushes his manhood into the secret place between a woman's legs and loses himself and his seed inside her."

"Nikolas!" Merielle pulled her hand back, her breathing ragged. She blushed, and perspiration formed on her brow.

He smiled. "I didn't invent it, so don't look so accusing."

"You would do this thing with me?"

Lately it was almost all he could think about. "I'd consider it."

"You'd plunge that 'thing' into me?"

"There's nowhere to plunge it, Merielle."

"That is how it is between a man and a woman?"

Did she really have to go on like this? Talking about it only made it too clear their attraction could only go so far. He had to get her well and get her out of here before she stuck to him tighter than a limpet on a rock.

"Let me help you dress." He pulled her gown over her bruises and turned his back on her. Her small fist hit the table.

"You said you do not run away."

Nik returned to his dinner preparations, refusing to look at the mermaid. He finished splitting the lobster and sprinkled the halves with herbs and lemon juice.

"Nikolas!"

Taking a deep breath, he met her gaze, stormy and accusing as it was. "There's no point talking about this. I can't 'be' with you and so I shouldn't kiss you. It's not good for either of us."

"We could give each other solace. Our first kiss was enjoyable. I would like to feel your hands on me, on all of me."

Nik choked on his indrawn breath and it was long moments before he could speak. "Not a good idea," he growled.

"When will you allow another being past your defenses?" she asked. "You are half dead inside, and Jon is only part of the story. The general confirmed that."

"Kain didn't tell you that!"

"It was more what he would not say, but I was right about one thing." Her eyes danced with mischief.

Oh, it would never be boring with this woman…mermaid. "What?"

"I knew you were a lord, no matter how you denied it. You have this air of command about you. It cannot be mistaken. But to have a queen for a cousin, that I never imagined. You are close?"

Frustration built within him, not helped by his barely controlled desire. *How do I get myself into these situations?* "Yes, Adriana is dear to me, more so because my own family is gone." The pain struck anew. The loss, the guilt, the resentment.

"If she loves you, she will come looking for me now, yes?" Merielle asked.

"She's a busy woman. I can hardly see her rushing out here to see the woman I have stashed. Anyway, I already told her why I wanted the clothes. Don't worry. I'll protect you."

Merielle looked deep into his eyes and Nik wondered what she saw there. *Too much for my liking.* All these questions designed to reveal his secrets. Why couldn't she just recuperate and leave him be?

"Who will protect *you*, Nikolas?"

"You talk nonsense, Madam. Your presence in my home doesn't give you permission to worm your way inside my head."

"I think they have left you alone for too long."

"I don't need them, and I certainly don't need you. I'm doing just fine, or I was, until I found you on the beach." He blew out a huff of air. "Sometimes, lady, I wish I had—"

"You wish you had left me to die on the beach?"

"No!"

"It *is* what you wish. How would that have helped you?"

"Well, I wouldn't have you here like a prickle in my sock, for one thing."

She shook her head. "You are too blind to see you are letting life pass you by. Is that what Jon would have wanted? Or your parents? Or whomever else you have hurt?"

"Why must there be someone else?"

"There is, I know it. What are you hiding from, Nikolas?"

He leaned his elbows on the kitchen bench and lowered his head into his hands. Even Adriana hadn't been this persistent in taking him to task. *Damned mermaid!* If he told her, perhaps she'd let it be. Perhaps she'd move onto some other poor man whom she thought she could save.

"Nikolas!"

He let out a long sigh. "I was a captain in His Majesty's Royal Navy. I already told you I shunned the wishes of my parents and took to the sea. I guess I was running away then too."

"Or running toward your destiny, perhaps?" Merielle suggested.

"Will you let me tell this? I was at sea for years, only home for short stretches. Jon would sit and listen to me tell my sea adventures for hours. He was much younger than I, and he was swept away by tales of monsters and pirates and battles."

"Mermaids?"

Nik glared at her. "No man was ever lost from my ship to a mermaid," he said. "I guarded those men with my life. I wanted to take them home to their parents, their sweethearts, their wives and children."

As usual, a great weight descended upon him as he recalled that time.

"When Mother and Father died, Jon took to the life of a sailor aboard my ship. I didn't try to dissuade him for I knew the fever that gripped him. I vowed to protect him as I had so many before. All was well for perhaps twelve months. Jon enjoyed the life of a sailor and rose swiftly through the ranks."

"He was like his brother?"

"Not in looks, but in heart."

"You loved him very much."

Nik was immersed in his memories. "We had a frantic week where storm after storm plagued us on our way back from a difficult mission. The crew was exhausted, and I had spent forty-eight hours awake, trying to negotiate a course along the Great Reef. Exhaustion I hope never to experience again overwhelmed me, and I gave over my watch to my lieutenant, entreating him to wake me should he have any concerns. He was an experienced sailor and a good leader. I felt safe leaving him in charge."

He fought the rising panic he always suffered when recounting that night, and disgust at the excuses he made for not being on watch. Merielle's hand reached toward him. He battened down the emotions and pushed on with his story.

"I fell asleep as soon as my head touched the pillow and woke to the sound of splintering wood and screams. The sea was rushing in somewhere close by, and I waded through knee-deep water out in the passage. The ship listed sharply to starboard and I knew we had hit the reef. Most of my men were asleep. I should have got as many of them to safety as I could, but my thoughts flew to Jon who was also below deck. I fought my way to his cabin, calling to my men as I went."

Oh Goddess, will this nightmare never end? He had lived it over and over almost every day since. The screams as the ship went down still tore at his gut. Sweat broke out on his forehead.

"I am sorry, Nikolas," Merielle said.

He hated the sympathy in her eyes. He didn't deserve it.

"I would not have made you relive this had I known the torment."

Nik wanted to fling the words back in her face, to grind her sympathy under his heel. What manner of trauma did she think sent a man into exile? But he stayed silent, swallowing the angry words that pushed their way from his heart. It wasn't her fault.

"I found Jon. He had fallen from his bunk when the ship collided with the reef and hit his head. He was unconscious. I hauled him from the cabin and up onto the deck, then found a boat and placed him in it. The deck was in chaos. My subordinate was trying to manage the men, but they were running everywhere. No one had been dispatched to wake me or the others, so I sent the lieutenant back below. I never saw him again.

"The ship gave an almighty lurch and buried itself further onto the reef. I knew if I didn't lower the boat Jon was in, he'd drown, so I sent it down the side of the ship to the ocean. Before I could retrieve any more sailors and usher them into boats or over the side, the ship began to sink further. If I didn't leap for my life I'd go down with it. I shouted for the lieutenant and dived off, reaching Jon's lifeboat in time to watch the ship break up on the reef. I rowed away some to avoid being caught in the maelstrom of debris. Calm descended after the ship broke up, and I was able to row through the area, checking for survivors. I found two men alive, but they died of their injuries before I could get us back to the shore. I gave them a burial at sea. Jon survived."

"What happened then?" she asked, her face white.

"I rowed for three days and two nights before a skiff picked us up and took us back to Wildecoast. Jon recovered enough to manage brief shifts rowing so I could rest." Nik huffed out a sharp breath, trying to pull his tattered emotions back under control.

"I hold myself responsible for the loss of life. It was one of the largest death tolls in the history of Wildecoast's Navy. Quite an achievement, huh?"

"And so, you turned your back on the navy," Merielle said, her voice a whisper in the room. "What of Jon?"

Nik gave an empty laugh. "As you can imagine, young Jon returned to the sea, against all my pleas for him to pursue another life. He visited when he was ashore, and each time I tried to lure him away from the navy. I didn't want him at sea if I wasn't there to watch over him. One day, I spied a visitor approaching, who turned out to be Jon's captain. He brought the diary and a duffle of belongings and informed me Jon was lost. I took to my skiff and sailed the entire region the captain described, finding no trace of him, no clues."

"I am sorry, Nikolas, for the wreck, and for Jon's loss."

"I don't deserve your compassion." His head throbbed as it always did when he relived the events that had devastated his life.

"No matter how you try to blame yourself, there is little else you could have done when the ship sank."

"The blood of one hundred and six men is on my hands. I was the captain, and as such I'm responsible for each one of them. More than one grieving relative asked me how it came to be that I was able to rescue Jon but not their son or husband. I had no answer for that. I still have no answer. It shames me to the core, except I could never be sorry I brought him out alive. It all seems for naught now that he also is dead. Perhaps it is the Goddess punishing me for choosing my brother over my crew."

"She does not work that way!"

"How do you know? Everything I built is gone - my family, my career, my pride. Do you know how many times I've said, 'if only'? If only I hadn't gone to sleep that night. If only I'd been able to rouse more of the crew. I chose my brother over a hundred men and it haunts me to this day."

"Nikolas!" Merielle's sharp tone cut through his pain. "Who do you help by thinking thus? Yes, things might have been different had you been able to stay awake. But tired men make mistakes. You knew that and wanted to have a fresher man on duty. Is that not so?"

"Makes no difference now."

"Ooh, you are so stubborn!" Merielle's fists bunched and bright spots of color flamed in her cheeks. "If I could walk, I would get up and slap you. You have suffered for over a year. Do you not think it is time to be kind to yourself? I do not think you could have saved more men, but we will never know. Would you sacrifice your own life now or will you make a difference in this world again?"

Nik was silent. No one had spoken to him like this since he was small. Merielle's words had made a chink in the black place inside him - a tiny crack of light into the darkness. Perhaps there was some truth in her words. Perhaps he did disrespect the dead by dwelling on the past and refusing to forgive himself. He took a deep breath, and when he let it go, his heart felt lighter.

"I'll think on what you've said. There must be a way to make these tragedies mean something besides sorrow and waste."

Merielle's face lit up like a beacon and he was drawn to her against his will. He righted the chair and sat beside her. He took her hands and placed them on either side of his face. Her fingers tensed as if they had never touched a man's skin. His eyes fixed on her lips and he was again drawn to their lush welcome, his tongue exploring the innocent warmth that lay beyond. Then suddenly her tongue battered past the barrier of his mouth and she plundered his secrets just as joyfully as he had hers. He thought again that she would never bore him.

Lust drove him to strip the clothes from her and take her there and then...But he could not. He pulled away.

"I think it is high time you returned to the sea," he said.

Her head jerked up and her eyes widened. "But I cannot return. I explained."

"I speak only of a dip in the ocean, my fine house guest. You're a wild creature. It can't be good to be cooped up in a cottage on dry land. Shed your gown and we'll ride down the cliffs so you can freshen up."

"I am fine, Nikolas. Do not trouble yourself."

"You gave me good advice. Now I wish to give you something in return."

"I cannot."

"What do you mean?"

"I am too afraid. I would rather do anything than ride that beast down the cliffs."

"But you've already done so."

"Please do not make me do it again."

"Merielle, I assure you Storm won't hurt you."

"You cannot carry me?"

"I told you that before."

He watched as she battled her demons. Her face, usually so composed, flitted through a range of emotions from terror to determination. He wondered what would win; her innate toughness, or the fear. She had already overcome it once, but perhaps that day her physical condition had numbed her. Now, with all her faculties restored, the thought of facing the horse again might be too much.

She let out a deep breath and her eyelids fluttered closed. When she opened them again, she stared at Nik and he knew her determination had won.

"I will ride to the ocean, but you must hold me as you did the first time."

* * *

Meri was naked, the gentle ocean waves supporting her body the way it had since her birth. No matter how this ended, the sea would always be a part of her, something ingrained in her very being. Nothing could ever erase that. Her hair floated past her face in crimson clouds, her tail plumped, and her heart uplifted. This was life, and a pang of deep sorrow struck at the thought she must leave most of it behind. It was unfair, but Meri dwelled in the hope that she would gain more than she lost, especially if Nikolas was the man who chose her.

Hope swelled. This morning she had almost lost faith in her tortured sailor, but he had returned more confused than angry, and he had admitted he cared for her. He was moved by her body, or at least the top half of it. If she could only entice him to forget they could not carry their physical attraction any further, perhaps there was a chance he would fall for her. He needed her, that was clear.

CHAPTER 7

MERI had made up her mind. It would be Nikolas. The very first human she encountered in fleeing her people was the man she would spend the rest of her life with. So savage he had been on the beach that first morning, but he had mellowed. The week since her dip in the ocean had been the best of her life.

Her shoulder slowly healed, and in mere days she would be fit enough to resume her search, or so Nikolas thought. At times when he didn't know she was looking, she spied a bleak expression on his face; she believed she was the cause. He was beginning to dread her leaving. But she would not leave, and soon she could reveal that.

She had not returned to the ocean over the last seven days. The thought of traveling down the narrow cliff trail on that wild beast was more than she could contemplate. Nikolas, brave and brash as he was, did not understand her fear, no matter how hard she tried to explain.

Each morning after breakfast, as Nikolas tidied the kitchen and swept the cottage, Meri sang her song of changing. She was happiest then; the two of them made quite the domestic picture. She was sure this must be how it was in human families. Nikolas did his chores in a daze as Meri sent the song swirling around him. And her efforts eventually bore fruit.

Tiny changes manifested themselves in her tail. The tips contracted and a valley appeared in the center, as though it would split to create legs. Indentations also appeared in the fins of her tail where the toes would emerge. The changes were subtle but painful, and she had to mask that pain or reveal to Nikolas what was occurring. He must not know, not yet.

But the changes told Meri she was winning. She would not be changing if Nikolas was unmoved by her. His regard for her grew each day and that was why her body altered. The combination of his feelings - dare she say, his love - for her, and the notes of the song were changing her into a human woman. Soon there would be no turning back.

The thought sent trepidation as well as joy into her heart. She wanted Nikolas to love her, not just so she could have this new life but so she could build a life with him and give him what he missed most: a family. But there were sacrifices. Humans seldom lived past seventy years. Meri did not know if she were truly ready for that. Could she live and love Nikolas enough in the next fifty years to make the sacrifice worth it?

Ticking away at the back of her mind was the realization she would have to reveal her plan. Soon Nikolas must be made aware of the changes to her body, where they were headed, and why. How would he react? Would his new love for her be enough to help him overlook her deceit?

She shook her head. They could be so good together. Already his kisses promised so much more than she had ever foreseen when she had contemplated life on the land. And when he placed his arms around her, she knew the thrill of being safe and protected. It was a feeling she had rarely experienced in the past. Oh, how intoxicating was the thought of spending a lifetime in his arms. But would it be enough?

* * *

Nik swept the cottage in time with the song that swirled around him. He loved Merielle's singing, foreign though it was. At first, he had tried to blot it out, but he just couldn't ignore the effect her voice had on him. It probed at the deepest reaches of his mind and swept him away to play with the dolphins and whales. The part of his mind that rejected anything linked with Jon's death rebelled, but that segment was becoming smaller day by day. He had been alone so long, and it was a joy to share his life again.

There, he had said the word: joy. Merielle gave him joy. Each day he became more accustomed to her presence and her strange ways. She was steadily working her way into his life and the thought of losing her was unwelcome. But leave she must. They inhabited different worlds, and he had to keep his mind firmly fixed on that.

But she had given him a precious gift. In such a short time, she had jerked him out of his introspection and grief and made him feel and think about other things. She had given him a different perspective on life. Even when Merielle moved on, Nik knew he'd be able to pick up his life and, in time, return to society. It was still waiting for him. Perhaps he'd even give the queen what she wanted and become her admiral.

Merielle's song ended. "Nikolas, could you carry me outside into the sun, please?"

He turned to her, his thoughts still upon his cousin the queen, and his breath caught. She was so exquisite it still surprised him. *Imagine her at court! She'd cast the other ladies into the shade.* But, Merielle in Wildecoast castle would be a risk too great to contemplate.

He walked over and bent to lift her, the plunging neckline of the purple gown she wore drawing his gaze. Such delights this mermaid offered! It was enough to drive most men insane. He lifted her, very deliberately dragging his eyes from the tempting cleavage on display.

"Are you sure you're eating enough?" he asked. "You seem lighter."

Her gaze was soft as it usually was after her singing. "Yes, of course, Nikolas. I have been inactive, that is all. My muscles have shrunk but they will return when they are used."

Her words reminded him of her imminent departure, and he stood gazing down at her, realizing he would never forget these days. "When will you leave?"

"I will be ready to travel any day now. You will have your cottage and your life to yourself once again."

"A poor bargain."

"I am sorry I could not give you what you wanted," she said, her eyes large with regret.

"That's not what I meant." He stood holding her, not wanting to let her go. She felt good against his body and it was torture.

"What did you mean then?" she asked.

"Having the place to myself is a poor exchange for your company."

She gasped. "Nikolas!" Her lips parted and he remembered their softness, how they had swept him away.

He carried her to his bed and placed her gently on the covers. He stood staring down at her, at the wonder in her eyes.

"I know this is wrong, Merielle, but I crave your skin against mine. Would you allow it?"

Her eyes widened further, as though this were the last thing she had expected. "Allow it?"

"Yes." Was he not making himself clear? "I wish to undress you and myself, and…touch you, have you touch me."

Nikolas knew he was probably torturing himself, but at least he would have this to remember when she was gone. *Idiot! Don't do this!* But he was beyond listening to reason.

He shed his shirt and stood, waiting for her acquiescence.

* * *

Meri's heart fluttered and suddenly the dress seemed to be choking her. Nikolas stood, his breathing ragged and his magnificent aqua eyes blazing. *Never mind his eyes, what about that chest!* It was broad, the glorious muscles defined from years of sailing and hard toil. Golden skin was sprinkled with blond hairs, so different from the hairless skins of the mermen. Her fingertips itched with the need to explore.

But the uncertainty within held her motionless. This was all she had hoped for; he was falling under her spell and yet she had so much hidden. What would happen when he learned she had deceived him? Lured him to love her by the notes of her song? He was a proud man, and moreover still grieved his brother. Meri swallowed the knot that gathered at the back of her throat. Could this ever really work?

His blazing eyes were hooded by a frown. "Merielle?"

"Dear Nikolas, to touch you would be wonderful. It is just that I…"

He lay beside her on the bed and brushed a strand of hair from her cheek. "I know, Lady, I feel it too. Nothing can come of this, except grief when we can't consummate the act. It's foolhardy to begin something we can't complete, and yet, I can't deny the urge which drives me."

Meri's insides clenched. He was such an honorable man. And she would manipulate him to suit her ends. But, when he found out, as he surely would, what then?

That was for later - she would not deny herself or him this pleasure. Nikolas had experienced so little joy over the past year. He deserved this. She pushed the guilt aside and ran her fingertips down the side of his neck and across his shoulder.

He shivered. Meri felt every small contour, every ridge, every dip, as she explored his shoulder and ran her hand down the bulging bicep. She allowed her other hand to wander in the same way. But what next? Why didn't he kiss her instead of staring as if he wished to eat her? At least then she would not have to think, she could just let her instinct guide.

He seemed content to watch, perhaps still uncertain they should venture further, but then his hand touched her throat and a bolt of desire speared somewhere low in her belly. That was new! She could not help but release a gasp as her eyes met his. He smiled, a lazy smile that sent another, smaller strike where the first had hit.

"Kiss me," she breathed, struggling to get the words past the lump in her throat.

Triumph flared in his eyes as his mouth swooped toward hers; then there was nothing else but softness, heat and desire. His arm swept beneath her and Meri was crushed to that broad, glorious expanse of chest. She took a moment to appreciate the hard ridges of his stomach, then lost herself.

CHAPTER 8

MERI awoke in the first light of dawn and for a moment didn't remember where she was. She pushed herself into a sitting position and realized she was naked, her gown discarded on the floor beside the bed. *The bed!*

A soft sound made her turn. Nikolas slept beside her, his handsome face relaxed and turned to her as he slept on his stomach.

She closed her eyes, reliving the ecstasy of intimate moments spent in her lover's arms, of his kisses on every part of her body. *He had kissed her tail!* Nikolas had worshipped her, loved her and run his hands from the tip of her tail to the top of her head. There was not an inch of her he did not know.

Heat rose in her cheeks at the thought of what she had done to him. Even now, she could not help herself. His firm, tanned buttocks beckoned to her, urged her to knead them. She reached toward his tempting rear and stopped. What was that mark at his hip? It looked like a tattoo.

She squirmed closer to Nikolas's hip, trying to get a better look at the mark. A tail? It was only small, and the rest was hidden. She traced the part she could see, and he stirred, pulling his leg up and flexing his hip so the tattoo became fully visible.

Meri froze, her heart pounding. She had seen it before - not on Nikolas, but on another man; a young man. The same tattoo of a tiny seahorse! Why did that familiarity strike terror into her heart?

Panic fluttered in Meri's brain like hunted bait fish. *Stop! Think this through.* She closed her eyes and cast her mind back. Memory struck like a bolt of lightning and she was transported to that night when she sat on the rock, the body of a young sailor in her lap - a sailor with the tattoo of a seahorse on his hip. Feelings flooded her: despair, anger, hopelessness. Raindrops of memory fell until she recalled the entire shameful chapter.

The handsome young sailor had been so smitten with her. The fear, the disgust at what she had to do swamped her anew. *Breathe, breathe.* Her family had so little trust in her, that two of her sisters were there to witness her first kill. He had seemed nice, the young sailor. He was about her age, full of the excitement of youth. She had swum closer than usual and spoken with him. He told her of his trip, of his kingdom home. Meri swallowed down the lump that threatened to choke her. *Breathe, breathe.*

"Merielle, what's wrong?"

Her eyes snapped open to find Nikolas kneeling over her. Shock swirled and she almost swooned. She closed her eyes and waited for the spinning to stop. *Time, I need time.*

"Merielle!"

"I need space, that is all," she said through gritted teeth.

"Open your eyes, talk to me."

Meri shook her head. She could not do this now. Not before she had it sorted in her head.

"It was too much for you, this intimacy," he said. "I should have realized it was a mistake."

She shook her head again, the ache in her heart spreading through her breastbone. "No mistake, Nikolas."

"Then why are you distressed?"

He will not give you time until you explain yourself.

She took a deep breath and opened her eyes, struggling to bring the chaos in her mind under control. "I do not regret what has passed between us, I merely require time to adjust. Do not be afraid."

He reached to brush the hair from her face, his gaze tender.

Oh, Nikolas, why must this happen to us?

His lips feathered hers for mere seconds before he pulled away. "I know just what will help," he said. "I'll make us breakfast and we'll talk. I'll even cut up some of that raw squid you love so much."

Tears sprang in Meri's eyes. He was so sweet, and she was going to hurt him, *again*. She nodded, unable to speak.

He lay her down and drew the blanket over her nakedness, kissed her on the forehead then left the room, taking his clothes with him.

* * *

Nik whistled while he kneaded the bread but inside his guts churned. He knew how Merielle felt, he thought. He hoped. For if she was feeling as he did, there might be hope for their relationship. He snorted. Who was he kidding? They could have no meaningful relationship. Nothing had changed. She was still a mermaid and he a human. So, she had changed his life in the short time they had been together. So, he now felt hope for the first time in years. So, he might now be able to move on with his life. What did it matter?

It mattered a lot. They had only just scratched the surface of what their relationship could mean. But she was a mermaid and he was confused. As he imagined Merielle was. This was not supposed to happen. He should be looking for a bride and planning a family. He should be taking the queen up on her offer and assuming control of the fleet. He should be helping to defend the kingdom's borders.

Instead, he was stuck out here. But thanks to Merielle, he could at least see that now. His hope, his enthusiasm for life, his feelings, had been reawakened by one beautiful, dangerous liaison. This might be love. It felt like love. How in hell had it happened?

As Nik popped the bread in to bake, he mused on the word, love. If he was in love with Merielle, where did that leave him? Stuck at sea without a paddle? Seemingly, when all they could ever be was friends. Talk about the ultimate frustration. Could he live like that? Would Merielle want to?

The sound of hooves came from outside. More than one horse.

Damn!

Nik checked the door to the bedroom was closed and moved to the front door. He peered through the peep hole.

Damn! Kain Jazara and a woman. At least it wasn't the queen. That much he could see.

Nik opened the door as Kain dismounted. He bowed to the lady still upon her horse.

"My Lady, General Jazara," Nik said.

"Ah, Nikolas, well met," Kain said, offering his hand. "How goes it?"

He shook Kain's hand, stretching his neck to ease the tension that had crept in with the arrival of his guests. *Damn, why had he done that? May as well tell these two he had something to hide.*

"It goes well, Kain. What could be better than a life by the sea, pleasing oneself?"

"Indeed, Niko." Jazara turned to his companion. "Are you acquainted with Lady Alique Zorba?"

Nik bowed. "I believe we've met on several occasions. You grow more beautiful each time I see you, Lady Alique. Are you now one of the queen's ladies?"

Alique's blue eyes speared Nik and he was instantly wary.

"That I am, Lord Cosara, and she has charged me with this duty."

"And that would be?"

"Help me down and I'll explain," Alique said, her eyebrows raised.

Nik groaned inwardly but what choice did he have? He approached the black mare and helped Alique dismount. She looked deep into his eyes and he steeled himself to withstand her scrutiny.

"You may remove the parcel from the packhorse, Lord Cosara. The queen has sent it to you."

He frowned at her words. A parcel? But he did as he was told and removed a soft lumpy bundle wrapped in cloth from the third horse. "Give her my thanks, Lady Alique. I'd also like to thank you and the general for delivering it."

"Are you not going to ask what it is?" Alique said.

This was going badly. Nik knew what the lady was building to, or he thought he did. He knew her type - nosy, caustic - and he liked to avoid them if possible. One advantage to living apart from the court, or so he'd thought. "Plenty of time for that later, My Lady."

She frowned. "The parcel contains more gowns for your friend. The queen thought she might grow tired of the three she already gave you."

"That's considerate of Her Majesty. I'm sure my guest will be most grateful."

"I am also to take the soiled gowns back with me for cleaning, Lord Cosara. I thought I might visit with your guest while I am here. She must be longing for female companionship after over a week alone with you, captivating company though I'm sure you are."

"That's kind of you, but I fear she's indisposed. We might have to defer your chat for a later time."

Alique stepped close so her perfume swirled around him. He held her gaze which was surprisingly difficult. She would make a fearsome adversary; one thing Nik didn't need. "I promised the queen I'd meet your guest. Would you send me back to her without having fulfilled my obligations?"

Your problem, Lady. Nik ground his teeth If he didn't acquiesce, they'd only be under more scrutiny. May as well get it over with. "If you'd please wait here, I'll make sure she's ready to greet you. You've had an early start. Please stay for breakfast."

Triumph flared in Alique's eyes, but she merely nodded and stepped backwards. Kain grinned.

You'll keep, Jazara! Nik reined in his temper and stalked into the house with the parcel, closing the door behind him. He found Merielle still naked under the covers. His gut clenched, reminding him of his earlier dilemma. Time for that later.

"Who is here, Nikolas?"

He tossed the parcel on the bed and began unwrapping it. "General Jazara and one of the queen's ladies-in-waiting. They've brought you a parcel from Her Majesty." He pulled a stunning golden gown from the wrappings, as well as a black and silver creation, and a red gown. These were not Adriana's cast-offs, even Nik could remember seeing her in the golden dress at court. She had no business sending garments such as these to his guest.

"Oh my," Merielle said, "they are more beautiful than the first three!"

"Put one on, they're coming in for breakfast. Hurry, they're waiting outside."

"Waiting outside? Can you do that to the queen's attendant?"

"No, but what else was I to do? I can't have you parading your tail before them."

Merielle shed the blanket, her glorious breasts almost inducing Nik to push her back into the mattress and kiss them until she moaned with ecstasy, as she had last night. The thought of what they had shared made him hard, but he pushed his urges aside and tossed the red dress over her head. In moments she had pulled the gown into position, scooped low over her shoulders and showing the perfect flesh of her cleavage. Her bare collarbones drew him. He tossed restraint aside and kissed her along one exquisite shoulder. She moaned and rolled her head over to one side, allowing him access to the pale flesh of her neck. He took full advantage.

Nik was gasping by the time he pulled away. He gazed at the darkened pupils of Merielle's eyes, seeing the same battle raging within her.

"You should finish dressing," he said, drawing the dress together at the back and fastening the many small buttons. Just as well he'd had practice the last week or so.

"There," Nik said, handing her the comb. Merielle's face was flushed and she still appeared far away after his kisses. *Damn visitors!* He had his cousin to thank for this. Serve her right if he never agreed to be admiral of her fleet.

When Merielle had combed her hair and washed her face, he drew her into his arms and carried her to her chair at the table.

"We should leave this seat for the queen's lady, Nikolas," Merielle protested, squirming a little in his arms. It fired his blood to have her move so against him. *I have it bad.* Hopefully Kain wouldn't notice his feelings for his house guest.

"This is my home and I decide who sits where," he snapped, adding when she frowned. "This particular lady we must keep in her place. Trust me."

"Very well, Nikolas," she said. "I am sure you know best."

Such meekness from Merielle was uncommon. Nik wondered what had brought it on as he walked out the front door and approached his visitors.

Lady Alique looked decidedly disgruntled. Kain had tethered the horses and was leaning against the cottage wall, at ease. Like most soldiers, he took his rest where he could but was always ready for action.

"Finally!" Alique said. "You took your time."

"Apologies for the wait. My guest was still abed, My Lady. She has dressed and is now ready to receive you. Please enter."

Alique mumbled something as she brushed past him into the cottage. Kain smirked.

"You could've given me some warning, my friend," Nik muttered to Kain. "My guest isn't used to receiving royal visitors, nor am I."

"Sorry." Kain didn't look a bit sorry to Nik. Amused, yes, remorseful, no.

"You'll keep, Kain, and so will Adriana. Now we'd better catch up before Merielle needs rescuing."

Alique had paused in the center of the living area and was staring at Merielle. Nik's heart leapt into his throat as he checked her tail wasn't exposed. Why was the lady staring?

Merielle's eyes were wide and her body stiff as if waiting for an attack.

"Lady Alique Zorba," Nik said, "may I introduce you to Merielle, my house guest. Merielle, Lady Alique."

"I am honored to meet you, My Lady," Merielle said. "Please forgive that I remain seated. I have an injury."

Alique approached the table, still appearing mesmerized. "Your hair, is it real?"

Merielle's eyes widened. "Ah, yes, it is."

Alique ran her fingertips down Merielle's bright crimson tresses.

Nik cleared his throat. "Lady, you forget yourself."

Alique blushed almost to the color of the hair she clearly admired. "Oh, please excuse my rudeness, Merielle. I don't know what came over me."

"Of course, My Lady." Merielle took a deep breath. "Please sit down." She looked at Kain. "And you too, General Jazara."

Kain bowed and pulled a chair out for Alique before taking a seat himself. He sat sprawled with his legs under the table, again appearing at ease even though he watched the ladies and especially Merielle, with the eyes of a hawk.

Nik went into the kitchen and took the fresh bread from the oven, setting it to cool on the bench. He made the tea, and selected his best cup and saucer from the shelf. This he gave to Alique, pouring her tea and offering the honey pot.

"Thank you, Lord Cosara," Alique said, taking a sip of her tea. "You make a good brew."

"No one else to make it, My Lady," he said, wondering where this conversation would take them.

"If you returned to your estate, you'd have an army of servants to make the tea. It seems a waste for you to live in this lonely outpost. Don't you miss court?"

Nik nearly growled. "In a word, Lady, no." Small talk had never been his thing, so if Alique expected him to partake, she'd be disappointed. He offered her the fresh bread and she accepted a piece. She buttered it, spreading it with honey.

Alique turned to Merielle. "And what of you? Do you not yearn for more company than the captain here? Handsome though he is."

Damned interfering nobility. This was why he had fled society in the first place. None of it was real. The only reality was here, on this lonely cliff, with Merielle. He nearly choked at the last thought. When had he included Merielle in anything? Best to keep his wits on the visitors.

"I am recuperating, Lady Alique," Merielle said. "It was good of Nikolas to take me in. I feel very fortunate to have his protection. Also, your queen has been most generous. You must thank her on my behalf. The gowns are wonderful."

"Thank her yourself," Alique said. "There is a ball the week after next and the queen has asked me to convey her desire that you attend, escorted by Lord Cosara. She will supply another gown for the occasion. Now I have seen you, I think I know just the style and color."

"Oh, I could not—" Merielle said.

"Out of the question—" Nik said at the same time.

They looked at each other, Merielle's eyes wide with what appeared to be distress. Nik almost laughed. Oh yes, he'd take his mermaid to the ball. What was this? A fairy tale? How did he get himself into these dilemmas?

A frown marred Alique's peaches and cream complexion. "Why ever not? I would hazard a guess Merielle has never been the guest of a queen."

"You'd be right in that," Nik said, offering Kain the bread and honey. "She'd feel out of her depth." *Ha, that was funny: a mermaid out of her depth.* He smiled at Merielle, but she merely looked annoyed. *What?*

Alique addressed Merielle. "Do you truly wish to turn down this offer? I think it most generous of the queen to provide you an invitation and a gown."

Merielle dragged her gaze from Nik to Alique. "I am most grateful for the invitation and gowns, My Lady, but I would have to speak with Lord Cosara before accepting. He may not be available to escort me."

"He's available," Kain said.

Nik glanced at his friend. He knew that look, it seemed he was Kain's next project. Nik quirked an eyebrow and Kain grinned. Oh yes, they understood each other alright.

He could see they were getting nowhere. "I'll think on it, Lady Alique."

Alique's gaze struck him like a spear. "I'll expect you both to attend the ball fourteen days from tonight, unless I hear otherwise. The queen's dressmakers will commence the gown and it will be ready and waiting for Merielle when she attends the ball." She rose from the table.

Nik and Kain stood as well.

"Lord Cosara," she said, "please bundle the other gowns and I'll convey them to the palace for cleaning. I'll return them once they are ready."

Nik gathered the two gowns that hung in the living area and entered the bedroom. He added the third gown he had stripped from Merielle's body last night and bundled them all into the cloth that had protected the gowns delivered that morning.

He emerged from the bedroom and followed Alique and Kain out to the horses. He strapped the bundle to the pack horse.

"Any news on the dark elves?" Nik asked.

Kain swung up onto his horse. "They've gone quiet again. Probably licking their wounds, at least in this part of the kingdom."

"Plans?"

"I prefer not to discuss them with you at this stage, my friend, that is until you resume your naval career. I told you, the kingdom needs you."

Nik battled down the resentment the snub created. Kain was arrogant, he should be used to that by now. Instead he turned to Lady Alique, who sat on her horse, flicking the reins back and forth. "I wish you safe travel, My Lady," he said, bowing.

"Thank you, Lord Cosara. Until the ball. I'll save you a dance."

Nik nodded. "Until then."

She turned her horse and galloped away. Kain cast Nik a despairing glance and followed, hot on the impulsive lady's heels.

Nik stood shaking his head, until the two riders were just a speck on the road back to Wildecoast. *A ball indeed! What am I supposed to do about that?* He returned inside to Merielle who was frowning into her teacup.

"Well, that was an interesting visit," he said.

Her gaze snapped to his, green eyes filled with worry. "Interesting! What are we going to do, Nikolas? I cannot go to a ball!"

"Obviously. We must make some excuse. Alique has seen that you can't stand. We'll say you haven't recovered sufficiently."

"Did you not hear her? She will come back to ask why!"

"You think?"

"Lady Alique is determined, Nikolas. You know her. What will she do when we do not arrive?"

Nik considered. "Mm, probably ride out here to check on us. Weren't you planning to be gone by then?"

Merielle looked guilty. *Why?*

"Merielle, you're sufficiently healed to leave this place and continue your journey."

She chewed her bottom lip. "You wish for me to go?"

"That's the plan." The thought of the empty days and nights ahead without her filled him with something close to despair. How had she come to mean so much in just a little more than a week?

"Oh…I thought, after last night…it was so…"

"Last night was magical, but we'd be unwise to invest ourselves in something that cannot be. I saw your uncertainty this morning, and you were right to feel it. As much as I enjoy your company, you must move on. You must find your destiny, your niche. Likewise, I must make some decisions about my future. I've wallowed in guilt and despair long enough and you've made me see I was wasting my life. You've given me perspective, and for that I'll always thank you."

A tear trickled down her cheek and his heart responded with a jagging ache, but he'd do her no favors if he allowed her to believe they could ever make each other happy, let alone fulfilled. He leaned over and kissed the wet track of the tear, and then her lips. When she deepened the kiss, Nik drew back. No use torturing himself.

"You are not running away again?" she said.

Funny how this woman could pierce his heart one moment and infuriate him the next. "This isn't running away!" he said, through gritted teeth. "Goddess, what future can we have? At every turn it's obvious, and yet you try to make me feel guilty. Haven't I had enough guilt?" The words were out before he could stop himself and he instantly regretted them.

"Yes, you have, and I would never try to add to it. You are right. I will make preparations to leave."

"Stay as long as you like, Merielle, just know we can never be more than house guests, friends, a port in a storm. Now if you'll excuse me, I must tend Storm and get fish for later."

* * *

Nikolas fetched his hat and left the cabin. Meri heard him clanging about fixing Storm's feed.

This was it, then, the moment of truth. He had said she could stay for now, but how to stay long enough for his love to change her permanently? How to deal with the fact she had been involved in Jon's death? She felt like a pearl in a clam, squeezed from both sides. On the one side were her goals, her feelings, her desires, and on the other, the consequences of her secrets. If she told Nikolas about Jon, he would never forgive her, but if she did not, how could she ever live with herself? He deserved to know the truth about Jon's death so he could say goodbye and lay that ghost to rest. What if she left and he never knew? Would he move on with his life, take up his career and never look back? Or would he be forever burdened with doubt over the disappearance of his brother?

She could lead him to Jon's final resting place. It was like a bell tolling in her ear. Imagining the scene where she would reveal to Nikolas that she had seen Jon die, Meri's heart beat like it would pound its way out of her chest. A roaring filled her, and the room started to spin. She laid her forehead on her arms against the table and closed her eyes. Gradually the spinning slowed.

Jon's final resting place. She could confess the truth, or at least part of it, and give Nikolas closure. Furious wouldn't even come close to describing his likely reaction. Would she even be able to explain she had not wanted Jon to die, had tried to save his life? Nikolas would not want to listen, would not be capable of hearing the words. All he would feel was loss and pain and betrayal. Would it be better to leave him as he was, never to know the truth about his brother? He was moving forward with his life and she had given him that gift. She had shown him the light at the end of the tunnel. He had more work to do if he was to forgive himself for the loss of lives on his ship, but at least he was considering returning to the navy, and that was a huge step.

Meri's heart ached. She was in very deep with Nikolas. She wanted to be the one to heal him, to lead him from the darkness. But she did not deceive herself. If Nikolas knew about her involvement in Jon's death, he would never forgive her.

And then there was her personal predicament. She was changing, and she had no experience to tell her if the changes now begun would complete themselves away from the source of love that had triggered them. She feared not. How could she turn her back on *her* light? This was her chance at a life she could be proud of, a worthy life, not a series of seductions and murders. She would not go back to that willingly, but the thought of revealing the truth to Nikolas filled her with fear.

CHAPTER 9

NIK quickly caught enough fish for their dinner and sat, the boat bobbing in the gentle waves. A friendly dolphin raised its beak from the water several times, but he didn't have the heart to notice this morning.

How did he get himself into these binds? At some stage he must start making good decisions instead of those that took him into disaster and unhappiness. By the age of thirty, as he was now, he should have learned life's lessons. Instead he kept listening to his heart, kept blundering in, instead of stepping back and thinking logically and clearly.

He had a gorgeous mermaid living in his cabin and she had to go before he got in any deeper, before anyone discovered the truth of her identity. He didn't want to lose Merielle and so he had briefly contemplated appearing with her at the ball, hoping the gown the queen organized would be long enough to cover her tail. He had quickly discarded the thought. There was too much risk. Even if the gown were suitable, there was still the chance disaster would occur. He smiled grimly as he imagined the uproar if her tail should come to light. *No, no, no.*

When would she leave? He had as much told her to go, but there was no need to hurry. The ball was two weeks away; two weeks during which he could enjoy her company, kiss her luscious curves and amazing mouth. He grew hard remembering. Merielle was a dangerous addiction - a dangerous, beautiful, mesmerizing dependence.

He swallowed hard at the thought. Did he depend on her? After only ten days was it true that he might be unable to live without her?

No! It wasn't possible. She was nice to have around, and she'd brought him part of the way back to his former existence, but she couldn't remain in his life permanently. It would never work. *Damn!* He'd known he was making a mistake that very first morning, when he'd agreed to give her shelter. Again, listening to his heart, not his head.

Alarm bells going off all over and I invite her to stay! Back then he thought she might lead him to Jon, but it had only taken days to realize she couldn't help. But she had made a difference in other ways, encouraging him to speak of his ordeals and making him see he was too hard on himself. He had a long way to go but at least he could imagine ending his self-imposed exile. Though Alique's visit had reminded him of the advantages of a life away from court.

Sea voyages would take care of that. He'd never be tamed. He'd caught a speculative look in the lady's eye when she had gazed upon him. As the queen's cousin, he'd fought off more than one advance by a woman hoping to improve her social standing and quickly told them he wasn't on the market.

A confirmed bachelor he had always imagined himself. Not for him the pain of losing a wife or children or leaving them alone to fend for themselves when he was away at sea. But Merielle, even though their union was impossible, had made him imagine what it would be like to love a woman and have her waiting for him when he docked; to return and find her round with his seed, and to contemplate the children who would carry on his name. Adriana had already begun to chip him about his lack of an heir, but he was her cousin, not her brother, and if he died heirless, the estate would revert to the queen's family anyway. From Nik's point of view, that was hardly a reason to hurry into matrimony.

Nik stirred, irritated by the way his thoughts jumped from one subject to another. Lately he had the attention span of a gnat. He couldn't hope to return to his former position in the navy while he suffered from this vagueness. But could Merielle be the cause of this mindset, or would she lead him out of it? He really didn't know anything except he would miss her. Instead of turning his world on its head, she had begun to restore him to humanity. But she couldn't be presented at court, and they could never be more than friends. Sooner or later, she must depart. The thought opened a deep pit within him.

* * *

Meri had worked herself into a frenzy after Nikolas left. She tried to keep busy, but the pain in her lower body was a constant reminder of the changes occurring within her. She was becoming human. As if to accentuate the fact, a blast of agony scorched up the center of her tail and flared out into her hips. That was the strongest one yet. The pain would be impossible to hide from Nikolas. She reached for the powders he kept on the kitchen table and mixed some into strong, cold tea. Gulping it down, she collapsed back in her chair, the combination of the medication and the pain making her sick to her stomach. Sweat broke out all over her. At this rate she would ruin the beautiful gown she had donned for the visitors this morning.

At least with pain like this, she couldn't dwell on the dilemma she faced - whether to tell Nikolas the truth about his brother. No matter how she looked at it, she could not decide the course that would give the best outcome for all concerned. Perhaps there was none.

She imagined living with Nikolas for the rest of her life knowing she kept the truth from him. It would eat at her, possibly drive her mad in the long run. Was it not better to reveal all now and allow him to decide if he could accept her? But Nikolas did not know she was changing, didn't know there might be a future, that she might be able to make him happy. And she could not tell him, with this other secret looming over them. Meri had to face the fact that, even though her change was proof of his new love for her, such a love was also vulnerable. It could die before it ever really blossomed, and her secrets would be what killed it. There was really nothing she could do to safeguard their relationship. He could still turn his back on her when he discovered she was changing, and she had sought that change without telling him.

As the pain faded to a dull ache, Meri came to a decision. There was only one course of action that could save her integrity, and it was to tell Nikolas about Jon, and to do so at the very earliest opportunity.

* * *

Nik whistled a sea shanty as he opened the door to the cottage, his eyes immediately seeking Merielle. She was seated at the kitchen table, slumped in the chair, her eyes closed. His heart picked up its pace, spurred by fear for her. What was wrong now?

Lately she had been showing signs of pain but every time he questioned her, she denied it. Nik knew illness well enough to understand what the frequent sheen of sweat on Merielle's brow meant. She suffered. Her lies itched at him because they spoke of a lack of trust. Surely he had done enough to earn her trust by now?

As he stood gazing at her, she opened her eyes and looked at him, her soul bared. Fear and self-loathing blazed there.

"What's wrong, Merielle?" he asked. "And don't deny it, for I see it in your eyes."

Not one hint of a smile graced her face. "I will not deny it, Nikolas."

"Then tell me."

"You will not like it."

Nik ground his teeth, his stomach bunching. He stalked past and placed the bucket of fish in the pantry then returned to sit at the table opposite her. No good to appear too intimidating. Already he felt the tension in the room.

"Tell me."

She drew a deep breath. "I learned something this morning."

A light flashed on in Nik's mind as he remembered her distress on waking. Such a glorious night. His manhood stirred despite his discomfort. "I could see you were distressed. What did you learn?"

"I saw the tattoo on your hip, the seahorse."

"Yes, go on."

"I have seen the same tattoo on another man."

Nik froze, his mind leaping back in time to the day Jon had begged his parents for permission to have the seahorse tattooed on his left hip, just like his big brother. "Jon?"

"I think it must have been, though he did not look like you. He had dark hair and was slender. When he smiled, he showed dimples in his cheeks."

A chill rolled down his spine. "Where did you see him?" He had tight control of himself, tighter than ever before. He couldn't jump to conclusions; must discover as much as he could.

"I saw him three times. I believe myself to be the mermaid in Jon's diary."

Nik surged up from his chair and it flew back and smashed against the wall behind him. "You!" Was she the killer he had first imagined her to be? Had he harbored the murderer of his brother in this very house for the past weeks?

She shrank back in her chair. "I did not kill him, Nikolas, no matter what you think. I have told you I fled my people because I could not carry out their wishes."

"Then how did he die?"

"Jon was to be my first kill."

"Merielle," Nik growled, his hands twisted into claws at his sides.

She closed her eyes and drew a deep breath while Nik struggled to comprehend what he was hearing.

"I seduced Jon, but I never intended to kill him. I thought I could fool my mother and sisters into thinking I had done the deed. But in the end, they sent witnesses - my sisters."

A crimson mist enveloped Nik's mind as he imagined the scene: Merielle floating seductively in the waves, singing her murderous melody, his brother leaning over the bow, gaze fixed on her charms. His breath came hard and tight, the air of the cottage choking him. "You lured Jon to his death!"

Her eyes widened and her bosom heaved. "No, Nikolas, please, you must believe me. I did not want to harm him."

"At the very best you played their game. My brother was besotted with *you*, not your sisters. So much for you not being able to help me.

All this time you've taken advantage of my sanctuary when you could have told me what happened to Jon."

"I have only just realized who he was when I saw the tattoo. I had blocked the memory."

"Oh, how convenient!" He sneered. "You could've told me everything you knew. You could've taken me back to the area and shown me. Instead you played me for a fool. Do you know how important this is to me?"

"I know you suffer, and I would do anything to help. That is why I spoke up."

"How can I believe anything that comes from your mouth?" Nik paced the confines of the cottage in a fury, hardly knowing what to do. He wanted to rage against Merielle, he wanted to hurt her any way he could. She had taken his brother; he didn't care about the details. This mermaid he had begun to love had been an integral part of his brother's death, and she wouldn't admit it. But what would it help if she did?

He couldn't hear any more of this. He must get away, to think, to calm down and decide what should be done. One thing was certain, Merielle would show him where his brother had died. She'd show him if he had to drag her out there trapped in a net.

"I'm going out."

"No, please Nikolas, don't leave me," Merielle said. "Stay here and let me explain."

"I can't do this now. I just can't."

"Where are you going?"

"I don't know, and I'm not sure when I'll return. You'll have to fend for yourself." He grabbed his hat and coat and stalked out of the cottage. He truly didn't know where he was headed, he just needed thinking space.

* * *

Nikolas was gone, and there was no telling when, or if, he would return. He didn't need to come back here at all. He had an estate, and the queen would see he was welcomed back into court with open arms. Lady Alique would look after him as well. Meri distracted herself by remembering the predatory gaze Alique had cast upon Nikolas. *Her* Nikolas! If she was not mistaken, the lady would happily get her hooks into the handsome sea captain and busy herself molding him as she saw fit. He would never be free then.

For what seemed like hours, she cried at the table. Nikolas had taken Storm, his hoofbeats fading away toward the city of Wildecoast. What if he fell, or Storm broke his leg in that wild dash? He could lie injured for days and no one would rescue him. His head was in a very bad place and it was thanks to her. *Poor man.* She had only been trying to help, and instead Meri had destroyed his developing faith in her. That might mean a permanent end to his recovery from the trauma of the shipwreck and the loss of his brother.

He would not listen, and she could not blame him. Her actions on that night had been wrong. She should have refused to go along with the kill and the seduction. But then her family would have cast a spell on her, which would have ensured her perpetual existence as a mermaid, ending all her dreams of another life. And Jon would still have died.

No, Jon's only hope had been her plan. Meri had thought she could fool her sisters, but they knew her better than she realized. They had anticipated her deception and taken the matter from her hands. All the details came back to her in stark relief.

The third night of her association with Jon was scheduled for his death. Meri had it all planned out. She left a few minutes early and bolted to the ship, anticipating where it would be after a day's sailing along the coast. It had been easy to find, and Jon was there as he had been the previous two nights. He leaned over the edge when she began her song and her heart had pounded at the risk he took. Fearing her sisters would catch up with her, Meri had sung with more power than ever before and Jon was completely swept away by her song. He had leaped into the ocean and swum toward her, his arms entwining her body when they met.

Meri smiled to herself as she recalled his face, innocent, trusting, loving, as he drew her into his embrace. As his mouth covered hers, she caught movement from the corner of her eye and feared she had an audience. She quickly sang the song of sleeping into his ear, and Jon stiffened, floating unconscious to the bottom of the sea. Meri knew he would be safe for a short while and she would recover his body and revive him, taking him to safety.

But she had not reckoned on the cunning of her sisters. They swarmed at her, accusing her of deception and immediately retrieving Jon from the seabed. They brought him toward the surface, waking him from his slumber as they did so. Meri fought them, as did Jon, with the last of the air in his lungs, but as he went limp, they dragged Meri away to the surface.

Still, she did not give up. When her sisters let her go, laughing at her distress, she immediately dived to Jon's body and conveyed it to a rocky atoll, where she breathed air into his lungs and sang the song of healing. It was too late. Never again did she see his chest move or his eyelids flutter. Meri sat with Jon's body for many hours on that rocky outcrop, reliving the horror of the night, filled with remorse for the life she could not save. It was that night that finally convinced her she must flee her family.

As the tide had rolled out, the entrance to a cave was revealed and she explored it, finding a dry cavern inside where she could lay the body of the young sailor to rest. And so, she had done this; it had given her some peace to know this was his final resting place, not some shark's belly.

From then on, she had tried to blot the night from her mind, focusing all her efforts on escaping her family. She'd watched many a sailor seduced and murdered since the night with Jon. Her sisters and mother hoped she would learn their ways, but she had been increasingly repulsed by the constant slaughter.

Finally, on the night she was destined to be brought before the mage and ensorcelled, Meri fled - straight into the face of a fierce storm that whipped the ocean into a frenzy. It had been a foolish but desperate act, her sisters in hot pursuit. They had turned back to seek shelter, but she had taken the risk and swum on, caught up in the violence of the waves, happy to perish rather than face the future destined for her.

Reliving the terror of the night, Meri realized if given the choice again, she would still swim straight into the storm.

And that had brought her to Nikolas. He loved her and was changing her into the woman she could be - his lover, his life partner. She was prepared to sacrifice two hundred years to be with him in his world, and now he might never return.

But then she realized something. He *would* return, because she was the only one who could lead him straight to his brother's final resting place. It seemed she had one last chance.

CHAPTER 10

NIK slammed his fist into the leering face of the sailor before him. The man dropped insensible to the floor of the tavern. His friends were momentarily startled, before they all rushed Nik. He didn't care. If one of them got in a lucky punch, all the better. Maybe when he woke up, he'd find this nightmare was only that – a bad dream.

Resting his weight on his toes, he prepared to meet the onslaught. He punched one in the face and another in the guts, but two more took their places. Now they were too close to land effective punches, so he charged them, knocking three down. The rage in his soul gave him strength, but there were too many. Despite his titanic struggles, they restrained him while they took turns using him for punching practice.

Nik found he did care about the pain, when it came down to it. One final killer punch hit his gut and knocked the last shred of wind from his lungs. He slumped in the arms of his opponents, and slowly the world went black.

He came to, spluttering, as icy water coursed over his head. He groaned. Everything hurt - his knuckles, his face, his shoulders, ribs, stomach, even his balls. There wasn't a place the bastards hadn't hit.

"Lord Cosara," drawled a crusty voice. "Of all the men I expected to drag from a fight tonight, you were not on the list."

Nik squinted up with his one open eye and recognized his friend, Grif Tyne, the Wildecoast gate sergeant. "Ho, Grif."

Grif snorted. "This place is covered with bodies, blood, and broken furniture, and that's all you can say?"

Nik growled. He wasn't up to this right now. All he wanted to do was crawl away and lick his wounds, both physical and mental. He tried to get up but as he tensed, sharp agony ripped through his ribs and he nearly passed out.

"Steady, man," Grif said, "you've taken a battering. Easy does it." He motioned for his men, who helped Nik to his feet and sat him in a chair.

The sergeant turned to the onlookers. "The bar's closing now, good sirs. Finish your ale and out you go. Nothing more to see here." He ordered two of his men to herd the patrons from the tavern. Then he pulled up another chair and opened a satchel.

Nik didn't care what he was doing. "Just pull out your sword and cut off my head now," he groaned.

"Don't be daft," Grif said. "You'll heal in no time."

"Humph," he snorted. "Rather die now."

Grif gently peeled Nik's shirt off and examined his bruises. He gasped as pain spread from a swelling over his left ribcage. "Broken rib here, mate. I'll have to bind it. The others feel fine though."

"Don't feel fine to me."

Grif set to work with bandages borrowed from the proprietor of the tavern. He wrapped them tight around Nik's chest after applying salve to the worst areas. Soon Nik was so trussed up he didn't think he could move. Breathing was easier though.

"This isn't like you, Nikolas," Grif said, moving on to tend to the cuts on his face. "You're no brawler. Makes me wonder."

"Well, stop wondering."

"You're on a downward spiral and that's for sure. Damn shame if you ask me."

Nik flinched as Grif stitched a cut on his cheekbone. "Lucky no one's asking you, then."

Grif paused. "You're a friend, man, and it's hard to see you do this to yourself."

"What? A man can't have a bad day once in a while?"

The sergeant pulled the thread through Nik's skin, none too gently. "One bad day is fine. A year or more of them, and you should take a long hard look at yourself. Talented sailor like you could be admiral, especially with the family connection."

"And I suppose that's going to make it all better?" Nik snapped. "I run the show and all past mistakes just disappear? You know it's not that simple."

Grif snipped the ends of the thread and gave Nik's face one last wipe. "Perhaps not, but the rest of us just get on with it. How come you get to wallow?"

"You wouldn't understand."

"Maybe not, but I bet there are those who would."

The remark made Nik pause. Merielle understood him, but maybe it was why he hurt so much. He had begun to depend on her, and she had shown herself unworthy. What was he to do now?

"I've patched you up as much as I can for now, man. I'll take you to the castle healer and let him care for you."

Nik groaned. Adriana would be in a fury over this. "Must you? I'm in no condition to deal with the queen."

"Yes, Lord Cosara, I really think I must. Lucky for you their majesties are away, attending Prince Zialni's marriage in Brightcastle."

He helped Nik to his feet and supported him out of the tavern and onto Storm. The ride to the castle passed in a blur of pain as Nik's injured ribs felt every jolt. His head ached from the tension of his gritted teeth. By the time they pulled up in the castle forecourt, he had called Storm all the names under the sun.

Grif appeared at his side. "I'm sorry, Nikolas, that must have been unpleasant."

Nik cracked open an eyelid, spying a spark of amusement in Grif's eyes, even in the uncertain light of the torches.

"Yeah, sure you're sorry," Nik said, trying to dismount. His body had stiffened, and he could barely move.

"Help here, soldier," Grif snapped to one of the young men on guard. The burly lad strode over and helped Grif haul Nik off Storm.

By the time Nik's feet hit the cobbles, the pain in his ribs and head was so intense he couldn't walk. Grif's amusement turned to concern.

Oh yeah. Better not let the queen's cousin die on his watch.

Grif helped the young soldier support Nik up the front steps and into the reception hall, where the steward took one look and sent a passing maid scurrying up into the guest chambers.

"Lord Cosara," the steward said, "what has happened?"

Nik tried to focus on the man but failed. He couldn't even gather his thoughts to answer the question.

"Lord Cosara has been accosted in one of the taverns and needs a bed for the night," Grif said. "I've tended his wounds, but I think the castle physician should be called."

"As you wish, Sergeant," the steward said. "The bronze room is being prepared as it's the closest available. Up the stairs and second on the right. I shall have a maid attend you, and food and drink brought."

"Thank you," Nik said, but the words came out as a muffled croak.

Grif and the young soldier helped him up the staircase, and never had a set of stairs seemed so high. He sighed with relief as he was helped onto the huge bed.

A maid pulled his boots from his feet and the shirt from his back before settling him under the covers.

Grif peered at the young soldier. "Thanks for your help. Return to duty."

He left and Grif turned to Nik. "I take it you'll be safe enough here for the night. No thoughts of getting back on that horse for the ride home?"

Nik imagined the pain involved and shook his head. Merielle would have to cope on her own. She had assured him often enough that she could manage without him. A twinge of guilt added to his pain as he thought of her sitting alone in the cottage, wondering when he'd return. And she would be doing that. Surely, she had to know he'd be back, that he'd force her to take him to his brother.

The shock of remembering Jon was really gone hit Nik again, as it did on a regular basis. Just when he thought he could manage it, all the loneliness, the guilt, returned. Merielle had made some of it go away, for a short while, until today.

"What's wrong, man?" Grif said, watching him.

Nik shook his head. "Not worth talking about, Grif."

"It's not like you to get into fights. You have this look about you, like you lost your best friend."

"It's just tough sometimes, Grif."

"I shouldn't wonder, out on your own in that cottage. You need people around you, people who care."

Nik grimaced. "I don't know what I need."

"The queen will see you right, if you let her help."

"That's what I'm afraid of," Nik muttered.

Grif chuckled. "She's really something, your lady cousin. Well, I can't stand around gossiping, got to get back to the taverns and kick a few more brawlers out. Look in on your way home, my friend."

Grif stuck out his right hand and Nik shook it gingerly.

"Thanks, Grif, I owe you one."

"Nothing you wouldn't do for me, My Lord." He saluted and left the room.

The maid bustled quietly around the chambers, stoking the fire and lighting the candles, then she brought him a drink and some broth.

He discovered he was hungry and finished everything he was given. The maid watched him from beneath lowered lashes but didn't speak.

"Thank you, Miss," he said. "You may go now."

"I've been instructed to stay and tend to you, Lord Cosara."

"I'm fine, Miss. No need to fuss."

The maid turned as a man entered the room, followed by a lady. Nik groaned inwardly, barely containing his dismay. *This is going to be so much fun!*

"Lord Cosara," the man said, "I'm Doctor Achan Mosard, the court physician. This is the Lady Alique Zorba."

"Lord Cosara and I are already acquainted, Doctor," Alique said, a triumphant smile on her face. "How are you, Nikolas?"

"I've felt better." He decided to ignore Alique as much as he could. "Thanks for attending me, Doctor."

"No trouble, My Lord. The night is but young and I was merely catching up on some reading."

"I, on the other hand, was enjoying a late dinner with a charming man," Alique said, a smirk on her lips.

She looked stunning in the candlelight, the golden waves of her hair glinting, her crimson gown molding her curves. Alique would have many admirers. *Poor sods.* But she was easy on the eye and there was no harm in looking.

"Don't let me keep you, My Lady," Nik said.

"My companion will wait, Nikolas," she said. "I just had to make sure you were in no danger and you were comfortable."

"You've seen, and now you may go," Nik said.

Alique's eyebrows shot up. "Oh no, Nikolas," she said. "I'm here as Doctor Mosard' apprentice. He is teaching me about herbs and the like. It's fascinating."

"Yes, Lord Cosara," the doctor said, "Lady Alique will tend to you under my instruction. I trust you are happy with this arrangement?"

Alique gazed upon him with wide, innocent eyes, but the smirk on her lips betrayed her. "I promise to take good care of you," she said, placing her palm on his brow.

Nik closed his eyes. *Great! I may as well get on Storm and head back to the cottage now. Better Merielle than this conniving woman!* "Fine."

Alique sobered as she examined her patient. Nik had to admit she seemed to take her task seriously. After feeling his forehead, she pulled back the covers and gently poked his ribs, before bending to listen to his chest through a long tube. She inspected the stitching Grif had done and pronounced it satisfactory. The fact she did all this under the eye of the doctor didn't seem to worry her in the least.

"Are you in substantial pain, Lord Cosara?" she asked.

"Hurts just about as much as any injury I've ever had."

"Then I'll mix you a powder to reduce the pain and help you sleep. The chest bandages are adequate, but I'll clean your abrasions and apply salve."

The doctor nodded. "You seem to have this well in hand, My Lady, and so I'll leave you and look in on the patient in the morning. Rest well, Lord Cosara." The doctor bowed and left quietly.

Alique hummed as she ground several herbs and mixed them into a half glass of wine. Her voice was soothing and surprisingly tuneful. It appeared she was not only beautiful but talented in other areas.

"How is your house guest, Nikolas?"

"Merielle is in good health, thank you."

"How will she fend for herself alone this night?"

"I'm sure she'll be fine for one night."

Alique stirred the goblet of wine with a hot fire poker and brought it to Nik. He sipped the warmed liquid, noting the bitter edge the herbs gave the wine.

"You're good at this," he said, beginning to relax under the influence of the medicine.

She gazed at him with eyes that appeared to miss nothing. "That remains to be seen," she said. "I've always had an interest in healing. The queen wishes to have someone trained in the medicinal arts close to hand. I'm fortunate to be able to learn from one of the best."

"I'm sure Her Majesty appreciates you."

"Perhaps. Regardless, I don't intend to waste this opportunity."

"My father was a healer," Nik said, and immediately regretted it.

"This I know. He wished for you to follow in his footsteps. Instead you chose the life of a sea captain. But now what are you?"

He frowned at her. How dare she speculate on his life?

But she went on. "Bereft of the life you knew, you wander directionless, and now you've been involved in a tavern brawl. The queen will not be pleased."

"This is none of your business, My Lady."

"I beg to differ, My Lord. You're here in this castle under my care and that makes it my business. Now finish your medicine and get some rest. I will see an attendant stays with you in case you require anything. I have ground more herbs to be added to wine if your pain returns."

Alique straightened his covers, laid her hand on his brow a second time, and left without another word.

* * *

Meri didn't sleep throughout the long, lonely night. The afternoon passed with her struggling to complete the tasks Nikolas would normally have done. Luckily the bucket of fresh fish gave her something to snack on when she felt hungry, and for once she could indulge her preference for raw fish. As she savored the flavor of the firm translucent flesh, doubt racked her. Would Nikolas return? Did he really need her to lead him to Jon's grave? Or was he so angry he didn't trust himself near her?

She couldn't answer any of these questions, so she got through the afternoon and night as best she could - alternating between singing and crying, and bursts of activity. If this was being human, she did not want it. And then she would think of Nikolas, alone out there, possibly injured, hurting, and she would be struck with remorse. She had done this to him. Right from the start it had been her fault. She should have said no to her sisters and swum away, taken her chances with whatever consequences came along. She should have been true to herself. Why, oh why, had she thought she could spare the life of her first victim? Was she doomed to fail at everything she attempted?

Stop feeling sorry for yourself. You have chosen Nikolas to share the rest of your life and you must have faith. If he does not return, you will deal with that.

Meri felt better after the stern talking-to. She did not sleep, but at least the crying and self-recrimination ended. She concentrated instead on positive thoughts of how she could make amends for her sins.

* * *

Nik didn't think he'd sleep after Alique left, but when he next opened his eyes, bright sun shone in the window. His first thought was of Merielle. Had she passed the night thinking of him? Had she eaten, drunk, bathed? Was she worried?

As though he was hearing it for the first time, he recalled her confession of yesterday. She had killed Jon; she'd been responsible for the death of his *brother*. He'd been right from the start to mistrust her, but like a fool he'd let his heart be swayed by her beauty and soft words. *Damn!* If he hadn't spent the last year stuck in that cottage alone, he might've had his defenses sharpened against that sort of feminine charm. He was vulnerable, lonely, and yes, desperate for company.

But how deep was he in with Merielle? Could he go back, finish what he had started and find Jon? The thought of never knowing the truth was unbearable. As painful as it might be to gaze upon the killing ground of his brother, and perhaps even see his grave, Nik knew he must pursue it. And the sooner the better.

He tried to sit up. Agony like repeated knife strikes rocketed through his ribs and he slumped back against the pillows. *Medicine, I need more wine and herbs.*

Gritting his teeth, Nik managed to sit up and swivel his legs over the side of the bed. He stood and gasped, stabbing pain tearing through his ribs. His head swayed but almost immediately his vision cleared.

He made it to the decanter, poured some wine over the herbs resting in a spare goblet, then mixed the concoction until much of the substance had dissolved. Sweat stood out on his temples as he threw the mix in one huge gulp down his throat and leaned on the table. Deep breaths - well, not so deep, that was agony as well - helped to settle the waves of nausea that came with every throb of his chest.

He stood like that for some time, not game to move, allowing the pain to settle as the herbs took effect. Soon he could breathe a little easier.

"What are you doing out of bed?" Alique's voice snapped from the doorway.

"Lady Alique, how nice of you to stop by," he said. "I'd bow, but I can't move."

He heard her bustle up behind him. Her small hands grasped his upper arms as she tried to usher him back to bed.

"Not the bed," Nik said, refusing to move.

She gave a lady-like snort. "You're so stubborn. Do you realize you could do yourself serious injury by moving around? You must stay still! Now back to bed." She tried once again to get him moving but she was no match for his bulk.

"And I said no, My Lady."

She appeared in front of him, hands on hips and fury in her baby-blue eyes. The hue of her dress exactly matched her gaze, and the neck and sleeves were edged with cream lace which didn't hide her impressive bosom nearly well enough, especially heaving as it was with indignation.

Nik shook the image of luscious creamy flesh out of his mind. *This woman is exasperating! Focus on that, man!*

"I thank you for tending my wounds last night, but you're not my keeper."

"You've been placed in my care by Doctor Mosard and he's a hard task master. Also, you are the queen's cousin. I can only imagine the grief she'll give me if anything happens to you."

Nik narrowed his eyes. Something didn't ring true. She was hiding something, something that unsettled her. From what he had seen, Lady Alique Zorba was not a woman easily disconcerted. But it was a problem for later.

"I'm sorry, Lady, but I can hardly loll around in bed all day. I must return to my cottage and my guest."

"Oh yes, your charming house guest, Merielle…What was her surname?"

Nik gritted his teeth. "I didn't tell you as it's none of your concern."

"Humph," she said, "you probably don't know either." Her eyes widened as she studied him. "Oh, wait until Queen Adriana hears of this! A house guest who hasn't even told you her name! I would be very careful, My Lord."

"What's all this noise about?" The commanding tones of Kain Jazara preceded his entry into Nik's bed chamber. "You'd think you were a married couple instead of physician and patient."

Alique went bright red as she stepped back to make room for Kain. Interesting, Nik thought, that Alique reacted so to the remark by his friend.

"Good morning, Niko," Kain said. "I hear you've been brawling. How do you fare?"

"Lord Cosara was set upon in a tavern last night," Alique said. "It was hardly brawling."

Kain's eyebrows shot skywards. "Oh, set upon, was he? The victim of some drunken sailors out for a bit of fun? My apologies, Niko, if it seemed I was blaming you for the ruckus."

Nik cast his friend a dirty look. It was pointless to deny anything. "I feel like death," he said. "Thanks for your concern."

"I'll return when you've completed your visit with General Jazara." Alique looked at Kain. "See if you can convince him to return to his bed, General." She curtseyed and swept from the room.

"You could do worse than marry her you know," Kain said, his eyes sharp. "She's half in love with you already."

"Surely you jest."

"You disagree?"

"I'm not about to discuss this with you. I've asked you and everyone to leave me be."

Kain held his hands up in surrender. "Hey, I only came by to see how you were doing. It concerns me you were brawling in a tavern, and before you say it, I don't believe you were set upon. I've eyes and ears all over town. What happened?"

"If you've spies all over town, then you don't need me to tell you," Nik snapped, leaning on the bed as his ribs burned.

"What sparked this need to lash out?"

"Not now, Kain."

"Niko, I worry about you. We don't see you for months and just when you seem to be getting your life back together, you do this. Why?"

"It's just about all I can do to breathe just now." Nik met his gaze with difficulty, gasping as he turned to face him.

"Then get into bed," Kain said. "Let me help you."

Nik swallowed the lump in his throat. This was exactly what he had tried to avoid by his exile, this sympathy and interference which only served to remind him of the tragedies in his life. At least out at the cottage he could forget the past, at times. He could revel in the majesty of the sea and the joy of its creatures. He could also suffer without anyone seeing, and without causing anyone pain.

"I'm not going back to bed," he grunted.

A muscle in Kain's jaw tensed. He wasn't used to people saying no to him. Then he shrugged, casting his gaze over Nik's bandaged ribs. "How are your injuries, really?"

"Ribs hurt like hell," he said. "I broke at least one. But I can't lie around here, as much as you wish for it. I must return to the cottage and check on Merielle."

"Ah yes, the beautiful redhead. You'll bring her to the ball?"

"I'm making no promises. It's likely she'll be on her way before then. Her injuries have almost healed."

"And yet she still couldn't stand when we visited yesterday?"

"I'll buy her a horse. She'll be fine."

"Why all the mystery surrounding this guest of yours, Niko?" Kain asked. "Have you fallen for her?"

Goddess, he was persistent, and too damn smart. "It's none of your concern. Merielle will soon be gone and it will be as though she was never there."

But he knew life would never be the same after Merielle. She would ever be in his thoughts, like a burr in his saddle blanket.

Kain gazed long and hard at his friend. "I wish we could return to the friendship we once shared. I don't like this wariness you cloak yourself with."

"Look, Kain, I value your friendship and I know you have my best interests at heart. But leave me to sort out my own life."

Kain looked long and hard at Nik who braced himself for more arguments.

"Fine. I'll see to getting you home, if that's what you want. Are you able to ride?"

"Honestly, I don't know."

"Then I'll order a carriage." Kain studied Nik for a little longer, but then he smiled. "Look after yourself, Niko." He turned and left without another word.

CHAPTER 11

MERI awoke, for a moment completely disoriented. Softness lay beneath her - that was unusual - and a comforting scent enveloped her. She was wrapped in something - also unusual, unless it was the seaweed off the coast. She took a deep breath and remembered. She was no longer a mermaid in the sea, but landlocked, and the comforting scent belonged to Nikolas. She was in his bed, in his shirt, and in trouble.

There was a sound outside and Meri pushed herself up. Her hair cascaded in unruly waves over her face and she groaned, her head pounding from the tears she had shed over the last day. Pain shot through her lower abdomen and she gasped. There was now a distinct valley where her tail would divide to become two legs, and her fin had contracted more. Soon the process would be complete, but what would she do then if Nikolas cast her out?

The outside door to the cottage opened. "Merielle?"

Nikolas sounded wary, and there was something else. His footsteps shuffled and there were still noises from outside. Someone else was here.

He appeared in the doorway and her heart lurched. He was injured! All her fears had not been unfounded. He leaned against the doorframe, his right arm clasped around his ribs, the left side of his face swollen and bruised. She would hardly have known him!

"What has happened?" she gasped.

He studied her for a moment. "I could ask you the same," he said. "What are you doing in my bed, in my shirt?"

Meri swallowed the fear that threatened to swamp her, that had been battering her ever since Nikolas walked out. "I did not think you would mind."

"You were wrong."

He tried to enter the bedroom and almost fell. His grunt of pain tore through her heart. *He is really hurt!* And she was about as much use as a beached fish.

"Nikolas, you are scaring me. What happened?"

He wiped his hand across his forehead and grunted with pain at the movement of his arm. "If you must know, I went to a tavern in Wildecoast and got into a fight. One of my army buddies patched me up and took me to the castle where I spent the night."

Meri studied him. Nikolas getting into a fight did not sound right. Had she caused this? Was this the reason he chose to isolate himself, so his temper could not get the better of him? She had seen no evidence of a bad temper since she had known the man, apart from her first meeting with him.

"Who is outside?" she asked.

"I was driven back in the queen's carriage. Storm was tied to the back, and he is now being stabled by the attendant who will then return to Wildecoast."

"You are still angry with me." She did not wish to discuss the issue that had led to their fight, but she needed to know what he would do.

"Damn right I'm angry. You're responsible for the death of my brother. It doesn't matter how long I live; I could never forgive you for that."

"Never?"

"I can't believe we're even having this conversation. Get out of my bed."

Her heart fell further. He was just as angry now as he had been when he left. "Please do not do this, Nikolas. Get the rocker and I will sit and keep you company. You can rest and I will tend your wounds."

"I'm the medicine man here, remember?" he said, but he did walk gingerly out to the kitchen, moving like an old man, and dragged the rocking chair to the bedroom. Then he fetched the teapot and his medicines.

Meri deftly flipped herself into the chair and Nikolas eased himself down onto the bed, sighing with relief when he had settled against the pillows.

"Hell of a trip from Wildecoast in that coach. Not sure it was better than riding Storm."

Meri mixed the ground powder in the tea and poured him a cup. He swallowed it in one gulp then lay back and closed his eyes.

"What can I do for you?" she asked. "I hate seeing you in pain."

"Funny that," he said, "since you've caused most of my pain lately."

"I would do anything to turn back the clock, to give Jon back to you," she whispered.

"You'd say anything to make me believe you weren't a willing participant in Jon's death."

"I was not willing, Nikolas. I cannot have you believe the worst."

"I'll believe what I like. I told you about Jon and you let me believe you knew nothing. How could you not have suspected?"

"I did not remember!"

"What do you mean? Have you been involved in so many deaths that Jon's didn't stand out?"

"I swear I've killed no one."

"How many deaths have you witnessed, Merielle?"

She closed her eyes as the faces of all the sailors flashed through her mind, some vague, others crystal clear. "Many, but Jon's only came back to me when I saw the tattoo."

"And you expect me to believe that?" His words were becoming slurred as the medicine took effect. *Poor man.* When she imagined the pain he must have experienced, bumping about in the coach to get back to the cottage…

"I hope you will believe me,' she said. "Just as I hope you'll believe I did not kill him."

Now was the time to explain, while he was vulnerable, half-asleep. Perhaps he would listen and understand.

"I met Jon three nights in a row, and I was expected to take his life on the third night. I left early for the rendezvous, thinking I could outwit my sisters. But they caught up with me just as Jon took me in his arms. I sang the song of sleeping..."

Oh my, this sounds terrible! Why should he believe me?

"My sisters and I fought, and Jon died. I tried to revive him. I sat with him on an atoll for hours, but he did not stir. All I could do was convey his body to its resting place in the hope that, one day, his family would discover it."

A gentle snore issued from Nikolas. Had he heard her? Or would she have to tell him all over? Never mind. She would tell him over and over until he understood. Meri knew she would do anything if he forgave her, including leaving his life. But she would have one thing from him first; her humanity. As wrong as it felt, she could not give that up. And so, she sang her song of change while he slept, weaving the magic through notes and words and feeling her body respond. At least she would have one legacy of the moments spent with her tortured hero.

* * *

Nik woke in the evening, refreshed. He opened his eyes and the first thing he saw was Merielle, her hair disheveled, green eyes focused on him. She looked as wild as the sea creatures.

Let's face it, she is wild. I should never have dreamed of her as anything else. Stupid, stupid man!

But he would have her do one last thing before he cast her off.

"Don't imagine for one moment I'm fooled by your sorry tale," he said, ignoring the hurt in her gaze. "Yes, I remember what you said before I fell asleep. I also remember you didn't tell me every detail. It doesn't bode well for your innocence."

"I will explain everything, Nikolas."

"Damn right you will. You'll also take me to Jon's resting place."

Dread swept across her face but was quickly gone. She took a deep breath and nodded.

That was too easy. "I thought you were afraid to return to the sea?"

Merielle chewed her bottom lip. "That is true, but this I must do. I care for you, Nikolas. I understand you must see where he lies."

He nodded. "We'll leave tomorrow."

Her eyes widened. "So soon? Are you well enough?"

"The rest has done me good." He sat up. "I have much less pain. It's almost like magic." He frowned at her. "Is this your doing?"

"I am no healer."

He rose from the bed, hardly able to believe all he felt now was a gentle twinge where his rib was broken. It felt half-knitted. He touched his face; the swelling was greatly reduced. He found a small sharp knife and removed the stitches from his cheekbone.

"You are almost your handsome self, My Lord."

"Stop the flattery." He walked to the door of the bedroom and turned back to her. "I'll prepare dinner." He left before she could reply. There was nothing she could say that he wanted to hear.

CHAPTER 12

THE small boat slid through the still water as Nikolas rowed away from the shore. Meri noted his grimace as he worked the oars. He was not healed properly and should not be taking this risk, but she knew better than to say so. He would not listen; he did not even wish to talk with her.

Last evening had been a terrible endurance test. She'd tried so hard to engage him in conversation until he had finally asked her to be quiet. The meal had been completed in silence, the kitchen cleaned, and Nikolas had retired to his bed. It was clear he did not trust himself around her. Perhaps he feared he might be overcome with rage if they discussed Jon's death.

His cold remoteness scared her more than his anger. At least rage could be combatted, worked through, but if he would not even engage with her... She watched the play of his shoulder muscles beneath the rough weave of his shirt. How she longed to feel those arms around her again. Fear spiked through her as she faced the very real possibility she would never feel them again; would not get to live her life with this man she had come to adore. Perhaps it was too much to ask that he forgive her for her part in Jon's death. Too much to ask...

Meri took a deep breath that drew Nikolas's attention to her. There was not only anger in his gaze but hurt. She had hurt him and destroyed his trust when he was just returning to normality. Her heart broke that he might never recover from this last blow. She had only ever wished to help Nikolas, to make him see his perception was flawed. He was a good man and his parents would have forgiven him for running off to sea. She may never make him understand that he could not be blamed for the choices he had made the night of the shipwreck, but at least she might have helped him come to terms with the loss of life. He was too good a man to be wasted out in that cottage.

She shook her head. Now she might never be able to heal his anguish. Once they found Jon, Nikolas would demand she leave his life forever; if they survived this voyage. There was plenty of risk. Her family would be searching for her, and Nikolas would not be safe around them, no matter what he thought. Meri tried not to contemplate what her fate would be if her mother and sisters finally caught up with her. Perhaps they could slip in and out of the region without attracting the notice of the *mer* people? Perhaps…

And then there was the ever-present danger of being at sea in a small boat. A sudden storm could wreak havoc, and at this time of year storms were common. Meri glanced down at her tail and swallowed a hot blast of fear. She drew the blanket back over her lower half, desperate to cover its evolution from Nikolas's gaze. He would notice soon enough but she was not ready to deal with that yet.

Nikolas rowed until the breeze picked up, and then raised the sails. The little skip slipped through the waves making its way toward the atoll and the cave, which was Jon's final resting place. That night, they dropped the sails and slept in the bottom of the boat after a cold dinner. Meri relished the raw fish she caught for herself after a leisurely dip in the ocean. She even dived for a crayfish on the reef below the boat. Nikolas feasted on dried fish and bread he had baked before leaving that morning.

It could have been an idyllic trip if not for the rancor between them. Nikolas spoke little and Meri tried to remain as inconspicuous as a mermaid with crimson hair could. Which was not very. She often felt his eyes on her, and it made her itch. She especially felt his scrutiny when she took her dip in the sea, but refused to allow him to spoil the delight she experienced as her body sliced through the water. A playful dolphin swam with her, laughing.

All too soon it was time to return to the confines of the boat and the intimidating silence. Nikolas bedded down immediately, leaving Meri to eat her dinner and watch the stars as they appeared. Her companion slept little during the long night for he was restless and did not snore. Meri dozed toward dawn and took another dip just as the first rays of the sun speared over the horizon.

Her shoulder had almost fully healed, easily good enough to continue her journey. The changes to the lower part of her body escalated day by day. That morning, she sang as Nikolas rowed, only ceasing when the wind picked up and he put the oars away. The pain in her lower half increased as she sang, and finally grew so strong she had to stop. Panting, she sat with eyes closed waiting for the pain to dissipate, but it kept coming at her in waves.

"Are you well?" he asked.

"There is considerable pain, Nikolas, but I will endure. Do not worry."

"How should I not worry? You look terrible, and you're sweating like Storm after a hard run up the beach."

"I am well," she said, through gritted teeth. "I must have overdone the swimming."

"So it's your shoulder that's causing this discomfort?"

She nodded abruptly as a new wave of agony shot through her. She did so hate to lie to him and had made such a habit of it lately.

"I'll get the pain medicine." He rifled around in his satchel and withdrew the powder, mixed it in wine and handed the potion to her.

This had to mean he cared for her still. Or was he just concerned she would die before showing him Jon's resting place?

They passed the day in awkward silence, Nikolas mixing her a glass of medicated wine whenever the pain grew too great. He seemed to know when she required more. Meri could not sing the song of change, so great was the agony in her lower half. All her energy went into trying to distract herself from the pain in order to appear as normal as possible. In this she only partially succeeded as his expression grew more worried by the hour.

Finally, midafternoon, he spoke. "I think we should turn back."

Meri frowned. "Why? You need to find Jon."

"You're ill and growing worse. I'd be a monster to put you through more torment than necessary."

She smiled. He did love her. "I will survive this, believe me. I wish to continue."

"Tell me the truth, Merielle," he said. "The pain doesn't stem from your shoulder. It never affected you like this."

Meri drew a deep breath and slowly released it. "No, you are right, but it is nothing to worry about. Just a mermaid thing."

Well, that was true. It was a mermaid phenomenon that caused her pain, and as difficult to bear as it was, she would get through it. But she could not tell Nikolas the truth yet. He was not ready to hear it.

He looked at her as if unsure whether he should believe her. "Really?"

"Yes, I will be well, and I will explain it to you soon." And the revelation would end their friendship, if it were not already dead.

"I'll hold you to that."

"For now, just ply me with your medicine and I will try not to let this affect our expedition."

"I appreciate that."

Meri sighed. He had become so stiff with her. She missed the easier relationship they had fallen into before she revealed her link to Jon. But she was getting what she wanted, wasn't she? Her body was changing, and now she was confident the change would be permanent. Even if Nikolas exiled her from his life, she would have the humanity she craved. A pity she might not have him to share her life with.

Might? There was no way Nikolas would accept her once he knew the entire truth of how she had lied to him and tricked him. It was a poor basis upon which to establish a relationship. She should have realized her mistake right at the start, instead of getting herself in so deep her heart would be broken - and perhaps his as well.

* * *

No matter how hard he tried to maintain his rage against Merielle, worry ate away at Nik's gut. She suffered, really suffered, and it appeared to be getting worse. The medicine he gave her every few hours only took the merest edge off as far as he could tell. At least she had admitted it wasn't her shoulder. At least she had told him that much of the truth.

He berated himself for caring, but her condition prodded away at the soft part of his heart that was vulnerable to her. He shouldn't concern himself with anything but finding Jon, perhaps bringing him back for burial. Maybe then this whole sorry chapter of the shipwreck and Jon's loss could be completed. Perhaps the relatives of the shipwreck victims, seeing his personal pain, could forgive him and move on. Or perhaps they would hate him and blame him forever?

No one seemed to understand how it weighed on his heart: the loss of his crew, the desolation of their families, the scorn of the seafaring community. Financially, he'd done what he could for the families, the funds coming from his own personal estate, against the queen's wishes. She seemed to think by doing that he was assuming blame. Hell, it was exactly what he'd done. If it enabled those people to feel they'd taken a piece of his life in return for their son, brother or lover, Nik was happy to oblige. It was only money.

He pushed thoughts of Merielle aside as far as possible - difficult when she sat only a yard away - and tried to concentrate on the movement of the wind in the sails and the boat over the water. The weather had been kind to them with moderate winds and gentle seas. They were making excellent time. Nikolas estimated they should reach their destination midmorning on the morrow.

* * *

Toward dusk, Meri's pain began to dissipate. She took a deep breath and felt her muscles relax for the first time in two days. It was such a relief that she smiled.

He raised his brows. "You're feeling better."

"Yes, the pain has eased of its own accord as I knew it would, eventually."

"Can you explain it to me?"

"I wish I could, Nikolas, but I would like to wait until after we find Jon. We must concentrate on him."

And Meri wanted to postpone her news for as long as possible after that, for fear her life with Nikolas would truly be over.

"As soon as we find Jon." The intensity of his gaze reinforced his words.

Meri tossed her concerns aside and settled down in the boat. "I will rest now while I can, it has been a difficult two days."

Surprisingly, Meri slept most of the hours of darkness. She awoke refreshed in the morning, to the sound of Nikolas's gentle snores. She pushed herself up and looked around, checking for landmarks. A way out to sea, she could just make out a small rocky outcrop - their destination, the place where she had kept vigil over Jon's body, never suspecting for one moment that his older brother would become so dear to her.

Her lower half had dried out over the last day, so Meri cast off the shirt and slipped quietly over the side. She expelled the air from her lungs and allowed her body to sink before swimming in a wide circle around the boat. Just as her body screamed for air, Meri surfaced and took in a great gasp. *Ah, that feels good.* Her muscles tingled as they were resupplied with their essential nutrients and already her tail had plumped up. Meri felt a pang of regret that she might no longer experience the thrill and freedom of a sea creature once she was human. But surely, she would retain some of her mermaid attributes.

Looking toward the boat, she saw Nikolas was awake and staring at her. Meri swam back and slipped effortlessly into the boat, quickly throwing a blanket over her tail.

He shook his head. "I'll never get over how you move in the water." His eyes ran over her and her face heated. She pulled her long crimson locks over her breasts. "How are you this morning?"

"Rested, and almost pain-free, thank you, Nikolas. I think the worst is over."

"Did you sleep well?"

"I did, which is just as well, as I believe today might be trying."

"Bound to be, when I have to collect the body of my brother." Resentment oozed from him.

Meri remained silent. Of course it was difficult for him, but she was also concerned about running across her people. All of them would be on the lookout for her, and they would not be happy with this human invasion.

"Please believe me when I say I did not seek his death," she said. "I did try to save your brother, but when my people have marked a victim, they do not give up easily."

"*You* marked the victim, Merielle, and for that I'll never forgive you. Why did it have to be Jon? Out of all the sailors on the ship, why did you pick my baby brother?"

"Chance?" She really did not want to discuss this painful subject with Nikolas, but she owed him in so many ways. "I am sorry. I did everything I could to save him but, in the end, it was not enough. I cannot bring him back, and I know you cannot forgive me. But if you could just accept that I never sought his death, I would be content."

"Content! This isn't about making you content. You forfeited your right to happiness when you targeted my brother and then lied to me!"

"So you will not accept I meant no malice toward Jon? You know me, Nikolas."

"I thought I did."

His words speared her heart deeper than Meri would have imagined. She swallowed the lump that threatened to choke her. "Please do not say that," she whispered.

"Well, what am I supposed to think? It's not so long since Jon disappeared, and yet you couldn't tell me details of how a young man you knew had died? Didn't you wonder a little about him?"

Meri wrung her hands, desperate to make him understand. "I know how it appears." She sought words that would convey something she didn't comprehend herself. "I blocked that night out and I swear I made no connection until the moment I saw your tattoo. When I saw the seahorse, it was as though a door opened and I witnessed it all again. I stared at that tattoo all night on the rock with Jon. I can only think his death was so traumatic I blocked it out."

"Or the other explanation could be that you deliberately didn't tell me because you had another agenda. You wished to ingratiate yourself with me for Goddess only knows what purpose."

"No!" The word came out strangled by the terror coursing through her. If this was how he felt, what would he say when she revealed her changes, her true plan? All his suspicions would be confirmed, and he would never, *never* let her back into his life. "Please do not say these terrible things."

"You refused to take me searching for Jon because you wouldn't reveal your part in the plot to kill my brother."

"Nikolas, no, please, I truly did not know until I saw the tattoo. You *must* believe me."

"I don't." His voice sliced through her, so devoid of any feeling, Meri felt all hope for them die.

"Please know I never wanted Jon to perish. If you cannot accept anything else, please believe that. I have tried to be a friend to you, and you have helped me so much. I cannot bear to lose everything we shared these last weeks."

Nikolas remained silent as he cast his eyes toward their destination and went about raising the sails. Silence prevailed as they bounded forward through the increasing swell. There was just the slap of canvas against the mast, the thrumming of line in the stiff breeze, and the wash of water against the small boat. Nikolas had locked himself away and Meri sat staring as the atoll loomed nearer. She also kept a look out for signs of the *mer* people who were sure to be patrolling this region. Her family.

The tension within her body mounted as they sailed closer to their destination, until Meri could stand it no longer.

"Nikolas, I must swim. Sitting is making me imagine all sorts of things."

He turned to her; his eyes flat, hard, disappointed. "Do what you must. You've shown me the site, so if you leave me here it's no concern of mine."

Meri choked down the sob his words caused and threw herself over the side.

* * *

Nik was torn. He knew he'd hurt Merielle, but he couldn't help it. She'd upset him so much he didn't think he could ever forgive her. She'd become important to him, essential even, but to think she could harm his brother and keep it from him, well, it was more than he could deal with. He didn't believe she could block the incident out so thoroughly that only the tattoo would trigger the memory.

He would never, could never, forget such a trauma. He recalled the events of the shipwreck in a waking nightmare that never ended. The groaning of the ship's timbers as it broke on the reef, the cries of the sailors, the bloodless face of his brother when he discovered him in his cabin; each detail was indelibly etched on his mind.

The only part of the nightmare that was fuzzy to him were the days afterwards when he battled to return to the shore, losing two more lives in the process. No, he didn't believe it could be so easy to forget the death of a man you sat with all night. Or *had* she sat with Jon? Was that part of her story as well?

He was so stupid. He should have followed his instinct weeks ago and left her on the beach to fend for herself. At the least he should have protected his heart, stayed aloof, done the minimum as her host. But she had slowly gotten under his skin and helped him see he could heal himself, that he didn't need to hide. Nik had been ready to return to society and give life another chance. Was he still ready to do that?

Even now as Merielle swam around the boat, fast as the dolphins, he kept an eye out for her. She compelled him as no one ever had. Perhaps it was always going to be impossible to stay detached from her. And now he loved her and couldn't imagine his life without her. But it was all over, their time together at an end. The sooner he made peace with that the sooner they could both move on.

At noon, Nik pulled the boat ashore onto a tiny coral island. He looked for Merielle and found her floating a few yards away, staring at him, her beautiful face sad, almost tortured. Perhaps she did care for him... Or perhaps she was more concerned about her people finding her and dragging her back to resume her life of murder.

Nik turned back toward the rocky outcrop on the far end of the tiny atoll. This was where Merielle had described the cave entrance to be. He walked toward the outcrop with Merielle tailing him in the shallows. The sea swept into the narrow opening of the cave. It would be necessary to swim into the entrance. He took off his shirt and breeches and entered the water, wading toward the opening. The water deepened until he had to swim. Sounds behind him warned him Merielle followed.

He stopped and tread water. "Stay here," he snapped.

Without waiting to see if she obeyed, he continued through the narrow cleft and, two strokes later, entered a small cave where the sounds of the waves were muted. Any other time he would have been delighted at such a find but today, his eyes flew straight to the pile of bones in one corner. Nik's throat tightened as he stood in the shallows, tears mixing with the seawater dripping from his hair. Jon, his baby brother, the last of his close family, and this was where he had lain the past two months. All the hope Nik had nurtured vanished, leaving an empty well in the pit of his stomach.

He stood, unable to move, needing to confirm this was Jon but fearing to be sure. The skeleton was largely intact, with only some of the toe and finger bones scattered. Heaving a great breath, he took one step and then another, forcing himself out of the water and onto the dry beach where the body lay. A small crab scuttled away at his approach.

Nik couldn't accept what he saw before him as the flesh-and-blood brother he had bid farewell that day on the pier. Jon had been alive and vibrant; a tall, muscular, easygoing sailor boy who took everything in his stride, who never believed the ocean could touch him. Surely this wasn't that young man? Nik stepped closer. The hair was the right color, dark, almost black, and shaggy. Yes, it could be Jon.

The gaping eye sockets gave no clue as to the man who had looked out from them. Nondescript sailors' attire clothed the body; no help there. The feet were bare, and the toe bones scattered as though crabs had carried them away and gnawed at them.

The hands. He remembered Jon's hands well. They were larger than average, strong, capable, able to hammer a nail and raise a sail or man an oar. But more than that, he'd worn a ring on the middle finger of his left hand. The ring was a gift from their father when Jon went to sea. It had been handed down in the Cosara family to the youngest son for generations, and their father had hoped it would keep his younger son safe.

So much for that. Nik moved around the corpse, careful not to step on any bones, until he could kneel beside the left arm of the skeleton. The hand was in tatters, most of the small finger bones scattered across the sand. There was no ring to be seen. He counted the bone sections and realized there was a whole finger missing. *Just my luck!* He stood, casting around the sand for more bones. It had to be here. He couldn't confirm this was Jon without the ring. He knelt and crawled from one end of the small beach to the other, casting his palms across the sand in case he felt something solid that had been buried. Nothing!

Next, he sorted through the small piles of seaweed and driftwood that had accumulated, his breathing increasingly frantic as pile after pile revealed nothing. *All this way! All this time searching and hoping!* He had to know for sure, not just take Merielle's word this was his brother. Something glinted in the reflected light from the water. *There!* Against the back of the cave in a crevice. He crawled over, hardly daring to hope it could be what he sought.

Tucked away in a small gap in the rock was a gold band. He reached a finger in and hooked it out, along with two finger bones. It was the Cosara ring indeed. He had found his brother.

CHAPTER 13

NIK cradled the ring and finger bones in the palm of his hand - the last contact he'd have with his baby brother. His skin tingled. It was as though Jon was trying to say goodbye; to tell him what had happened all those weeks ago.

Jon was really...*dead*. The word thudded in Nik's heart. Even though he'd told himself repeatedly his brother was dead, there had always been hope...until now. Now he'd have to come to terms with Jon's passing, with not even the faintest ray of hope to soften his days.

Nik placed the finger bones near Jon's left hand and the ring on his own left middle finger. Immediately, he felt connected to his brother. He knelt beside Jon's remains, placed his hand on the empty chest, closed his eyes, and said a prayer to the Goddess. It was late, but he fervently hoped Jon had entered the hall of heroes and was in the company of his parents. Believing his family was together comforted him.

He stood, sad but feeling more at peace than he had in weeks. He must find a way of conveying Jon's remains to his Wildecoast family estate for a proper burial. It troubled him to think of disturbing the remains, but he could see no alternative than to load Jon into a sack and convey him that way. Better than leaving him for the crabs.

He waded into the water and swam through the crevice into a blustery overcast. While he had been in the cave, the sky had clouded over, and rain threatened. He waded up to the island beach and looked for Merielle. He couldn't see her; perhaps she was taking another dip.

Nik scanned the waves as he walked over to the other side of the island. Four redheads bobbed in the water, several yards from the shore.

Two mermaids were struggling to haul Merielle out into deeper water. A chill raced through him, and it had nothing to do with the blustery wind. Merielle was locked in a frantic struggle against the sea nymphs who gripped her upper arms and hauled her between them. Ignoring a more mature nymph who floated nearby, watching the proceedings, Nik raced into the waves, shouting for them to stop.

"Let her go," he snapped, grabbing the arm of one of the mermaids. She turned on him and snarled, a high-pitched note slicing through his head. He let go, holding his skull and breathing hard as agony throbbed through his brain.

"Who are you to order us, human?" the older mermaid said.

Still gasping to rid his head of the rebounding waves of pain, Nik turned to the speaker, whose green gaze blazed into him. Was this Merielle's mother?

"I am Nikolas Cosara," he said, injecting every ounce of authority into his words. "I've cared for Merielle these last weeks."

"Well, now she no longer needs you. I extend my thanks to you for tending to my daughter, Cosara. Now it is time for you to depart, if you value your life."

Dread settled heavily in his gut. He had no defense against these sea nymphs if they used their songs. His eyes met Merielle's and she gave a tiny shake of her head. What did that mean? Did she wish for him to stay or go? She tried to pull her arms from the grip of her sisters to no avail. He looked back to the mother.

"Your daughter seems unwilling to return with you, Madam."

"That is none of your concern. You have had quite enough influence over her already."

The remark struck Nik as odd. How had he influenced Merielle? He had tended her wounds and taught her some human ways. They had given each other comfort. Perhaps the matriarch saw him as a corrupting influence? Perhaps she thought Nik was the source of Merielle's reluctance to return to the sea?

"I can't allow you to take her against her will. Merielle has no desire to live with you."

"Believe me, Cosara, there are ways of making sure my daughter accepts her life with us."

Something deep in Nik rose up at her words. "You'll force her to accept a life which is repugnant to her? Merielle has told me of her fear but I didn't understand until this moment. You're her family but I see you care nothing for her."

"Caring is not part of our purpose. We exist to carry on our species. Merielle has told us your brother's body lies in that cave and how he came to be there. Perhaps it might help you to know his spirit now exists in a *mer* man. He lives on."

Her words smashed the comfort Nik had gained from finding his brother's resting place. The idea of Jon, trapped in a body he hated, being made to carry out abhorrent tasks that ran against his very nature… He pushed the thought from his mind. He couldn't let them make him angry – it was what they wanted. Merielle might have lied to him, but she'd also helped him from a dark place. He couldn't let them do this to her. After meeting her family, he could see how different she was. He focused on getting himself and Merielle to safety.

"Leave Merielle with me, Madam," he said. "She has chosen a life apart. If you take her, she'll cause you endless grief. Do you wish to have a family member who fights against you every step of the way?"

Merielle's mother hissed. "Why should you care?" She turned to study her daughter, her eyes running over every inch of Merielle's form. Her sisters studied her too.

"Perhaps he is right, Mother," one of the sisters said. "Look at her. She is almost ruined. The damage may be irreversible. We do not want a freak amongst us."

The other sister piped up. "I agree with Pearl. Merielle has been nothing but trouble, and now she is perhaps forever corrupted. Give her to the human and let him deal with the consequences."

The matriarch considered. "This is new, this corruption. She would be little use to us this way. It is a risk bringing her back. If she has chosen to live with you, Cosara, I might consider it."

Nik could tell a bargain would have to be struck. "What do you want?" An uncomfortable feeling up the back of his neck warned he wouldn't like it.

"You must take Merielle and depart immediately."

"My brother's remains lie in the cave. I wish to take them."

"Then you must choose," Merielle's mother sneered.

"Choose what?"

"I will allow you to take that pile of bones; all that is left of your brother."

Anger blasted through Nik. His brother was a pile of bones instead of a vigorous young sailor because of this mermaid and her kin.

Merielle's mother continued. "Take your bones, but you must leave Merielle with us."

At her words, Merielle keened. The sound sliced through Nik, so full of fear and pain and dread was it. He'd never heard anything like that from her. But what did he owe her? She'd been involved in Jon's death, and she'd lied to him. In time he'd forget the connection they had made, and he would have Jon's bones to bury, and a grave to remember him by. And Merielle would be with her family: cold, heartless *mer* people whose only desire was to perpetuate their race by murdering humans. Merielle was one of them, and yet she was neither cold nor heartless, quite the reverse.

The thought of her back in their merciless clutches hurt him. Merielle should be free to choose, no matter who she was. If he turned his back on her, the sound would haunt him forever. He wouldn't be responsible for the loss of even one more life. The thought of leaving Jon's remains behind brought a burning to the back of his throat, but they were only bones, not Jon. He knew what had become of his brother now, and one day he might return to claim what was his.

He sought Merielle's gaze. The desperation in her eyes sealed his decision. He could choose her life, and it was what he would do.

"I'll fetch the boat and Merielle will return with me. You may keep my brother's bones, for now."

As Nik crossed the island and waded out to the boat, he was tempted to have one last look at Jon's final resting place. But he fought the impulse. Instinct told him to take Merielle and flee, before they changed their minds. He climbed into the boat and sailed it around the island to where the mermaids waited in the shallows.

Merielle wrenched her arms from her sisters' clutches and swam over to the little skiff. One graceful leap brought her into the boat, and she covered her tail with the sheet as she had on the journey out.

As Nik prepared to depart, Merielle's sister, Pearl, cleared her throat. "Not so fast, human," she said. "I have one further condition. It is unprecedented that a human," her words dripped with venom, "should enter our company and leave in safety. There must be a penalty."

Merielle gasped and her mother's eyebrows shot up.

Nik looked at Pearl. "You have a condition?"

"In the years to come, I will succeed my mother, who grows old and infirm."

The matriarch turned her glacial eyes on Pearl, but she ignored them, continuing. "So yes, I have a condition, which you will fulfil if it should pass that you and Merielle wed."

Nik snorted. A crazy picture of Merielle in a wedding gown - her tail protruding from the hem - leaped into his mind. *Of all the insane ideas...*

"If you wed, you shall bequeath to us your first-born daughter on her sixteenth birthday. You shall bring her to this spot and leave without her. We shall take her and teach her the life of the sea nymph, and she shall be very powerful." Pearl was in a trancelike state. Her voice had changed until it seemed a higher power spoke through her. "This you shall promise, or you and the changeling will not be permitted to leave this place." Pearl blinked and shook her head as if awaking from sleep.

He and Merielle? It was preposterous! Merielle clutched his hand and pulled him close to her.

"We cannot agree to this, Nikolas. It is too much. Our daughter, we cannot bargain with her life."

"Merielle, it's not even possible for us to have a child. What's the harm in bequeathing a daughter who'll never draw breath?"

"I am telling you, Nikolas, there is power in her words. You saw it. Please, we cannot agree to this."

"How can we not? It's either that or leave you here. Are you willing to stay? It's nothing to promise a daughter's life who will never exist. Surely you see that?"

Merielle stared at him and he could see her mind worked furiously. Nik would have laughed if there wasn't so much at stake. That she could take this phony prophesy seriously!

Finally, she nodded.

Nik turned to the mermaids. "We agree."

Pearl's eyes lit with triumph.

Stupid nymph! Nik realized he was witnessing a changing of the guard in Merielle's family. Perhaps he could truly win out of this. "We bequeath to the *mer* people our first-born daughter at the age of sixteen," he said. "In return, you'll allow us to leave this place, and ensure the safety of the sailors on any ship I am captain of."

Fury flashed from Merielle's mother, but Pearl clutched her arm. "Let me speak, Nerissa." She stared at Nik, her eyes narrowed. "I agree to your terms. Any ship you captain will be safe from our people, until the sacrifice is presented."

Nerissa appeared to be choking on something and Nik wondered if the treaty would last when the current matriarch didn't support it.

"Can I trust your word?" he asked, looking at Nerissa.

Again, emerald fire blazed from her gaze. She nodded once.

Nik bowed to the mermaids, furled the sail, and the little skiff darted forward over the waves. As he sailed away, he felt the hard eyes of the sea nymphs on his back. He drew a deep breath and turned to Merielle.

"Don't think this means I've forgiven you," he said.

She ignored his statement. "I truly hope we don't regret this."

"I do too, but I couldn't leave you at their mercy. They have none."

"I am glad you see that," she said. "But our first-born daughter, Nikolas? It is too high a price."

"There'll be no 'first-born daughter'," he said. "We have nothing to lose."

Merielle's jaw tensed as though she battled with herself, but she remained silent.

"Now, I wish to put as much distance between us and your family as I can, before the wind drops."

CHAPTER 14

MERI sat huddled in the bow of the skiff, her changing lower half hidden by the sheet. Her mind buzzed with the events of the afternoon and she still found it difficult to believe Nikolas had chosen her over his dead brother. Perhaps he was not as furious with her as he wanted her to believe, or perhaps he just could not leave anyone to the mercy of her family.

At least he had seen the extent of the fate she faced if she stayed with them. Meri shuddered at the thought. They were more than capable of forcing her to undergo a mystical brainwashing which would render her useful to their cause, even as it deprived her of any real ability to function independently. It was a fate worse than death and certainly worse than her choice of becoming human, short though that life would be.

She allowed herself to dream of a future with Nikolas for a few moments. He would protect and cherish her and perhaps give her children to love. If there were no daughters conceived, all would be well. The bargain he had made struck fear into her heart. Of course, Nikolas did not yet know that a daughter for them was eminently possible, but he soon would. Meri would have to tell him before he observed the changes himself.

She would tell him soon; perhaps tomorrow. After his unpredictable behavior today, she couldn't imagine what his reaction would be. He would certainly be angry, but when she explained it was his love that had wrought the changes, perhaps he would have a different perspective.

The wind slowly dropped, and Nikolas furled the sails and pulled the food bag from under his seat. He handed Meri the watered-down wine and she drank long and deeply. A pity it was not full strength. She could certainly use something stronger.

He offered her bread, but she shook her head. "I am not hungry."

"You must keep up your strength."

"I am fine, Nikolas. I will break my fast on fresh fish in the morning. Do not concern yourself."

"But I do concern myself with you, and that's the mystery," he said, frustration oozing from every part of him. "Since the day I found you on the beach, I've been concerning myself with you and I don't seem to be able to stop it."

Meri hid the smile that tugged at her lips, grateful for the fading light. "I am truly grateful you chose me over bringing Jon home, Nikolas. I know how important finding him was."

"Important, yes, but I found him and satisfied myself it was indeed his body. I spent time with my brother, and hope he is now in the halls of the dead with our parents. Bringing him back was only a small part of that. I couldn't allow those creatures to take you, not when I know how much that would hurt you."

Meri smiled. "Always the honorable man."

He snorted. "It has nothing to do with honor! You might have lied to me, but you don't deserve to be tortured. Your family are cruel in the extreme. Whatever has passed between us, I couldn't sentence you to that."

"What *is* between us, Nikolas?"

"Before I learned of Jon, I believed we were becoming friends."

"And now?"

"Now, I don't think I can trust you, but you did help me to see I was letting life pass me by. I'll be forever indebted to you for that. I bargained for your life and now it's yours to do with as you wish. You're fit and well enough to continue your journey when we reach Wildecoast."

Meri closed her eyes and let his voice wash over her, soaking up the comfort for the long days ahead. "What if I wished to stay with you?"

"I don't see how you can."

"Would you allow me to stay with you if it were possible?

He was quiet for a moment, then shook his head. "I couldn't trust you."

Meri controlled the white-hot blast of temper that swept through her. "I did not remember Jon; I swear it to you."

"It doesn't matter."

"It matters to me. I do not like you thinking so poorly of me when I love you." Oops, she had blurted that out and now there was no taking it back.

Nikolas stared at her, a muscle twitching in his jaw. What would he say to her declaration?

"Impossible, out of the question."

She stared. "What do you mean? I am telling you how I feel, and you throw it back in my face?"

"If you expect me to make a declaration of my own, you'll be waiting a long time."

"I need no words from you. I know how you feel, and I have proof." Now was the time to reveal everything. No more secrets. If their union was meant to be it would survive this. The trouble was, a proud man like Nikolas might never recover from being tricked. Her secret, when revealed, had the power to destroy them.

Meri tossed aside the cover to reveal her truncated tail. The demarcations of her toes could clearly be seen, even in the rapidly fading light. He stiffened and looked up at her, eyes wide.

"I am changing. Soon, thanks to your love, I will be human."

* * *

Nik clutched the sides of the boat for support. His eyes must surely be playing tricks, his ears deceiving him. She couldn't have said she was becoming human; her tail couldn't really be altered so much. "Say it again," he snapped. "I can't have heard you correctly."

"You heard me quite well," she said, wariness oozing from every pore. "I think there is enough light to see I do not lie."

He ran his gaze over her lower half again. The dolphin-like tail he had come to accept over the last two weeks was much altered. Was it truly possible Merielle was becoming human? And what had she said? Thanks to his love? What sort of statement was that?

"Can it be true?" he asked.

"The evidence lies before you, Nikolas. Believe."

"Now I understand why you've kept it covered these last few days."

"I feared how you would react."

"And your recent illness? It was because of this?" He pointed at her tail.

"It was."

"Why couldn't you have come straight out and told me?"

"You have been through so much of late and you did not trust me at first. Then when you began to open up and speak to me, I feared damaging that trust."

"Would you say we've ever been friends, Merielle?"

She drew herself up and looked him boldly in the eye. "I would. You mean a great deal to me."

"Then tell me the truth. Everything."

She sighed and her shoulders drooped. He realized he wasn't going to like what she had to say.

"Most of it you already know. I fled my people and now you understand why. I wanted to be free to follow my own will and I knew that soon the choice would be taken from me forever. And so I fled, but not before the time for my first kill arrived."

"Yes, that's right, the killing of my brother which you conveniently forgot."

"It was the most distressing moment of my life," Merielle said, obviously upset at his sarcasm. "I thought I could trick my sisters into sparing him. If they thought he was dead, they would leave me to retrieve him from the ocean bottom and I could wake him. But I was wrong, and they made sure his death was taken from my hands." She paused, breathing deeply and wiped her hands across her eyes.

He followed the convulsive movements of her throat as she swallowed once, then again.

"Go on," he said, when the silence lengthened.

She glanced at him, but her eyes shied away. "I sat with Jon's body on that rock all night, hardly believing what had happened. I can't remember much of those hours except staring at the tattoo and Jon's face. And I remember how he looked at daybreak when I laid him in the cave." She wiped a tear from her cheek and Nik steeled himself to feel nothing for her torment.

"What about the rest?"

"I must have blocked it out after that. I don't remember much of my time with my family until I fled. I was involved in more seductions and my sisters made me witness several deaths, but that time is unclear. Finally, I knew I had to escape or face the witch who would enforce the mermaid law on me. After that, I would be one of them, body, mind and soul. I had to get away. I had it in mind I would flee to the land and find a human man to love me. There is a spell, a sung spell, that incites bodily change in my people. If they can bring a human to love them, and sing the song in his presence, slowly the spell will induce the change. And that is what you see before you. Soon I will be human."

Nik was silent for a long time. He'd never heard of mermaids becoming human.

Wait! She had said the spell could only work in the presence of human love. "You're trying to tell me I've been a party to this? That this means I love you?"

Merielle nodded, hope shining in eyes that glinted with moisture.

"I could never love you." *You've already admitted to yourself you do, idiot!* "Whatever has induced this transformation, it's not my love." His chest contracted and a burning grew in his sternum. He wished, more than ever, he had walked right by Merielle that morning on the beach.

"I knew you would fight this, beloved, and that is why I kept it from you," she said. "There is so much between us already, not least Jon's death. There was never a good time to tell you of my metamorphosis. But I am excited to be changing, even though my life will be much shortened. I can finally be true to myself."

He stared. "Don't call me that. I'm not your beloved. You've used me, tricked me, and if you think I'll overlook that, you're mistaken. I was developing a fondness for you, but that was before I learned of Jon. Now you tell me you've been using me these last two weeks, not just for shelter but for your other plans. How can you expect I'll forgive you?"

"We can have it all, Nikolas. I wish for you to follow your dreams, to forgive yourself, and return to the full life you deserve. I wish to give you a family. I will always love and support you. Now all you must do to seize that opportunity is forgive me for not telling you everything."

"You're delusional, Merielle. I admit I find you attractive, more so than any other woman I've known, but there must also be trust. How could I ever have that with you?"

"Have I not tried to help at every instance? Nothing I have hidden has harmed you."

"That's your opinion!" he snapped. "I can't talk about this any longer. Take your rest, and I'll row for as long as I can. I wish to be home where I can think."

"But Nikolas…"

"No more, Merielle. I can't," he said.

She frowned at him and bit her lip as if to stop the words from escaping, but at least she acquiesced. She made a pillow of her arm, pulled the sheet over herself and closed her eyes.

Nik sighed. Thank the Goddess! Now he could do some serious thinking about this situation without her eyes on him.

* * *

Meri closed her eyes but did not sleep. How could she when her life with Nikolas hung in the balance? She had no idea where things would lead now. There was relief he finally knew the whole truth, but he had reacted just as she suspected. Her honorable sea captain could not stand the idea that she had kept her plan from him. But surely, he had to recognize his feelings had caused her transformation? Would he have fallen in love with her had she revealed all to him at the start? Of course not! He would have tossed her back into the sea.

She was grateful for the chance he had given her. Now it was her turn to fight for a future with him. It would be difficult, but it would be worth it. This short new life of hers could be rich and wonderful if she could convince Nikolas to share it with her.

CHAPTER 15

TWO and a half days later, at dawn, Nik steered the skiff toward the beach below the cottage. He was relieved to be home, to have some space to escape. Merielle had accused him of running away from his problems, and he saw now she had been right. He did run away, but usually came back. He needed space to sort through his difficulties, that was just the way he worked.

Spending time with Merielle in such close quarters, after she'd revealed her secret to him, had been agony. Her body attracted him more than ever, especially with the promise of fulfilment he had never thought possible. However, her secrecy disgusted him, and the knowledge she had tricked him into spending time with her so she could hatch her plan to become human, infuriated him.

Merielle sat with her back to him, watching the approaching shore. He liked it best that way. Her gaze was too compelling and the hurt in her eyes wounded him. He felt responsible, just as he always had. It was what had gotten him into this in the first place: feeling responsible.

She slipped from the skiff and swam in the shallows beside the boat. Over the last two days of their return journey, she had steadfastly refused to speak to him except for the most necessary discussions based around meals and travel. He supposed she thought she was giving him space, but the silence chafed.

The sand grated on the bottom of the skiff and Nik jumped into the shallows and pulled it up the beach above the high tide line. "I'll fetch Storm," he called, gathering the bags from the bottom of the boat and striding toward the path that wound up the side of the cliff.

He reached the top and went in search of Storm. The horse was happily munching hay at a net strung from the tree in his paddock. Everything looked in order around the outside of the cottage. He opened the door and stepped inside. The smell of fresh baked bread and flowers greeted him. Someone had been here already this morning, but who?

The thought had no sooner crossed his mind than Alique entered the living area from the bedroom.

"Nikolas!" she said. "I wondered where you had gotten to."

He stared at her. She was wearing a royal blue riding habit. It accentuated her blue eyes and blonde hair and showed off every tempting curve. Realizing he was staring, Nik bowed.

"Lady Alique, your visit is unexpected."

"I thought I'd see how you fared. You look better than I expected."

"I heal quickly."

"And Lady Merielle?"

"She's taking a dip in the sea."

"You must have had an early start indeed this morning."

"No earlier than you, My Lady," he said, trying hard not to grind his teeth. If she suspected he didn't want her here, he'd never get rid of her. The thought of Merielle swimming, oblivious to the threat above, made his stomach spasm.

"I couldn't sleep for worrying about you," she said. "You left my care too early and I just had to see your healing was progressing well." She looked him up and down. "I must say, you seem to have made a full recovery." She stepped closer and ran her finger along his cheekbone where the flesh had been puffy and bruised. "I'd never have known." Her gaze fell to his lips and Nik froze. Her lips drifted to his, her right hand wrapped around the back of his neck and she pressed her body against him. Everything male within stirred.

When their lips met, Nik's arms swept around her and he crushed her to him, wanting her. But he feared if he allowed this, Alique wouldn't let him forget, and he might never be free of her. His lips moved in tune with hers, and he ran his hands down her back, molding her soft curves to his hard muscles. After so long without the pleasures of the flesh, it was good to have a woman against him. The drive to strip the gown from her and carry her to bed was almost irresistible. *Almost.*

Merielle waited for him. He couldn't indulge his desires with the intriguing Lady Alique. It would be a mistake even greater than forgiving Merielle for deceiving him. Alique most definitely had designs on him, and if he allowed her to get her claws into him, he knew he'd regret it. The last thing he wanted was to sire a brat with her. And that wasn't the only reason he had to deny her. He sensed they would never be compatible.

"Lady Alique," he said, having gently prized his mouth from hers. She clung to him as if her life depended on it. He tried again. "Alique!"

"Mm?" she said, eyes still closed, and lips swollen from his kisses.

"We can't carry on like this, My Lady."

"Who is there to stop us?" She opened her eyes and fixed her piercing gaze upon him.

Imagine waking up to that scrutiny every day. She'd never let him do anything remotely enjoyable, except for the obvious pleasures of the flesh they'd indulge in. "We both have obligations. I must saddle Storm and convey Merielle from the beach."

That made her pause. "Oh, she's waiting for you?"

"Yes, I should go." He remembered the bread and flowers. "Thank you for the baking and for tidying the cottage. We'll enjoy our fresh bread for breakfast."

"How homey it all sounds. But will your country guest be able to hold her own at court? I suppose we shall see."

"Whatever the future holds for Merielle, it doesn't concern you." He fixed her with a stern look. "The same can be said for myself. Believe me, you don't wish to be burdened by one such as I."

Anger flashed across her lovely face. "I was simply after a little fun, Lord Cosara. You're a handsome and virile man, and I'm a woman, who must have certain needs satisfied. You can't blame me for seeking you out."

"I'm flattered, but you really should go, My Lady, before we indulge in something we'll both regret."

"I would never regret an affair with you, Nikolas. I believe I'd find it most…stimulating. And I know the queen wouldn't object. She approved my trip out here."

Nik gazed down at the entrancing young woman, eyes full of hope, and a vulnerability he was startled to see. He swallowed. "Again, I must decline. You're beautiful, and once upon a time I'd have welcomed you with open arms. But now…it would be wrong of me to encourage this flirtation."

Nik was again surprised at the hurt that swept across Alique's face. She drew herself up, the hurt replaced with anger. "I will not ask again, Nikolas. It's your loss." She curtseyed.

Nik bowed deeply in order to assuage her embarrassment. "You have honored me, My Lady. Please, I beg you not to be discomforted. I wish you a safe return trip."

He bowed again and Alique swept from the cottage. He heard her horse gallop away moments later.

That had been awkward. His body still thrummed from the feel of her pressed against him. In the past he would have welcomed her, but to say life was a little more complicated now would be an understatement. The last thing he needed was a fling with Alique; with that young woman, an affair would never be simple. She very definitely came with complications, no matter what she said about having "a little fun".

The thought of romantic attachments reminded him Merielle still waited on the beach. He stalked from the hut, caught and saddled Storm, and made his way down the treacherous narrow path. He found Merielle luxuriating in the shallows.

Nik watched the waves caress her body. In the sunlight, her skin had taken on the faint greenish hue typical of all mermaids. Her perfect breasts greeted the early morning rays and the sight of them made him hard. He forced himself to examine her lower half. What had once been a dolphin-like tail had changed dramatically - the shape of long womanly legs appearing and the tail fins shortening and dividing into delicate feet and toes. She rolled a little in the gentle surf and Nik gasped. A delicious rounded feminine backside was rapidly shaping itself. His hands itched to explore the new territory.

Merielle's eyes flew open at hearing him. "Do you like what you see, Nikolas?"

He spluttered. "It doesn't matter what I like. Let's get you up to the cottage before someone comes along."

"Or we could lie together in the surf and enjoy each other for a time."

"Out of the question." He reached down and drew her into his arms, trying to block the thought of her luscious curves from his mind. That was difficult when she was pressed up against him. She'd set out to trap him, but he wouldn't let her succeed.

"You were not so reluctant last week," she said. "I am the same person now as I was then."

"Last week I didn't know about Jon or that you set out to deceive me."

She lapsed into a petulant silence as Nik carried her up the beach to where Storm stood.

He paused beside the horse. "Are you ready?"

She breathed deeply, battling the fear that always came with exposure to the horse. Nik didn't understand it, but it was a fact that had to be dealt with.

Merielle nodded. "I am ready." She closed her eyes and Nik lifted her onto Storm's back, her new legs facing him and her bottom in front of the saddle. Then he vaulted up and placed his arms either side of her, hands grasping the reins. Clucking to Storm, they ascended the steep and narrow cliff path, Merielle's arms gripping his chest and her head buried into his shirt. He kept up a soothing monologue for both horse and mermaid and they reached the top once again without incident.

Nik dismounted and drew Merielle down, striding with her into the house. He placed her in the rocker and fetched her one of his shirts, before walking back outside to unsaddle Storm.

On re-entering the cottage, he found Merielle slumped with her hands covering her face, breathing deep, shuddering breaths. Trying to ignore her struggle, Nik threw some more wood on the fire, that Alique had started, and boiled a kettle for tea. He sliced thick slabs of fresh bread and spread them with butter and honey before setting the plate and a cup of steaming herbal tea in front of her.

"Eat and drink," he said, hating the sound of his voice. He was doing the best he could under the circumstances.

She uncovered her face. "The only thing that will make me feel better is for you to understand me, to forgive me."

"Not going to happen any time soon, Merielle."

"I love you."

Nik gasped. "You don't love me. If you loved me, you could never have used me."

Fresh tears pooled in her eyes. "I never set out to use you. Right at the start, I never considered you might love me. You were so hostile and filled with anger for my people. I thought I would accept your hospitality to heal and then move on to another man."

"So you say."

"It is the truth!"

Nik almost believed her. "Say I accept that," he said, "what about when you began to sing the song of changing? You did it to induce your metamorphosis. Why didn't you say something then?"

She had the grace to look guilty. "You are right, and I should have told you. I started to have feelings for you, and you kissed me, so I knew you were not unmoved. But I could not trust you would allow the process to complete itself. I did not want to lose my chance at freedom. Even if you eventually cast me out, at least I would have a chance at a life. Don't you see I could not take the risk, Nikolas?"

"I can see how it would've been difficult, but what relationship can exist without trust?"

Her eyes dropped. "I am ashamed. I do not deserve you."

"Now we're getting somewhere."

"I would have told you sooner except then I remembered about Jon and you were so angry. How could I add to your dismay by revealing my plan?"

"You're a coward, Merielle." Nik knew he was being harsh. "I've been through hell because of you and your family." *Now she's destroyed a relationship that had begun to mean something to me.*

"I know that, and I am truly sorry. Can you forgive me?"

"I don't know. I truly don't." He entered the kitchen and began preparing lunch. "Eat up."

* * *

Meri forced the delicious fresh bread into her mouth and tried to chew it. She wasn't hungry but didn't wish to anger Nikolas further. She took a gulp of the herbal tea and it aided the passage of the bread down her throat. *Fresh bread?* She looked at the table in front of her and noticed the flowers for the first time.

"Where did the flowers come from?" He blushed and Meri's interest was further piqued.

"Never mind," he said.

"And the fresh bread?"

"I said never mind."

"Nikolas—"

"For the love of the Goddess, woman, Alique was here this morning."

Meri stared at the flowers. Alique? "What did she want?"

"Me, it seems," he said, sending her a smug look.

Fury flashed through her. *That hussy is moving in on my man.* "And?" she said, trying to keep her voice level.

"I sent her packing."

"She would not have liked that," Meri said, imagining the haughty lady being rejected by Nikolas. She could prove a powerful enemy. "Why did you send her away?"

Nikolas frowned. "Not that it's any of your business, but I think I have enough to deal with now. I have a band of angry mermaids ready to lynch me, a human-mermaid hybrid using me for her own agenda, and a heap of crap from the past to steer my way through, plus a queen who wants me back under her thumb. I don't need another bossy woman trying to command my time."

She frowned. When he described his life like that, it did sound daunting. "I wish you would not see me like that. I want to help you, Nikolas."

"We've exhausted this topic. I need to work through my feelings without pressure from you."

Meri ate a little more bread. "I am still hindered by my form. I have to know what you intend."

He stopped chopping vegetables to look at her. "I'll see you through to the end of your change, until you can fend for yourself. I haven't decided what I'll do after that."

Meri did not know how to take his words. He was not casting her out, but equally had not embraced her in his future. What did she expect? That he could put aside his feelings about her involvement in Jon's death? That he could forget she had lied to him? But she could not overlook the fact that he cared for her.

"I know you loved me once," she said. "You can do so again. Your love has changed me, and I can never forget that. Can you?"

He looked uncomfortable. "I only have your word that my feelings for you played a part in your metamorphosis."

"Nikolas! You have experienced feelings of love for me. Remember them! Do not deny what we have found."

He shook his head. "I won't deny I was developing an attachment before you told me of Jon, but everything has changed."

"I love you, Nikolas. I love your honor, your caring and strength. I adore everything about you, and we will be together."

CHAPTER 16

FIVE days had passed since their return from the sea voyage and Nik was no closer to deciding if his future would include Merielle. He'd never canvassed the possibility of a life with her when she was a mermaid. Getting his head around Merielle as a human woman was proving difficult. For her, the days passed in a haze of agony, her body accelerating toward the time when she would truly be mermaid no more.

Nik felt helpless as he watched her suffer and tried to ease her pain any way he could. His supply of powders dwindled and still she suffered. It seemed there was no end to the agony of her transformation. Would she think it was all worth it when it was over?

He lay back beside her after a particularly difficult night. If he was this exhausted, how must she feel? She spent most of her day writhing in agony, interspersed with short periods of unconsciousness. Her brow was continually wet with perspiration and his days filled with washing and cleaning, bathing her skin to keep her cool and calm her agonized breathing.

It seemed to help when he tended her. She settled a little and even smiled occasionally, although she didn't seem to recognize him.

Her lower limbs were almost formed. Perfect small feet with dainty toes had emerged from the flippers of her tail. Thighs and calves had sculpted themselves as an artist reveals a form from stone.

Nik watched, fascinated, for hours at a time as her lower body slowly changed. He fed her but she would only accept the fish broth he made fresh each day. Nik had a real sense that, left unsupported,

Merielle could die during this process. Her ribs were more prominent and her lovely face gaunt as he had never expected it to be.

And so, he redoubled his efforts to help, keeping the fluids up and spooning the broth in whenever he could get her to part her lips. He had gone beyond tired, for she woke him whenever the pain became too great and he would do whatever he could to relieve her suffering. Dust had begun to coat the cottage, but Nik couldn't afford the time away from his nursing duties. He could barely afford the short trip down to the beach to gather vital food for his broths.

He was not cut out for this and yet what other choice did he have? Merielle meant more to him than he had bargained for on the day he found her washed up like a piece of debris. Still, he wondered what would become of them when she emerged on the other side of this haze of pain. No matter. There would be time for that decision later.

All that day, Merielle seemed to battle her own body. Nik had never been so sure she would die. She tossed and turned and at times screamed his name as though he could take the pain from her. She never woke and, in between her restless fits, she dropped into a deep sleep where she couldn't be stirred. It was virtually impossible to get any sustenance past her lips.

She shrank before his eyes, her once-glowing skin becoming dry as parchment, her beautiful eyes sunken, lips cracked. Merielle was near death, he knew that now. He had done everything humanly possible for her and it had only slowed her death so far. Should he call the doctor, or Alique? Even as he had the thought, he discarded the idea. It would take too long to reach them and bring them back. She didn't have the time and he couldn't leave her untended.

Was it even possible for her to live a human life? Would she truly be human or just some curious hybrid? Would she still eat raw seafood and require a regular bathe in seawater? Was it just the metamorphosis doing this? Or had all the potions he had poured into her crippled her? He couldn't bear to have another death on his conscience, especially Merielle's.

Something in his thoughts made him pause. There was a clue in there he'd overlooked. There had to be. What manner of human was

Merielle now? Was it possible she'd always need the special things the *mer* people required? *Seawater!* Nik cursed at his own stupidity. He'd completely forgotten! She hadn't been anywhere near the ocean since their return six days ago.

He raced from the cottage and grabbed Storm from his stable. The horse seemed unsettled by Nik's haste and nudged at him as he threw the saddle on.

"I know boy," he said. "I'll feed you later."

He led Storm out, positioned him by the mounting block near the door of the cottage, then raced into the bedroom and lifted Merielle into his arms. She whimpered as he pulled her from the sheets and strode with her out to Storm.

"It'll be fine, my love," Nik said. "Just hold on."

He stepped onto the block and managed to get himself and Merielle into the saddle, cradling her against his chest. "Take us down to the beach, Storm." He gripped the horse tight with his knees and held the reins loosely, giving the horse his head so he could navigate the treacherous trail.

Many nervous moments later, they reached the sand and Nik pulled Storm to a halt. His arms and shoulders burned from the tension of keeping Merielle safe. The trip down the cliff had been foolhardy with an unconscious woman, but what choice did he have?

He threw his leg over Storm's wither and slid off the horse with Merielle in his arms. He landed cleanly and stepped into the shallows, wading out a little until he could lay her gently in the water. He knelt beside her. Now she was bathed in sunlight, he could see how fundamental the changes in her body were. The slight greenish tint to her skin was almost gone. Her tail had become two long legs, separated to the knee and finishing in two delicate feet, the toes of which were almost fully separated from each other too.

He closed his eyes against the sight that tempted him. And now she was changing, the temptation was all the stronger. Would he be able to resist her? Should he?

Nik opened his eyes to study her. She lay unmoving, pushed to and fro by the water as she floated in the shallows, her head supported on his lap. He leaned over her to shield her face from the sun.

"Merielle, can you hear me?"

There was no response, not a fluttering eye, a turn of the head or a twitch of her foot. *Nothing.*

"Merielle, come back to me." His voice cracked with emotion and he cleared his throat. "You can't let your family win. There has to be something more than this."

His heart ached for his stupidity. He should have asked her how this metamorphosis should be managed before she was lost to him, but he hadn't anticipated the severity.

"Come back to me, Merielle." There was still nothing. They sat thus for many long minutes, perhaps nearly an hour, until Nik's muscles cried out for release. He sat in the shallows then and pulled her onto his lap. She sighed and his heart nearly stopped.

"Merielle?"

"Mm?"

"Open your eyes, or at least squeeze my hand." He grabbed her hands in his, but they were limp.

"Merielle!"

There was a tiny flutter of her eyelids. It was something at least, a small indication she still heard him. *Just be patient.*

His stomach growled. Perhaps two hours had crawled by since they had left the cottage. The sun beat down on his unprotected head and his throat was parched. Damn his lack of preparation! But he was stuck here until she awoke. He had no choice but to wait it out.

Storm nickered. "Find shade, my friend, but don't stray." Nik clapped his hands and Storm ambled back toward the cliffs, settling under a small shady tree that protruded from the rock.

His attention returned to Merielle as she took a deep breath and moaned. Her skin had wrinkled and taken on more color. Perhaps this hadn't been a crazy idea after all.

"Meri, come back to me."

She moaned again and stretched her legs. "Nikolas?"

His heart beat fast at his name on her lips. "I'm here." He leaned over her so she could see his face. Her eyes were open, brilliant green orbs that locked onto him, sending a spike of fear into his heart. *I care too damned much about her.*

"Where am I?"

"You're at the beach."

"Why?"

"I hoped it might revive you. You've been so very ill."

"Oh." She smiled. "You were afraid."

He frowned. "Yes, I admit I was. Nothing I did seemed to help. You've been in and out of delirium for five days. It came to me that perhaps the sea might revive you. This was my last hope."

"It seems to have worked," she said, smiling again. She touched his face with her fingertips and smoothed the lines on his forehead. "I think all will be well." She gazed down at her body and gasped. "I am almost complete!"

Merielle sat up and then fell back into his lap. "Oh, my head spins."

Nik held her against him and trickled cool water over her brow. "Take it slowly. You've been near death for days."

She took a long, deep breath and sat up slowly. "I think I must swim for a while." She took more breaths, then rolled over and swam slowly into the deeper water. Nik stood so he could follow her progress.

At first, she swam slowly as if she was getting her sea legs. Gradually, she swam further and quicker, until Nik knew she was swimming faster than he ever could. He marveled at her grace through the water and wondered if she'd miss this very important part of herself. Would she retain some of the amazing characteristics of the mermaid? She rarely surfaced for air and as he watched, her body shot from the water in a short leap, sliding back into the waves with barely a splash. Despite the difficult week he'd had and his conflicting feelings for Merielle, he found himself grinning as she disappeared beneath the water.

* * *

At first Meri's body was slow to respond when she embarked on her swim, but it wasn't long before the energy was zipping through her limbs once more. The seawater was a balm to her aching body, and she could feel the toxins draining out and being replaced by the vigor of life. She surfaced, took a deep breath and dived again. She swam as fast as she could up the beach, out a little, and then back down the beach. Every two laps she took a breath. She could not hold her air as she once had, but perhaps that would return when she recovered. Or perhaps it would never be the same as before. She had known there would be losses and gains to life as a human.

As she swam, Meri mulled over the last week, which was only a fuzzy jumble of images and words. She had sensed the fear in Nikolas as he bent over her. He had expected she might die. There was no other explanation for it.

Where would their lives lead from here? Her transformation was almost complete. Soon she would be able to fend for herself and could start adapting to being human. Would Nikolas stay to help her, or would he run again? She surfaced and looked for him. He had shaded his eyes and was gazing at her from the shallows. He was keeping an eye on her. Perhaps she could count on him to see her through this transition. It was a lot to ask.

Meri floated on her back, gently kicking in a loop and looking at the clouds floating in a blue sky. She had spent plenty of time thinking about his feelings for her over the last weeks, but she had rarely stopped to examine her own feelings for him. Was this love she felt? Having never experienced love before, it was a difficult question to answer. Could she see herself living the rest of her life with this man? Could he give her what she needed?

The number one requirement for her was freedom to live her own life, not be dictated to. Nikolas had never tried to curb her freedom. When she refused to take him out to search for Jon because she feared her people, he had agreed the risk was too high. He respected her refusal. But then when he learned of her involvement in Jon's disappearance, he insisted on her help to find Jon's resting place. It had been only right and fair that he expected her to help him. She would do anything to remove the stain on her life that her involvement with Jon had left. Truthfully, Meri realized she could toil for the rest of her days and never repay the debt she owed Nikolas. And now he had saved her life, again.

So, where did that leave her? In debt to Nikolas, a man who desperately needed to be loved, and who needed to forgive himself for past tragedies; attracted to a man who perhaps still saw her as a monster; loving, *yes loving*, a man who might never let her into his heart. Had she already ruined any chance they had to be together because she didn't trust him enough to be completely honest? This opportunity at a new life meant so much to her, and now she had to wonder if her life would be bearable if it did not include Nikolas.

She rolled onto her stomach and kicked off in a final sprint away from the beach, then back to Nikolas in the shallows. She paused at his feet and looked up. He did not look at her but gazed out to sea as if afraid to meet her eyes. Then she remembered she wore no clothes. Carefully, she arranged her hair, so it covered her breasts, and then spoke.

"Thank you for looking after me, Nikolas. I will forever be in your debt."

Finally, he looked down, his eyes flickering over her backside where it was exposed.

"You're welcome." He cleared his throat. "I'm only glad the sea has revived you. It was a close-run thing."

"I will never forget what you have done for me."

Nikolas looked up and down the beach as if aware they could be discovered. "We had better go." He called Storm and the horse trotted to him. Nikolas picked Meri up and balanced her on the horse. She stiffened, panic blazing through her. Storm seemed to sense her fear for he snorted, which only made her more nervous.

"Nikolas," she warned, gripping his arms when he would have let her go.

His voice was low, soothing. "Storm would never hurt you, Merielle. Let me go and I'll soon be up behind you. Breathe, relax."

Slowly, she loosened the grip on his arms, and he vaulted up behind her. Immediately Meri turned her head into his chest and wrapped her arms around his waist.

* * *

Nik only had half his concentration on negotiating the path up the cliffs. The rest was on Merielle, who had her head burrowed into his chest and her arms tight around him. Her hair tickled his chin and she smelled of the sea. She was soft in all the right places and so damned enticing; he had to keep reminding himself that perhaps he could never trust her, and if he couldn't trust her, she didn't deserve a place in his life.

But no matter how often he told himself that, his eyes drifted back to her face against him and the trust he felt coming from her. How could she place all her cares at his feet when he couldn't do the same? They were such a mismatch it would be funny if it weren't so tragic. No, if he wanted a romantic attachment - and it was a big "if" at this point in his life - he should pick a woman who wouldn't bring the kind of complications that Merielle had.

With everything that had happened, Nik wondered if she could ever be truthful. Was it just a part of her makeup that she kept things from him? He couldn't live his life wondering if she was telling him everything.

Just the fact he was considering a life with her staggered him. He, Nikolas Cosara, was contemplating casting all caution aside and inviting a mermaid-turned-woman to share his life. But that was all he was doing: considering. There was time enough to mull this over and make the right choice. First, he had to ensure she was out of danger.

They arrived at the cottage and Nik would have dismounted only he had a trembling woman attached to him.

"It's fine to let go now," he said. "We've arrived and you're safe."

She opened her eyes and the look in them rocked him; part terror, and part trust that he'd rescue her from that terror. Could he handle the responsibility she'd bring?

"It is so difficult, Nikolas."

"What's difficult?"

"This human life. Is it worth the struggle?"

"Ah, the age-old question humans have been asking since time began. Only you can answer that for yourself."

"But what do you believe? It is such a short life, and full of difficulties and dangers."

Nik stared at her. "I thought you'd have contemplated that before you became human. Surely it's too late now?"

Her shoulders slumped. "You are right. But where is the reward for this difficult life?"

Nik heaved a great sigh. "The Goddess rewards us in the afterlife. This life is a test to see what that reward shall be. That's what I believe." Even to him, it sounded grim.

"That is truly what you believe?"

He nodded. "Now, could we climb down off Storm before he tosses us off?"

Her eyes bulged. "He would do that?"

Nik cursed silently, regretting his words. "It's unlikely, but horses can be unpredictable."

He slipped from the horse and drew her into his arms, then conveyed her into the cottage and installed her in the rocking chair. "I'll prepare the shower so we can wash the salt from our bodies."

She blushed beautifully and her eyes fell from his. Her skin had taken on a delicate alabaster sheen since her metamorphosis, making her even more exquisite in his eyes. He sighed. How was he to resist her? With each passing moment, it became more difficult.

He walked outside, unsaddled Storm and placed him in his paddock. All the while, he tried to keep his mind on the task at hand. He filled the shower pail with fresh water from the tank, trying not to anticipate the moment when the cool water would sluice over her body, washing the sand and salt away. He positioned a stool below the pail and walked back inside.

"Are you ready?" he asked, pulling a towel from a rail beside the door. He slung it over his shoulder.

"You are angry with me?"

Her words again made him huff out a breath. "I'm not angry. Could we please just get cleaned up? There'll be plenty of time for talking later."

"Of course."

He lifted her back into his arms, carried her out the front door and deposited her on the seat below the pail. He handed her the soap and pulled the slide from the bottom of the shower pail, so the water rained down over her body.

She immediately lifted her face and raised her arms to drag the water through her glorious crimson hair. Nik stared as the water tumbled over her, drinking in the sight of her wet nakedness. *Goddess I have it bad.* He had no idea how to defend himself against her. As Merielle began to run the soap over her body, clearly reveling in the delicious experience, he dragged his gaze away and reached for another pail. He filled it from the rain tank and climbed the ladder to top-up the shower pail.

"Nikolas, will you soap my hair, please?"

The groan that rose to his lips almost made it out, but he bit it back. He wouldn't let her see how she affected him, at least not the full extent.

Nik finished filling the pail and slid the base closed so the water was cut off. He descended the ladder and took the soap from Merielle, working up a lather in her long thick tresses. Goddess, she'd cause a stir if she ever made it to court. *Stop thinking about it!* As his fingers massaged her scalp, she sighed.

"Of all the things I have discovered since I came to stay with you, soap and a shower must be the most wonderful. There is truly nothing like it for restoring the soul." She sighed again, her eyes closed, the expression on her face peaceful, contented; the fragility of this morning fading fast.

"Glad I can be of use," he said, dismayed at his bitter tone.

She opened her eyes and stared up at him, her brilliant green gaze spiking his heart. He returned his attention to her hair to avoid her scrutiny. He was soon finished and reached up to open the sluice of water again. Merielle washed the soap from her body and hair, and Nik tried to avert his eyes as the soap bubbles ran over her breasts and coursed down her belly and thighs, but he just couldn't look away. *Oh man!*

Finally, the water ran out and he reached for the towel and wrapped it around her. He picked her up and carried her into his bedroom, seating her on the edge of his bed.

"Do you need help to dress?" he asked.

She looked up at him as she rubbed the towel through her hair, her breasts moving with her arms. Nik gulped to swallow down the desire that swept through him. She must have seen the effect she had, for she stopped and leaned back on her hands, which brought her lovely breasts front and center. He couldn't help staring.

He took a step toward the bed, propelled by the wave of lust that stormed through him. His second step brought him up against the bed and he kneeled on its edge, looming over her, wanting to feel her against him. Moving slowly, he leaned in to kiss her pale red lips. They parted in a gasp, so he deepened the kiss, exploring the warm depths, flirting with her tongue, surprised when she responded with some exploration of her own. At first, she was tentative but when his fingers found her nipple, she arched into him and her lips and tongue became melded with his in a fury of desire.

He fell to one side and pulled her around to face him, without losing contact with the soft lips that drove him wild. Her curves beneath his hand were different now, softer, more pliable. If only the process were complete, they might consummate this moment. His hand slipped down to the place where her newly developing legs met her body. The cleft there seemed to deepen as he explored but, despite

159

the rapid changes taking place in her body, it was too soon. Groaning in frustration, Nik flung himself on his back, tearing his lips from hers.

She gave a little cry and reached for him, unbuttoning his shirt and leaning to kiss first one nipple and then the other. Her hot mouth on his skin sent a wave of longing to his groin. She licked his nipples until he could stand it no longer and then her hand touched the bulge in his breeches and he nearly climaxed at the shock. She fiddled with the fastening of his pants then pushed them aside and he sprang free.

He was watching her face when his manhood escaped its confines and if he were not under her spell he would have laughed. Her eyes bulged at the sight of his straining rod and then she licked her lips. Perhaps it was a completely innocent gesture, it probably was, but all he could think of was her lips giving him pleasure, and release. It had been so damn long. His dick bounced at the thought and Merielle grasped it in her hand. He gritted his teeth to stop himself from crying out as he watched her mouth descend.

Her mouth closed around his shaft, her tongue exploring the tip and then flicking backward and forward. Then her lips began sliding up and down as her tongue performed its magic and he was lost. His body had a mind of its own and thrust against her as she claimed his shaft again and again until he was fit to burst.

"Merielle," he croaked. "I'm at my limit. If you don't want my seed in your mouth, stop now." He panted to force down the wave of release that had built, not sure if he could stop it.

"Your seed?"

"It is how we reproduce. I told you once before. Liquid."

"Will I like it?"

"Some women do."

"Will you like it?"

Her words were nearly his undoing. "Yes." The sound came out even more strangled than before. *Oh Goddess, let her put me out of my misery.*

She smiled before turning back and her lips descended, sliding up and down his shaft until he came in blinding, astonishing delight, his seed spraying into her mouth, her tongue and lips sucking down on him as she swallowed. He bit back a cry as she withdrew and lay beside him, her arm propping up her head, her damp hair cascading over her shoulders.

He had to say something to let her know how astonishing the experience had been, how he appreciated what she'd done.

"Thank you," he said and cursed silently. *Not good enough, man!*

"Is that what a man usually says to a woman after the sexual act?"

Nik huffed out an exasperated breath; exasperated with himself. "Sometimes. It's appropriate here as I've not been able to pleasure you. When there is both the giving and receiving of pleasure, that's usually enough without thanks."

She smiled. "You did give me pleasure."

"How so?"

"I enjoy loving you. There has been little enough I can do for you since I came to stay. I have given you far more pain than pleasure."

The admission seemed to cause her sincere distress.

He reached for her, threaded his fingers through her hair and pulled her in for a kiss that had her moaning and pressing her body against him. *Bad move.* Now he wanted her again.

"You confuse the hell out of me, Merielle," Nik said, tearing his lips from hers and struggling to breathe away the desire flooding him. This was wrong, so wrong.

She frowned and her small, perfect teeth chewed her lower lip. Even that fueled his desire.

"There is no need for confusion, Nikolas. Just give into your feelings."

He pushed up from the bed and paced back and forth across the small room. "I'm drawn to you, and yet repulsed by what transpired between you and Jon. Your deceit angers me, but I'm grateful to you for showing me there might be light at the end of my struggle. This can't continue or I'll drive myself crazy."

He hated the look of sympathy she fixed on him. Of everything she could offer him, it was the last thing he wanted. He could deal with this, damn it, and no amount of coddling from Merielle was going to make it easier. "Don't look at me like that!"

Her eyes widened and she gulped, appearing confused and dismayed. "Where does our next step lead, Nikolas?"

He sighed loudly and looked to the ceiling; better that than try to make sense of it all when she was lying naked before him. "Honestly, I don't know if there can be a future for us. That will depend on if I can get past the anger and distrust."

Her eyes blazed at him. "You will not get past the anger until you do trust me. I have told you over and over - I tried to save Jon. I will have the stain of his death on my soul for the rest of my days. How do you think I will live with that? It would be easier to forget if I had nothing to do with you, his brother, but I love you." She sat up on the edge of the bed, pulling her hair over her breasts like a shield. "Perhaps it would just be better to leave you now while I think I might be able to do so. You are a stubborn man, and I fear you will never believe me."

"You know it's not just about that. You lied to me."

"And what if I had told you of my plan to become human?"

"Honestly, I don't know, but at least you would've been able to say you didn't keep it from me."

Merielle thumped her fists on the bed. "You love me, Nikolas. The changes in my body are proof of that. Accept there is love between us and move forward."

Nik closed his eyes, still not willing to accept any of it. She had lied before. He was only relying on her word that his love had linked with her song to create her transformation. It all came down to trust. "Which dress will you wear? I'll help you into it."

Merielle scowled, seeming to want the matter resolved, and opened her mouth but closed it again. "The black and silver," she snapped.

He pulled the gown from its hanger and dropped it over her head, then helped her with the fastenings. The dark fabric made her skin appear even more fragile and his heart ached at the hurt in her eyes. She shouldn't be able to move him so, but he couldn't deny his feelings were strong when it came to the bewitching mermaid. Could they build a life together? The thought of a relationship built on the death of his brother and a trick scared him. But could he move on without her? Could he cast her out of his life and never know if she were dead or alive? Never know if the men she encountered would treat her with honor?

"I'll go fishing and prepare a meal while you rest," he said, grabbing his shirt and putting it on. "It's been a long week and an eventful morning."

She gazed up at him, the hurt still large in her eyes. "I do feel tired."

"Then rest. There'll be time for talking later." He left the room, not willing to gaze at her stricken expression any longer. As he grabbed his fishing rod and headed down to the skiff, Nik wondered how he was ever to negotiate his way out of the mess of his feelings for Merielle.

CHAPTER 17

MERI awoke to the delicious aroma of baking fish and she lay there, anticipating the moment when the soft white flesh would sate her hunger. But then the events of the past week or more tumbled in on her. Nikolas loved her but he would not admit it. Even if he did, he might not risk a future with her. Could she continue without him? What would happen to her body if it was not nurtured by his love? She did not know the answer to that question, and the thought of the painful metamorphosis reversing terrified her. She could not go through that again and live.

She shook her head. So many problems to be worked through, not the least was learning to walk once her change was complete. Would Nikolas help? She did not think he would expel her from his home, but he was unpredictable.

He appeared in the doorway and she propped herself into a sitting position.

"The meal is served," he said. "I'll carry you out."

"Not yet," she said. "Could I see if I can stand?"

His eyes widened. Her heart beat faster as she imagined being upright on her own. Could she do it? He walked slowly to her and helped to slide her lower limbs over the edge of the bed.

Limbs! The thought of having legs filled her with all kinds of emotions - fear, excitement, anticipation, hope, fear again. What would it be like to walk and run and dance? To make love with a man. Whenever she imagined that moment, it was always Nikolas she saw. And he was now waiting patiently while she hesitated, lost in her daydream.

She reached out her hands and he took them, pulling her to her feet and transferring his hands to her waist to help her balance. She closed her eyes for just a moment and reveled in the feeling of his hands on her body, and her feet - *her feet* - on the cold floor. She looked up into his eyes. He seemed to appreciate what a momentous occasion this was for her.

"I offer my sincere congratulations, Merielle," he said. "This is what you've waited and hoped for. If I hadn't seen your transformation with my own eyes, I'd never have believed it possible. And here you stand before me."

"Thanks to you, Nikolas," she said.

His face hardened. "So you've told me."

Meri resolved to drop the topic, at least for the next little while.

He grasped her hands and pulled her back and forth, so she swayed on her stationary feet. "You mustn't expect too much. Just get your balance this first day. Human babies spend months and years before they can master walking and running. In fact, they learn to crawl first."

"What is crawling?" she asked.

"It's when you go down on hands and knees and move with alternating hands and knees. Once you have full separation of your legs, I'll show you."

Meri's heart leaped with joy at his words. He was going to let her stay and teach her all she needed to know. She couldn't help beaming at him.

He frowned. "How does that feel? Are you ready to stand on your own?"

"If you let go but keep your hands nearby in case I fall, that will be best."

He did as she said, slowly removing his support until she stood on her own. The thrill of it ran through her like the current of the eel. She could stand on her own. Soon she would be walking, and then the world had better watch out. Nikolas had better watch out too. In that moment, Meri resolved to pursue him to the ends of the kingdom and beyond if she had to. She would never give up.

CHAPTER 18

IT had been two days since Merielle stood for the first time, but it felt more like a week. Nik suffered. The pressure built within him to flee the entire situation. The push and pull were agony. He'd lost his appetite and Merielle had noticed. She cast him anxious glances when she thought he wasn't looking, but she hadn't mentioned it.

He tried, he really did, but the mounting pressure of their history couldn't be ignored.

And now it was the day of the ball. The queen would be expecting them, but he dreaded Merielle's first foray into society. He'd taught her to crawl, to walk, but not to dance, and now it was too late. There was nothing for it. When the queen commanded, her subjects didn't spurn her, even if when they were her cousin.

He pulled his best breeches and tunic from the wardrobe and laid them on the bed, then grabbed a towel and went to take a shower.

As he stood under the cool stream of water, he decided Merielle was right. This shower and a good soaping were one of the best things in his world.

He dried himself as he walked back into the cottage wrapping the towel around his hips. His gaze met Merielle's.

"When are we leaving?" she asked.

"A carriage will be here to convey us to the ball in an hour or so. The queen has an afternoon of pampering in mind for you. Do you think you can manage that?"

She frowned. "What is pampering?"

"I don't really know; maybe a bath, scented oils, a maid to dress you and do your hair. Will your body stand up to the scrutiny of strangers?"

Her eyes hardened and Nik realized he could have put that more delicately.

"You would be a better judge of that than I, Nikolas." Her tone was short, angry.

Yes, I've offended her by asking about her body. "Goddess, I was only checking that your transformation wouldn't raise questions," he said. "I didn't mean to insult you."

Her chin came up. "Well?"

He huffed out a breath. "I think you'll pass the scrutiny of the maids who attend you. Whether you can pass yourself off as a fully-fledged human woman remains to be seen."

"Considering I have had little experience of human women, it might be difficult." Her voice was still frosty.

"Just keep your mouth shut and keep it simple. We'll talk on the way in the carriage and make sure our stories coincide. I'll try to stick close to you tonight. Obviously, I'll be unable to help during your pampering."

"There are no men allowed?"

He frowned. Perhaps he had underestimated the magnitude of the task before him. "No men are allowed in a lady's chambers, though there are communal baths under the castle. I doubt they'll take you there. The queen knows you're from the country and unschooled in these things." He paused. "I caution you against trusting Lady Alique. Since I spurned her, she might think you're her competition."

Merielle fixed him with her penetrating emerald gaze. "And am I?"

"I'm not interested in Alique Zorba."

"You didn't answer my question."

And I'm not going to. "You'll do fine at court," he said. "Keep your wits and don't complicate your story."

She frowned but didn't look nervous at the thought of appearing at court. Perhaps it was because she had no idea what to expect. He truly didn't know if she'd hold her own or be eaten alive.

"Is this gown suitable for the trip to Wildecoast?" She wore the dress which almost exactly matched her hair.

"You look beautiful. No need to further prepare. I'm sure Adriana has thought of anything else you might need. Now I must throw on some breeches and make sure all is ready for our departure."

* * *

Meri watched Nikolas stride through the front door, taking deep breaths to still the fluttering of her heart at the sight of his bare torso and tight breeches. Now the change was almost complete, her interest in him had escalated to almost unbearable intensity. At times it was a battle to keep her hands from him. He would not welcome such attention at this delicate stage in their liaison.

But now she was human, she truly appreciated his appeal to the opposite sex. How would she endure the long hours alone with him in the carriage? And he had said he would stay close to her at the ball as well. Meri did not think her overstimulated senses would cope with Nikolas in close quarters.

To distract herself, she tried to imagine what she might experience at the ball. With no understanding of human customs, she did not know where to begin. Instead, she swept the cottage and dusted the few objects Nikolas kept on the shelves. Then she washed the dishes from lunch and ensured all their food stuffs were stored away from invading ants.

Nikolas walked in the front door. "The carriage is here, Merielle. Are you ready?"

She removed the apron and tidied her hair. She collected the small bag with the few belongings she had accumulated since coming to stay with Nikolas.

"I am ready." She exited the cottage, walking slowly to keep her balance. Nikolas had said it would just look dignified, even regal, to move with slow deliberateness, but it mortified her to think she might fall flat on her face at court.

The carriage attendant's eyes widened when he saw Merielle, and he continued to stare before Nikolas cleared his throat behind her. The attendant, who looked to be the same age as Nikolas, stepped forward to help her into the carriage. His palms were moist. Nikolas steadied her from behind, his hands on her waist. Unused to stairs and flustered by the gawking attendant, Meri was grateful for the support. The door closed, and she sank onto the seat, surprised it was somewhat soft. She pushed her hand against it, testing the give.

"This is comfortable," she said, arranging her skirts and smoothing them.

"Nothing but the best for the queen's ladies," he said. "The seat is stuffed with horsehair." He continued to study her. "You mustn't mind the attendant. He was staring at your beauty. You're going to turn more heads when you arrive in Wildecoast; best brace yourself for that."

Her heart fluttered at the thought she would be the center of attention. She could not imagine it after trying to be inconspicuous for the last month. It was almost enough to stop her from imagining herself in Nikolas's arms. He had not touched her at all over the last two days, except to support her when she tottered, and her skin ached for his caress, her lips for his kisses.

"We must talk, Merielle."

Her heart beat fast. He sounded serious. Maybe he wanted to resolve what was between them, once and for all? Suddenly she was not ready to hear his words. What if he told her he could never make a life with her? They were traveling to Wildecoast. He might leave her there to fend for herself. Desolation enveloped her at the mere thought of a life without him.

"Yes, Nikolas." She swallowed hard, squared her shoulders and folded her hands in her lap. That was how ladies conducted themselves.

"We must get our stories straight."

Relief swept over her, immediately followed by frustration. Still he delayed the inevitable decision he must make. Or had he already decided his feelings for her? She had spied a tortured look on his face many times over the last two days. Perhaps he had not made up his mind yet. Perhaps tonight would be a magical night when she could show him what he would be missing if he rejected her.

Meri hoped none of these thoughts showed on her face. As a mermaid, she'd learned to control her feelings, so they stayed hidden, so she seemed cold. Most mermaids had no issue with this, but Meri had always had to work very hard at it. Now it might pay off. She could not allow the court to see she loved Nikolas completely and irrevocably.

"Merielle?" he said, a frown on his face.

She jerked back to the present. She should not be daydreaming when such an important occasion loomed before her. "My apologies. I am just a little tired. You wish to speak of our plan?"

"I do," he said, his sharp turquoise gaze examining her. "But perhaps you should try to get some rest?"

"No, I am quite well. Our story, Nikolas."

He nodded. "We've already told General Jazara you arrived on my doorstep, injured, and I took you in."

"Perhaps I was fleeing a man? My husband? You have said that is the word for the man a woman enters into a contract with," Meri said, fighting the fear she would never have that bond with Nikolas.

"Correct. Were you escorted?"

"Would a lady set out by herself?"

"No, that would indeed cause gossip. You might have been traveling with a small merchant caravan that was attacked by bandits, robbers. You fled into the forest, hit the coast and made your way north, and finally came here to me."

Meri nodded. "That is a worthy story. I am concerned only about one thing."

He raised his brows.

"Will people not gossip about my husband? Would such a man not search me out?"

Nikolas nodded. "Yes, you're right. Perhaps you're fleeing an arranged betrothal. That would mean you had no attachments."

"Betrothal? What is that?"

"It's the promise of a future marriage. Arranged unions are common - the parents of the woman and man offer their children for this union. There are usually benefits for both families."

Meri couldn't help the shudder that coursed through her. Was she fleeing the coldness of her race only to encounter equally cold customs here? To think all choice could be taken out of such a personal decision saddened her. "You speak so lightly about that, Nikolas. Would you not be angry to be involved in such a relationship?"

"I said arranged unions are common, not that I approved of them." He shrugged. "It's a fact of life for many of the upper classes. The queen would arrange a marriage for me in a heartbeat if she thought I'd countenance it. Hers was arranged." He fell silent.

"In case I might receive an offer from a lord at court, I would not want any perceived encumbrances." Meri fired the barb, hoping it would strike home. It did.

Nikolas stiffened even though he quickly hid it. "I'm not sure I'm comfortable with the thought of the lords of Wildecoast seeking your hand in marriage."

Meri lifted her chin. She hoped he lost plenty of sleep worrying about that. "You have had ample opportunity to make me yours over the last two weeks. I cannot wait around forever."

His hand whacked the seat beside him. Meri almost smiled.

"You know damned well why I haven't committed to you," he snapped.

"You cannot use that excuse forever," she said, assuming a lofty air. "I am not blameless, but I have apologized for the harm I caused you. Continuing to do so will not help."

He stared at her. Was he lost for words or had she finally penetrated his frustrating stubbornness?

"You're right. I must decide once and for all. But for this day and the next, let's enjoy the luxuries Wildecoast Castle has to offer. You'll be amazed, Merielle."

"Call me Meri," she said, unable to quash the wistful tone from her voice.

He frowned. "That would be inappropriate."

"Nikolas," she said, "you have touched me in places no one else has. You have given me the gift of life. Why should you not call me by the name I use for myself?"

"Meri?"

She nodded. "Meri."

"I'll try, but perhaps not at court. There'll be enough gossip as it is when you're presented."

A thrill of excitement coursed through her. She was going to be presented at court. A beautiful ball gown awaited her and pampering she couldn't even imagine. "So Nikolas, we have our story straight?"

He nodded. "You were escaping an arranged betrothal when your caravan was set upon by bandits, and you were injured fleeing the danger. You made your way to the coast, and then north to my cottage where I took you in. As for the rest, I think it better to be vague. Are you comfortable with that?"

Meri had been lulled by the sound of his voice and had not paid full attention. "Yes, I will be vague."

For the remainder of the trip, Nikolas pointed out the countryside they passed through, describing events that had occurred at different points along the way. At a castle ruins, the last battle for the kingdom had been fought and the castle destroyed by fire. That was when the king's new seat at Wildecoast had been constructed. He pointed out farms and described the produce grown there. It was all fascinating to Meri, and her excitement increased with each mile.

Nearing Wildecoast, they came upon a small patrol of soldiers. The sergeant knew Nikolas.

"Nikolas Cosara," he said, pulling his horse up beside the window of the carriage. "I suppose you and the lady are here for the ball?"

His eyes roved over Meri whose face grew hot. What had happened to cool and composed?

"Fin!" Nikolas said, reaching to shake the hand of the soldier. "It's an age since we've crossed paths. How are you?"

"Still raising hell, Cosara. And you?"

"No hell to be raised out where I live," Nikolas said.

"So I heard." He dropped his voice. "Seems you managed to pick up a lady friend though, man."

Meri noticed Nikolas stiffen. "The lady was in need of help," he snapped. "Would you have me turn her away?"

The sergeant looked again at Meri. "No man, *I* couldn't."

"Are we cleared to pass into the city?" Nikolas asked.

"There'll be another checkpoint at the gates as usual. You'll have to satisfy Grif, but I'm sure that won't be a concern."

Nikolas saluted and tapped on the roof of the carriage to start it moving forward.

Meri sat in silence. "Will it be like that at the castle?" she asked, finally.

The gaze he turned on her was sympathetic, or was it pitying? "Worse, Meri. The court feeds on gossip, and your arrival will be the biggest event since Lady Benae and Squire Ramón arrived unchaperoned last month."

Her excitement turned to fear. "You could have tried to set my mind at rest, Nikolas."

"I'll be by your side. Just smile if you don't know what to say."

The carriage rolled on toward the castle and they were soon at the outer gate. The sergeant, Grif, waved them through without more than a glance, but Meri caught the wink he sent Nikolas's way.

"A friend of yours?" she asked.

"Grif and I go way back."

Meri barely heard, so transfixed was she with the crowds lining the streets inside the gate. "Who are all these people?"

"Townsfolk come to see the high and mighty arrive for the ball." Nikolas stuck his arm out the window and waved in the general direction of the crowd. A roar went up and people waved and jumped up and down, men holding small children above their heads so they could see the approaching carriage. A few closer folk frowned and brandished their fists in the air.

"Looks like some haven't forgotten my past," Nikolas muttered.

Meri grasped his hand. "They will forgive in time."

Her words only served to deepen his frown. She turned back to the view, never imagining there could be so many people in the world. This was just one city of the kingdom, and the Kingdom of Thorius was only a part of the larger continent, and that was only one part of an entire world. *There are so many lives squashed into this place!* Meri could swim for miles in the ocean without coming across another mermaid, and it was rare for them to congregate in numbers larger than the family unit. *How will I ever cope with this overwhelming accumulation of people?*

A large warm hand squeezed hers and she turned to Nikolas.

"Try not to worry," he said. "Just wave back and enjoy the view."

"There is no danger?"

He pointed to the rooftops and Meri spied men atop the gables, arrows nocked, sharp eyes scanning the crowd.

"They're Wildecoast's top archers, trained by Kain Jazara, and paid to keep the guests safe. I'd place my life in their hands in an instant."

Meri released her breath and tried to relax back in her seat. She even waved occasionally. "What do the women wear? It is quite different to the gowns the queen sent me."

He laughed. Meri was glad she amused him. Honestly, how was she supposed to learn if he laughed at her questions?

"That's their holiday best. The head cover is a bonnet, the flowers are always worn in the hair, and the aprons are decorated with frills and embroidery. Their dresses are made from cotton - it's all these women can afford. The dresses my cousin sent you could never be owned by these folks."

"I had never thought there could be such a chasm between your peers and the common folk. It seems they live in two different worlds."

Nikolas frowned. "In a way you're exactly right. I know it must seem wrong that some have so much while others have comparatively little, but I've lived on both sides of the divide and there's much to be said for the simple life. If you have a roof over your head, food on the table, and someone to love you, that's all you really need."

Meri felt the power of his words, and knew he absolutely meant them. Nikolas would gladly give up all the trappings of his life and the power he wielded if he could be happy. But Meri suspected he would not be left alone for long. He had been given the space to grieve and brood, but the queen would one day demand his presence back in Wildecoast, and he would again have to take up his responsibilities.

"The upper classes have the responsibility to protect those less fortunate," she said.

"That's how it's supposed to work." He stared at the hordes of excited townsfolk whose numbers grew larger as they drew closer to the inner gates of the castle. "Sometimes those in power use it to advance themselves. I hope I'll never be such a person."

"You are a good man, Nikolas," Meri said, suddenly gaining an insight into what had really upset him about the shipwreck. "If you could have, you would have saved every last one of those sailors."

He had fallen into a brooding silence.

"What would you do differently if you had the time again?" she asked. "Would you not take your rest, knowing you were too tired to trust yourself? Would you not go looking for your brother and see him to safety?"

His face tightened as he contemplated her questions. "Of course I'd rescue Jon. How could I leave my brother? But would I take the break? Knowing what I know now, I'd have to say no. Would it have made any difference to the outcome? I suppose I can never know that." He stared at her as if a revelation had suddenly hit him.

"You cannot look back in the past and say, 'What if I did this, or that?' All you can do is move forward and try to be a good man. Please do not torture yourself. It does not help, and it will not bring all those people back."

"Somehow I must learn to move past all of that," he murmured, seeming lost in thought.

At last he sees the error in his thinking! But it would take more than that for Nikolas to truly move forward. Meri just hoped he would allow her to stay by his side as he healed.

She had no further chance to contemplate, for the carriage had stopped at the inner gates, where another sergeant spoke to Nikolas. Meri heard little of the discussion, for her attention was focused on the castle. It was gigantic, or so it appeared to her, constructed of weathered blocks of gray stone, and rising at least five stories into the air, with turrets much taller than that. Nikolas had told her the turrets were for defense of the castle, and Meri could only imagine the view she would enjoy should she be brave enough to climb one.

The carriage rolled through the gates and into the castle forecourt, drawing to a halt before the imposing stairs that led to the front door. She peered from the window, eager to catch her first glimpse of royalty - apart from Nikolas, of course.

He turned her around to face him. "Follow my lead, Meri. Walk slowly, remember, with dignity. Smile often and… Damn!"

"What is it?"

"I forgot to teach you how to curtsy." He poked his head from the carriage, speaking to someone outside, perhaps the bored-looking man who stood near the foot of the stairs. Nikolas turned back to Meri and she took a moment to admire how his frame filled the space inside the carriage, his shoulders brushing the ceiling. "It's too small a space but let me show you what a curtsy is." He placed his hands as if to clutch an imaginary skirt, took one leg behind the other and bent his knees, dipping his head at the same time.

Meri giggled. "When should I do this?"

He cursed under his breath. "Whenever you meet or take leave from those who might be considered your betters, you should curtsy. The higher the rank, the deeper the curtsy - you can offend by not dipping deeply enough. Then again, you don't want to go too far the other way."

She stared, aghast at the potential for catastrophe this simple gesture could cause. "How is it possible for me to stay out of trouble?"

"Keep an eye on the others around you and follow their lead. Most of them will be above you in social standing so just show more respect than they do."

Tremors raced through Meri at the thought of being thrown into this ocean of potential mistakes.

Nikolas reached for her hands. "It will be fine, you'll see. They know you're from the country, and they'll be so transfixed by your beauty no one will notice."

"I hope you are right."

"I am. Are you ready?"

"No, I will never be ready for this."

"Take a deep breath. Let's get this adventure started." He opened the door, leaping to the paving stones and turning to hand Meri down from the carriage.

She hesitated, aware that when she alighted, there would be no turning back. Nikolas looked up and his smile shot through her, warming the cold block of fear that had settled in her stomach. Without words, he seemed to be saying all would be fine and he would be right beside her to protect her.

Meri squared her shoulders and straightened the folds of her skirt, then stepped from the carriage, placing her hand in Nikolas's as she did so. It was harder to alight than she had contemplated and as she stepped down, she stumbled. His hands came around her waist and he lifted her, ensuring she had secure footing before slowly releasing her.

"Watch your step, Meri. You're not used to stones underfoot, and they can be slippery."

He smiled again, the warmth in his gaze holding her attention, creating a private moment that locked out the rest of the world.

Someone nearby cleared his throat, and Meri turned to find the man she had noticed earlier, frowning at them, at her.

"Lord Cosara, My Lady," he said. "Welcome to Wildecoast Castle and to the Royal Court. Queen Adriana sends her apologies that she cannot greet you herself. She has some last-minute matters to attend to. I will have the housekeeper show you to your rooms." He bowed to Nikolas and turned to Meri. "My Lady, you will be shown to your chambers where staff will prepare you for your entrance into society."

Meri heard his words, but they made no sense. What was he talking about? Entrance into society indeed! But she curtsied to the officious little man and smiled.

The man's eyes widened but Meri didn't know what might have caused his alarm.

"Please follow me, Lord Cosara, My Lady." He turned and hurried into the castle.

Nikolas caught her elbow. "Don't ever curtsy to a servant, no matter how important their position." His voice was soft, but Meri still heard the censure.

Her temper instantly warmed. "I am doing my best," she snapped. "I am sure it will be the least of my errors this day."

He frowned. "Just think before you act. Be polite to the servants. That's all the respect they seek. Anything more will cause gossip."

"The court will know I am a rustic, Nikolas."

"You must keep them guessing. Act like a princess, expect much, say little. Smile a lot…" He stopped as they caught up to the steward.

"I'll show you to your chambers, My Lord," the steward said, "and then escort the lady to hers. A repast has been delivered to your room, and the baths are ready for the gentlemen. The ladies have already availed themselves of the facility this morning, but of course, Lady Merielle will bathe in her room."

Meri felt her face heat. *All this talk of bathing!* These people placed great store in being clean, obviously. The thought of the man commenting on her bath seemed wrong. And what were these baths the gentlemen were going to this afternoon?

They reached the chamber assigned to Nikolas and he left her with a bow. Meri remembered to offer a moderately deep curtsy and was rewarded with his gentle smile. This time she had done well. She allowed the happy thought to warm her as she followed the steward along the hallway and into another wing. Meri lost her bearings in the maze of corridors, but soon they arrived at a door made of golden wood.

"This is your chamber, Lady Merielle. The queen has bestowed an honor upon you by assigning you these rooms." He laid his hand reverently upon the door. "This is golden oak, very rare in the kingdom, and some would say the most beautiful of all timbers." He stroked it, then pulled a cloth from his pocket to polish the surface where his hand had been.

Meri wished he would open the door to allow her first glimpse of the chamber. And that is what the steward did when he was satisfied the timber had resumed its former sheen. The door swung open to reveal a sitting room paneled in the same golden oak as the door. The effect was warming. A fire crackled in the grate of a much grander fireplace than she was used to back at the cottage.

A young woman in a black dress hustled out from another doorway and dropped a low curtsy before Meri. "Lady, I am Somata, your maid while you're here."

Meri didn't curtsy this time but smiled at the pretty blonde woman. She was only young, perhaps late teens, and her eyes were an open and friendly pale blue. "Hello, Somata." Meri wanted to say more but she could almost hear the words of Nikolas, guarding her against revealing more than she wished.

Somata smiled. "I have your luncheon laid out, and after that I will bathe and dress you. There is so much to be done, and only six hours left before the ball!"

Meri could not conceive it would take all afternoon to prepare and yet Somata seemed to think such a long time would only barely be enough.

The steward cleared his throat. "You're in good hands, Lady Merielle. I hope you enjoy your stay in the castle."

Meri turned to the steward and smiled. "Thank you."

He bowed and left.

Meri allowed Somata to usher her from the cozy chamber into a dining room where a bath was set up at one end. Another door stood open in the opposite wall and Meri assumed this must be the sleeping chamber. This set of rooms was twice the area of the cottage. She was a little daunted by the sheer size of her chambers, let alone the castle itself.

"Come Mistress, you must be tired and hungry," Somata said. "Please sit and eat. Then we'll heat your bath and prepare you for the ball." Somata gazed at Meri, blushing, and then drew out a chair at the small dining table.

Meri perused the meal before her. There were fresh warm rolls and butter, and hot herbal tea, a cheese platter and a spiced seafood broth. The chunks of fish floating in the soup still had the pearly sheen of uncooked fish. They must have been tossed in at the very end of cooking. *Nikolas.* He had made sure the food was to her liking. She loved him for giving her this special gift amid all the strangeness. He could not be as angry with her as he appeared, could he?

It did not matter how much he cared for her, if he did not wish to have her in his life, if he did not trust her, then there was nothing more she could do to convince him.

* * *

Nik lay back in the steaming water of the underground cavern and felt some of the tension drain from his shoulders. This was something he'd missed during his exile, the long hot baths he used to take in this very cavern. The unique hot springs beneath the castle had been opened by hacking through the rock of the mountain many centuries

180

ago. An ingenious system of locks and canals allowed fresh hot water to flow in, and the spent water to be drained on a regular basis and used for watering the castle gardens.

He had company. Kain Jazara had appeared at his door within minutes of his arrival, shared his lunch and then insisted on escorting him to the baths.

"This is the life," Nik said, letting the air escape from his lungs in one long sigh.

"Thought you might need something to relax you," Kain said. "I saw you arrive. You looked tense."

Nik ignored the comment.

Kain didn't take the hint. "She's still living with you, then? You said the fair lady was on her way weeks ago."

"Her recovery has taken longer than anticipated."

"She looks fine to me, more than fine."

"Merielle is almost fully restored to good health."

"Then say goodbye and move on with your life. She's not good for you."

The tension that had eased from Nik's shoulders was suddenly back with a vengeance.

"You know, Kain, this has nothing to do with you."

"I want to see you happy… and back in the navy. Everyone does."

"Why is this about what you want? Surely it's my decision?" Nik snapped. He should know better than to allow Kain to get under his skin.

"Look, I know you're in pain, my friend. Sometimes it's easier to see the facts from the outside looking in."

Nik swallowed the angry words he wanted to hurl at Kain. This was his business, not anyone else's. It was unfair of his friend to stick his nose in and think he knew better. Merielle was good for him in some ways. It was just a pity she couldn't be honest. But she had her own cross to bear, her own adjustments to make.

"Back off, will you? I know you mean well, but this doesn't help. I'm working my way through this in my own time, and that includes Merielle."

"Does that mean she's helping you, or that she's part of what you have to work through?"

He shook his head. "I'm not going to discuss this with you. Now leave me be." He closed his eyes and laid his head back against the stone edging, willing every muscle to soften. With a great heave of warm water, Kain left the pool and Nik listened to his wet footsteps as they left the chamber. *Now maybe I can relax.*

CHAPTER 19

THE time of the ball had arrived, and Nik was more nervous than usual for such occasions. Traditionally, the queen would line up a bevy of suitable ladies to parade before him; an endurance test he had no patience for this night.

But his gut swirled with a strange excitement as he walked toward the wing that housed Merielle's chambers. As much as he tried to quash the anticipation, he couldn't ignore the connection he felt to her. He swallowed, clearing his throat as he knocked on the golden oak door. The maid swung the door wide, but he barely noticed her.

Merielle. A vision in cream and gold. Her body was sheathed in cream satin studded with pearls and trimmed in gold thread. The full skirt, falling from her hips to the floor, was overlaid with golden lace. Her shoulders were bare, the neckline plunging to reveal the top of her shapely bosom, and her arms encased in more gold lace. Nik stared, his mouth dry, breath stolen, every thought fled from his mind. The luster of her skin was complemented by kohl to the eyes and a light blush over her cheeks. He wanted to race her away, ignoring the ball and everyone at it.

And then she presented him with a deep and perfect curtsy that showed her bosom to its best advantage, and very nearly brought him undone.

"Lady Merielle," he said, his voice as hoarse as an adolescent. "You're exquisite."

Her eyes widened, surprised. Had she even looked at herself? She'd attract every eye at the ball - all the women would be in her shadow; every man would crave her company. The thought wasn't welcome.

"Thank you," she said. "You look very handsome." Her eyes darted down past his chest and back up to his face as though she was afraid to look at him too closely. "You have cut your hair!"

"Merely a trim, My Lady. The queen's fussy about these things, and it's long since these unruly locks have been pulled into line."

She stepped closer. "I like your unruly locks, Nikolas." Her gaze lingered on his.

He cleared his throat, unwilling to believe she was flirting with him. "Let's join the company, Merielle." He offered his arm, which she took. "The queen will be anxious to meet you."

He guided her out of the chambers and down the hall.

* * *

Meri's heart beat faster than she had ever imagined as she walked with Nikolas toward the ballroom. She hardly paid attention to the halls they traversed or the people they met along the way. How she longed for her old life in that moment - even the horror of being chased by the killer whale would be preferable to being the center of attention tonight. *Perhaps Nikolas is wrong, and no one will notice me?*

Even as she had the thought, she knew it was impossibly silly. She was with Nikolas Cosara, and every person at the gathering, including the queen herself, would want to spend time with him. *Why did I ever agree to this?*

They descended a level and her steps dragged. Nikolas stopped and turned to her.

"What's the matter?"

"I cannot do this," she said, leaning against the wall.

"That's not an option now, Meri. You should hear the buzz around the castle," he said, amusement dancing in his blue-green eyes. "You're big news. These people are bored, so they make the most of every event that comes their way."

She frowned. "How can you stand it?"

"Why do you think I've spent the last year and more out at the cottage?"

Meri huffed out a breath. This must be nearly as hard for him as it was for her. Nikolas was a loner and he had suffered so much loss. *If he can bear this, so can I.*

"You are correct," she said. "I can endure this for one night."

As he gazed at her, his expression softened. "I'm not going to force you, Meri."

She squared her shoulders. "The queen has given me much and she is your cousin. I will not bring shame upon you by throwing her kindness in her face. Just do not stray far from me." The fear returned as she uttered the words and she wondered where her brief show of bravado had come from.

Nikolas smiled and they continued, soon arriving at the top of a grand staircase. The buzz of many people talking rose to them from the open doors that led off the foyer at the base of the stairs.

She groaned. Why did there have to be so many stairs? She was sure she would trip and fall head over heels before the end of the night. But she did not hesitate as Nikolas stepped off, holding his arm out for her. He went slowly, and about halfway down, Meri heard an announcement.

"Lord Nikolas Cosara, the Queen's cousin, and Lady Merielle."

By the time they arrived at the foot of the stairs, every eye in the ballroom was trained on them. Meri felt like the air had turned to honey. She could hardly move, let alone breathe. Nikolas escorted her to the doorway where he paused. A stunning, dark-haired woman in a crimson gown and silver tiara approached them, trailed by an assembly of young ladies. Meri had never been in the presence of such regal grace.

Nikolas bowed to the queen and then turned to Meri. "Your majesty," he said, "this is Lady Merielle. Merielle, this is Her Majesty, Queen Adriana Zialni, mistress of Wildecoast."

His elbow bumped Meri out of her stupor, and she dropped into a deep curtsy. *At least I can now execute that correctly!*

The queen reached for her hand and drew her upright. "I am pleased to make your acquaintance, Merielle. I hope you are now fully recovered?"

"Yes, Your Majesty," Meri said, sounding to herself like a simpleton. How was she ever to survive this night? "Um…it is an honor to meet you. You have a lovely home."

Adriana's laugh was like sweet bells ringing. "Thank you. I quite like this old castle, though the maintenance is a killer." She laughed again and so did Nikolas. The queen turned to him.

"You are looking good, cousin," she said, drawing him closer and kissing him on both cheeks. "I hope this visit means we will see more of you around here."

His jaw tensed. "We'll see, Adriana. Where is the king?"

"Changing the subject will do you no good," Adriana said. "Beniel will return shortly. There were some matters he had to attend to. It has been so busy of late, what with the sudden wedding of his brother."

"Yes, why was that?"

"I do not think it wise to discuss it here, cousin. Suffice to say, Jiseve has always been impulsive, unlike my Beniel." Adriana smiled, and Meri thought that for all the rumors of the queen's arranged marriage, she seemed truly fond of her husband.

A buzz gripped the far end of the ballroom and they all turned to see what the fuss was about.

"Ah, there he is now." The queen beckoned, and an older blond man, dressed in a red tunic, approached.

Adriana drew him alongside and turned to Meri. "My husband, King Beniel Zialni, please meet Lady Merielle."

Meri dropped into another deep curtsy and was mortified when she staggered a little on rising. All this up and down motion was difficult when she had only just learned to walk.

"Hello, Lady, and where do you hail from?" the King asked, his startling blue eyes full of kindness.

"I am from the south, Your Majesty, and have been staying with Lord Cosara as his guest. I was injured on my travels and Nikolas took me in. He has been most kind."

Beniel turned to Nikolas, studying him with narrowed eyes. "Most kind, indeed, My Lady. It seems he was in the right place at the right time. These are dangerous days to be on the road."

"And you have been on the road of late, Beniel," Nikolas said. "You're both just back from Prince Zialni's marriage. Did you come across any dark elves?"

"One hundred soldiers have the effect of clearing the road ahead, Nikolas. We had no concerns. My men did flush out several pockets of the vermin, who were holed up in the woods some way from the main road, but they were quickly taken care of. I have initiated regular patrols between Brightcastle and Wildecoast, with occasional forays into the forest surrounding, just to monitor elven movements and keep their numbers under control." He glanced to Meri. "But this talk of elves and soldiers must surely distress the womenfolk." He smiled at the queen. "Might I suggest we ask the musicians to play their first tune and we lead the gathering in a dance, my love?"

Adriana bowed low before her husband and the two swept away, seeming not to have a care in the world.

Nikolas turned to Meri. "Your first dance, My Lady. I hope they don't play anything too difficult, for you or for me."

Meri smiled. "Something tells me you will have no difficulty with anything the musicians play."

His gaze warmed at her words and she drew in a sharp breath. If only he would gaze at her like that all the time.

The music began. It was a lively tune but with simple steps. They watched for several bars before joining the dancers. Meri was tense at first, head down, concentrating on her feet. But after a while, Nikolas gently tilted her chin, so her eyes met his, and she was able to be confident in her steps without looking at her feet. It was then that she could enjoy the feel of his arms around her and the press of his hard thighs against her hips, reminding her of everything they could now share, if only he was willing.

The dance finished and amid the polite clapping, Meri realized she had taken her first steps into society. She was feeling proud of her accomplishment, when Lady Alique swept up to them. She wore a gorgeous royal blue gown, but Meri was shocked at how much bosom her plunging neckline revealed.

"Merielle," Alique said, "that dress looks gorgeous, almost bridal."

Meri fingered the lace on her skirt and tried to smile. "Good evening, Lady Alique. Thank you for your part in organizing this."

"Oh, I did nothing. Merely kept the process moving while the queen was in Brightcastle. It's pleasing you were able to attend." Her gaze slid to Nikolas, roving over his impeccable dark gray tunic and breeches. What she saw seemed to delight her. "Good evening, Lord Cosara. I hoped you might have saved this dance for me."

Nikolas seemed torn between Meri and the buxom Alique. "I've promised this dance to Merielle, but you may have the next, Lady Alique."

She sniffed, her eyes frosty. "I'll find you later, Nikolas. If my card permits, we shall dance then." She gave Meri a small nod and swept away.

Nikolas took Meri into his arms, but she could not relax, thinking he was only staying with her because she needed him, while he really longed to dance with the golden-haired woman whose charms were so much on display.

She pushed back a little from him as he guided her onto the dance floor. "Nikolas, you did not have to choose me when you obviously wish to dance with Alique."

His eyebrows rose. "How did you come to that conclusion?"

"It was clear. What if she doesn't come back?"

He drew her body tight against his and it was almost enough to make her forget her misgivings. "I'm here with you, and my duty is to see you're cared for. This is a big step for you, literally. What kind of man would I be to throw you to the wolves after one dance?"

Meri frowned. *Duty.* Was that all she was? Well, what did she expect after their history? She was stupid to dream of anything more, even though he loved her. Sometimes, perhaps, love was not enough.

Nikolas watched her closely. "What have I said now?"

He continued to guide her around the dance floor, and Meri found she could rely on him to steer her safely between the other couples. She also noticed many admiring glances from the men, and other less friendly looks from their partners.

"It does not matter," she said. "Thank you for staying with me. I would be frightened on my own."

"When I do leave you, I'll find you a safe dance partner and ask them to be gentle."

"Is that what you have been, Nikolas? Gentle with me?" Meri injected the words with a note of censure.

He frowned. "Obviously not if you have to ask."

"Can you not see how good we could be together, if you would only forgive me?"

"Get off my back, Meri. This is a night for us to enjoy."

"Children, children," a voice purred from behind them. "You squabble like an old married couple."

The queen and General Jazara danced alongside and, before Meri knew what had occurred, she was in Kain's arms, and Adriana had danced off with Nikolas.

"We meet again, My Lady," he said. "You are exquisite this evening."

The same could be said of Kain, whose black dress uniform sat snug across broad shoulders. If she were not so smitten with Nikolas, she would find Kain attractive.

"Thank you, General Jazara. I must admit to feeling somewhat out of my depth."

"Is that why you were arguing with Niko?"

"That is private, General," she said, stiffly. Meri was rather proud of herself for standing up to him. He was intimidating, somewhat dark and dangerous.

"Nik is my friend," Kain said, "and I intend to stand by him and protect him to the best of my ability. I'm yet to decide if you're a threat or not, My Lady."

Meri gasped. That he would just come right out and say it...

"I would never do anything to hurt Nikolas," she said. But of course, she had hurt him deeply, and deprived him of the dearest person in his life. She began again. "I would never *intentionally* hurt your friend. He has been good to me and I am trying to help him through his loss. He needs to heal and move on. I hope I have helped him see that."

As they danced, Kain studied her. He guided her as expertly as Nikolas, but she did not feel as safe as she had with her sea captain. This man was ruthless and, if he decided she was a threat, she might never have Nikolas.

"I see you do not trust me, but I will show you I only have his best interests at heart. And I know you will be watching me to ensure that." She injected a hard edge into her voice that she had heard her mother use on occasion.

Kain's head jerked backwards. "Ah, the beauty does have a brain and a mouth to match. You're right, Lady. I'll be paying close attention to you, and don't think I'll hesitate to step in if I see him in trouble."

"We want the same thing," Meri said, "for Nikolas to be happy. Please do not treat me as the enemy."

The song ended and Kain escorted Meri from the floor and over to the food tables. She wished he would leave her alone so she could rejoin Nikolas. She almost groaned aloud as Alique slid up beside them.

"Good evening, General Jazara," she said. "I'll take care of Merielle now. I think the queen wanted to speak to you about some security matter." Alique watched him go. "That man infuriates me at times. So secretive." She turned back to Meri. "You have secrets too, don't you?"

Meri swallowed the sudden fear that clawed its way up her throat. "Don't we all have secrets?"

"Ah, yes, but I am talking of the secrets that get people hurt. I see the way Nikolas looks at you. He doesn't trust you and yet he is drawn to you. I can see why. But if he doesn't trust you, I have to wonder why he has had you in his home for so long."

"You will have to ask him, My Lady," Meri said, now desperate to escape the clutches of the beautiful Alique. She looked around for Nikolas and saw him way across the other side of the room with a lady and a whiskery lord.

"There is some mystery, and I will discover it," Alique was saying. "I'll not have you sweep in here and take the man I love."

Meri turned to the blonde goddess. "Nikolas will make his own choices, Alique, and there is nothing you or I can do to change that. Now I would appreciate it if you could leave me alone to enjoy my supper." She turned to the table, collected a plate and filled it with food, most of which she could not identify.

Alique stood with her mouth slightly open, as if she had never been spoken to like that, which Meri found difficult to believe.

"This is not over," she said, and swept away in a cloud of blue satin and indignation.

"My, my, what has crawled up her ladyship's nose?" a deep voice drawled beside her.

What now? Meri turned to find a stocky young man her own height. He had dark blond, wavy hair and laughing caramel eyes.

"You seem to be creating quite a stir, for a country lass," he said. "I'm Lord Tomas Hen and hail from the lands south of Wildecoast." He bowed deeply, much deeper than Meri felt she deserved. She gave a curtsy of equal depth and hoped it was correct.

"I am Merielle, Lord Hen, and I am very pleased to meet you."

Tomas wore a dark green tunic and breeches and was handsome in his own way. "The pleasure is very definitely all mine, Lady Merielle." He sent her a sly look and warning bells went off in her head. "You do come from the south, do you not?"

Oh no, not another tricky conversation! "Yes, that's right, Lord Hen." *If in doubt say as little as possible.*

"And that would be where, specifically?" he asked, fixing her with eyes that no longer laughed.

191

"Oh, it is such a small place, you would never have heard of it, My Lord." *Please, please someone rescue me.* "It is so unpleasant to think of my past. Could we perhaps discuss something else?" She was rather pleased with herself for coming up with that.

Meri spent the next hour falling into and out of trouble as she moved around the room and danced with what felt like every male there. Nikolas had been kept at bay, first with the queen, then a string of ladies, including Alique, whom he had danced with on three occasions. Meri had been groped on the backside by Lord Korert, had her hair mistaken for a wig by Lady Feolinde, and been flung around the room on the arm of so many lords she had wanted to throw up. The only thing that saved her was having an almost completely empty stomach. She had not been adventurous enough to try any of the foods on offer. By the time Nikolas finally caught up with her, she was in a foul humor.

"I'm sorry, Meri. The ladies have conspired to keep us apart," he said, his blue-green eyes full of concern, and more than a little wariness.

She almost fell into his arms, so relieved was she to be back with him. "That is exactly what they have done, and Lady Alique is to blame. She wants me out of the way. She even told me as much."

He frowned. "I'm sure you misheard her."

"I did not. She said she loves you."

"Well, I don't love her."

"She would make a perfect wife, would she not?"

A muscle tightened in his jaw. "Meri, I won't discuss this." He swept her onto the dance floor and held her close, his lips grazing her hair. She felt at home in his arms, and safe. Now to convince him they belonged together.

She looked up. "I am very tired. Do you think you could escort me to my room?"

"The night is only half over. If you leave now, there will be gossip."

"Please, Nikolas, I don't think I can bear this a moment longer. I am sure you can orchestrate a reason for us to leave." His mouth was close, and his cologne embraced her with a musky outdoors scent that was all Nikolas. It took real control to stop herself from reaching up and planting a kiss on those full lips.

He stared at her for a moment, then swept her up into his arms and strode toward the doors. Lord Korert grunted as her slippered feet bumped his shoulder.

"What gives here?" he snapped, spinning around. When he saw who had collided with him, he laughed. "Imbibed a little too much mulled wine has she, young Nikolas?" His ruddy face implied that, when it came to mulled wine, he was an expert. "Thought I noticed her a little unsteady earlier." He looked at Meri. "Never mind, young lady, you'll be right as rain in the morning. Nikolas will look after you." He nudged Nikolas with his elbow and winked. Meri felt her face heat.

Nikolas smiled and nodded as he resumed walking. Lords and ladies parted until Alique stood before them, her eyes narrow and hostile.

Meri turned her face into Nikolas's chest, desperate to block out the startled faces of the other guests and determined not to deal with Alique again that evening.

"Goodnight, Lady Alique," Nikolas said, his voice low. "I may see you in the morning."

"Come back down when Merielle is settled in her room," she purred. "I'll save a dance for you."

"As you wish," Nikolas said.

Meri felt them move on. Nikolas carried her as if she weighed nothing. They moved up the staircase and into increasingly chilly corridors. He seemed to be miles away.

"You may put me down now," she said, looking up at him at last.

He stopped abruptly. "Oh, yes, of course." He placed her gently back on her feet and held his arm around her until she had her balance.

"Thank you for making everyone think I had consumed too much wine," she said, her voice oozing sarcasm. "That is sure to keep the gossips happy for days."

"Lord Korert handed me that one at a most opportune time, don't you think?"

"No, I do not!"

"I'm stunned you're angry. You asked me to get you out of there and I did. Lord Korert gave us the perfect excuse."

"In what way was it perfect?" she asked, hands on hips.

He gazed down at her, a smile playing on his lips. "Let's not stand in this draughty hall arguing. I'll escort you back to your chambers." He took her arm and she had very little alternative but to go along with him.

They arrived at her golden door and Nikolas reached past her to open it and ushered her inside. A fire crackled in the grate, making the room cozy. Meri turned to him and the words on her lips died. Nikolas seemed to be suffering the same fate, as if he wished to say something too.

"What is it, Nikolas?" she asked.

"You were beautiful tonight. The men lusted after you and the ladies were green with jealousy, even Lady Alique. I'm sorry you were embarrassed by the excuse I used to extricate us. I'll correct the rumors tomorrow."

Meri stepped closer and placed her hands on his chest. He swallowed, and she knew her nearness affected him. *Excellent start!* "I don't really mind about the rumors, Nikolas. But there is something I do care about, and that is you...and me."

He stared down at her as if mesmerized, his pupils swelling until they almost eclipsed the blue green of his eyes. "There is no you and me," he said huskily.

"There is if you would just admit it," she said. "I love you. Your love has literally changed me into the woman before you. I know you are attracted to me, so why fight it? Let us consummate this love we share and move forward together."

He walked away from her. "If only it were so simple," he said, staring out the frosty window. "I've thought on this and every time I keep coming back to your deception. If I can't get past that..."

Meri only half listened to his words as she worked at divesting herself of the creamy gown. She would only get one chance and she was not going to waste it.

He turned and froze, his gaze sweeping her from bottom to top as she stood with the gown at her feet. Heat pooled in her core at the look of naked desire in his eyes.

"Meri," he began, and stopped as if lost for words.

She stepped from her slippers and away from the gown then began unlacing her bodice. "This is all for you, Nikolas," she said. "This," she pointed to her half-clothed body, "is what your love created. Come and claim what is yours."

* * *

Nik stood as if turned to stone. Meri had all but laid herself before him, was offering herself up to him. Most men would leap into her arms and take what she offered, worrying about tomorrow later. She was offering herself, wasn't she? No strings attached. But he was smart enough to know there was always more to it than that.

She crossed to a chair by the fire and seated herself, then continued to undo her bodice until it gaped, showing most of her breasts. She was as perfect an example of womanhood as he'd ever hoped to find. Her skin was alabaster, her breasts full and firm, waist tiny and hips ripe for childbearing. Her limbs were long and muscular, and her face…her face was the most beautiful thing he had ever seen.

If their history had been different, had she not been a mermaid, Nik could happily have settled with Meri and fathered her children; if it were even possible. But her unearthly beauty meant she might never fit happily into his world. Tonight, had been a good example of that fact.

Perhaps he should just take advantage of what she offered. She had come into this with her eyes wide open, unlike he, who had been deceived from the very first. Anger bubbled again at the thought, tempting him to have his fun with her, and then hurt her just as he'd been hurt by her lies.

Her striptease continued, not that Meri would know that's what she was doing. She was innocent in that way, or was she? After all, part of her training had been in luring sailors. She had the skills at her disposal. Nik's mouth went dry when she settled back in the chair, legs spread, flimsy pantaloons hiding little of the pleasure-house at the juncture of her thighs. She had to know what this was doing to him. He glanced at her face and found her studying him. She knew sure enough.

His manhood swelled until it was just shy of painful. It had been so long since he'd enjoyed the pleasures of the flesh. His recent romp with Meri didn't really count, but tonight he'd be able to lose himself in her body, perhaps reclaim some of what she and her people had taken from him. His gut tightened at the thought this might be some sort of vengeful act. It was coming from a black place, a place he had dwelt too long in the past and knew he would visit in the future.

Nik took a step toward her, and then another, until he knelt at her feet. He parted the remaining threads of her corset and tossed the garment on the floor, then caressed her breasts, sweeping his fingers over them until the rosy nipples stood erect. Meri flung her head back, eyes closed, a pulse pounding at her throat. Her breathing quickened and Nik bent to kiss the side of her neck before sliding his tongue down over her chest to her nipples. Taking first one breast and then the other into his mouth, he sucked and then flicked the hard bud with his tongue. Meri thrust her chest at him, moaning his name, her hands reaching for him.

He pulled his lips from her breast, stood, and divested himself of his clothes. She lay back, panting, her eyes on his body. His gaze was drawn to the moisture between her legs. She was ready to receive him, but was he ready to take the step that would join their bodies and possibly their lives?

* * *

Meri *was* ready, and instinctively knew she had to seize this moment. She caught the wild look in his eye as though he was trapped against his will. One false move and she would scare him away.

196

And so, she lay before him, admiring the man whose love had changed her. There was not an aspect of him that did not inspire desire. His bronzed skin covered shoulders broadened by years as a sailor. His glorious chest was covered with a smattering of fair hair that ran down over ridged stomach muscles to long, muscular legs. His arms were huge, sculptured, the fists opening and closing as he stood gazing down at her. And his manhood seemed large. Meri suppressed a spike of fear as she imagined it penetrating her as Nikolas said it must.

She would not trap him. It must be his choice to come to her. "Do not fear. Nothing we do this night can ensnare you."

He snorted without amusement. "You don't know the power a woman can exert over a man."

Meri thought of the influence this man had wielded in her life. Her very form was dictated by his love for her.

"I love you," she said, "but I would never force you to stay with me. It must be your choice."

He took a step forward but then closed his eyes. "Jon would hate this power you have over me." He opened his eyes and stared at her, his torment obvious. "But I must join with you, I must know your body if I am ever to make a choice about the future." He fell upon her, tore the pantaloons from her limbs then gently picked her up from the chair and laid her on the rug before the fire.

Meri forgot where she was, and all her fears, as Nikolas loved her with his mouth, and ran his hands over her breasts, her waist, her soft moist places, until she panted with desire. She had never imagined the act of coupling could bring so much abandon, delight, release. As he kissed her breasts, his fingers sought the newly formed folds between her legs, and he gently inserted one and then two fingers, exploring. Meri's hips jerked as his fingers discovered a hard nub that sent her rocketing into the stars, her whole body tensed and aching, rising higher and higher before reaching the peak and toppling over. She lay panting, and when she opened her eyes, he was gazing down at her.

He gave her a tight look of intent before rising, pushing her legs further apart and spreading her folds. She gasped as Nikolas pushed himself inside, gently, gently, then broke through with a sharp sting. He paused, looking down at her, but she raised her hips and that was all he seemed to need. He thrust into her over and over, groaning, panting, muttering her name. Meri relished the connection; knew she was experiencing intimacy she could never have enjoyed as a mermaid.

She thrust against him and soon was not thinking of the act, but spiraling higher and higher until she crashed over the cliff again, Nikolas calling out and shuddering against her in wave after wave as he emptied his seed.

When his breathing had returned to normal, he rolled to the side and she felt bereft without him. She cried out in protest.

"Was it very painful for you, Meri?" he asked.

"No, my love, it was just a tiny sting and then I forgot all about it." She rolled onto his chest and kissed the sensual lips she had first admired so many weeks ago. They had given her unforgettable pleasure. He responded and she felt him harden beneath her, but still she could not rejoice for she read the wariness in his gaze.

"I meant what I said. I would never force you to stay with me. And I am so very sorry about all that has gone before."

He opened his mouth to speak but Meri could not bear to hear him reject her apology. She placed her finger on his lips.

"No, do not speak yet. I will not make excuses, and I can never repay your loss, but I can spend the rest of my days loving you and trying to prove you can trust me with your heart. All I ask is that you consider this. Because of my change, I know you love me. I know you care for me and you would not want me to suffer. But I also want all of you, not just the part that feels responsible for me. If you cannot give me all of you," Meri paused, gathering her resolve, "then I will not take any of you. Nikolas, you must decide, and I will accept."

He pulled her down and kissed her lingeringly and lovingly. Meri rejoiced he could express his love for her so freely, but she also knew this was far from decided. If Nikolas could not move forward and forgive her past sins, then she would lose him.

* * *

Nik woke near midnight, gently extricated himself from Meri's limbs and slipped from the bed. He dressed, all the while gazing upon the woman who had infiltrated every niche of his life. Could he now go forward without her? Despair gripped his heart at the thought, but anger at the past still ate him up. With one last lingering glance at his sleeping mermaid, he slipped through the anteroom and out the chamber door.

Back in his room, a fire had been lit, and Nik chose to sit before it rather than seek his rest. He had thinking to do.

Meri had been changed by his love, and the changes were profound. She was now human, and the night had been a revelation. He wanted her more than he'd ever wanted anyone or anything. But he owed it to her and himself to be able to completely forgive her for the past, and he wasn't a man who found it easy to forgive. If he couldn't, he'd poison their relationship. And so, the impasse. He needed to dispel the angry knot in his gut that grew whenever he remembered Jon; that festered when he thought of how he'd been tricked. No matter how much he enjoyed her body, her mind, her love, he harbored anger toward her.

On the other hand, Meri had taken full responsibility, and he appreciated that. There was nothing more she could do; it was up to him. The trouble was, Nik doubted he could absolve Meri.

He gave a great sigh and rose, shedding his clothes and climbing into bed. Perhaps in the cold light of day it would all be clearer.

When Nik awoke next morning, he lay quietly as the events of the previous evening came back to him - the ball, Meri, and the incredible connection they had made. She was imprinted on his skin, and his fingertips trembled with the need to stroke her. It would be so easy to dash over to her room and take her again, to make their love a permanent thing in his life. He wanted that, or at least his body did. Perhaps even his heart wanted it.

As he dragged on his clothes, his body hummed with a yearning to be near her, and it made him nervous. He had no room in his life for such dependence. Better to have always wondered about Meri and what they could've shared, than to know what he might never have. But was that true? Was she an impossible dream?

* * *

Meri stretched in her bed and realized Nikolas was absent. The sun was well up, if the brightness of the rays coming through the chink in the curtains was any indication. She wondered why the maid had not been in to wake her. Perhaps the entire castle was having a late morning after the festivities of last evening. Queen's orders?

Maybe it was just as well Nikolas was not here. She would be mortified if he should be found in her room. There was already enough gossip about her in the castle. Well, soon it would not matter. Last evening Nikolas had stamped his possession of her, and Meri had been transported to heights of ecstasy she had never imagined existed. Oh, how wonderful it would be to have that bliss every day! Now she had no doubt she had done the right thing in leaving her other life behind. She smiled, anticipating the moment when she could be with him again.

She rose and dressed in the lavender gown she had found in the wardrobe yesterday, assisted by the maid who came to tend her. The exquisite dress molded her body all the way to her knees, and then flared out into generous ruffles to the floor. The sleeves were similarly fitted and there was a low rounded neckline that left her shoulders and neck bare. It fitted her as though it had been made for her. The maid pinned Meri's hair into a twist, and then applied kohl around her eyes, and rouge to her cheeks and lips.

Meri was pleased with the woman she saw in the mirror. This was a woman who could hold her own at court, for that was what Nikolas would require. No matter what he had chosen over the last year, he would soon have to return to his career.

The maid left and Meri sat down to breakfast. As she uncovered the tray, there was a knock at the door.

"Enter."

Nikolas stepped into the room and closed the door behind him. "Good morning, Merielle," he said. He seemed to be wary of her.

She stood, overwhelmed with love for her man. She closed the space between them and enfolded him in her arms, her cheek against his chest. "I love you. Last night was magical."

"I too enjoyed it," he said. "I want you to know that."

It was an odd thing to say, and she looked up at him. "You cannot hide that from me, my love. I could see how profoundly affected you were by our coupling."

"Our joining was important to me as has been the last weeks we've spent together."

"Yes," she said carefully. "Now kiss me." She pulled his head down and kissed him with abandon, felt him respond, his manhood grow hard.

He groaned and pulled back from her. "We can't do this, Merielle."

"Why not? I can lock the door and we shall not be disturbed."

"That's not what I meant." He walked across the room.

A cold hand clawed its way around Meri's heart. "You are making me scared, Nikolas. I thought after last night—"

"Last night was fun, but this is the cold light of day and we have to be practical."

Shock hit her like a cold pail of seawater. "Fun! Last night was not fun, it was profound - at least it was for me. Perhaps it was not so for you?" Desperation drove her to frame the last as a question so he might reassure her.

"I imagine it was life-changing for you, but for me it was a moment of joy that can't be repeated. I must consider many things when I look for a life partner, Merielle. I'm afraid you may never integrate into this life and I can't be worried about you all the time, fearing you'll do something to give your past away. And that's if I could forgive you for Jon, and for the lies. You ask too much."

Meri clutched her throat to stop herself from keening. She was ice cold from head to foot. He could not be saying these things. Not after the most wonderful night of her life. They had connected, she knew they had. Meri could not find words to reply to his rejection.

"I'm leaving the castle for my estate this morning," he said. "You may have the cottage. Kain will escort you safely back there. I'll see someone visits twice a week to tend to Storm and check on you. Goodbye, Merielle." The last was said in a whisper as he brushed past her and out the door.

Meri did not know how long she stood in that spot, but the ice inside her would not allow the tears to flow. Eventually she summoned a maid to help her pack.

CHAPTER 20

THE weeks had dragged since returning to the cottage. Meri went through the motions of cleaning and cooking, not that she needed much of the latter, preferring raw seafood as her staple diet. Nothing brought her joy - not the simple sea creatures, nor the sunrise, or the daily swim in the ocean. Nothing had any purpose without Nikolas in her life. She wondered if he felt the same…but she could not allow herself to dwell on that or to hope he had not meant all he said.

Everything in the cottage and surrounds reminded her of him. His tools put her in mind of his hands and the magic they had wrought with her body. His clothes smelled of him, and so did his bed. Whenever she worked, she remembered Nikolas completing his household tasks while she sang the song of changing. Every place in the cottage held memories of something they had shared, reminding her of her dreams of a life with him. Meri had imagined growing old with Nikolas and even having his children, though she did not know if it was possible.

Even Storm, who still terrified her, reminded Meri of the times when she had been so dependent on Nikolas, when he'd ferried her up and down the cliff and she had clung to him for fear of the beast. But she forced herself to stand near the horse to fill his water, although his snorts filled her with fear.

When the sadness was particularly bad, she sought refuge at the beach. But there were memories there too, especially of the first time she had ever seen Nikolas as he stood over her, ready to take her life. And her heart broke, again and again, every moment she was apart from him.

Meri tried to tell herself she should be grateful for the life she had been given, that she was greedy to want more. But she could not convince herself. A life with Nikolas was all she desired and if she could not have that, there really was no point.

Kain came twice a week or sent someone in his stead if he was busy, but she learned little from him. Nikolas had returned to his estate, as he said he would, and the queen was expected to make him admiral of her fleet. Kain looked forward to working with his friend again, but would not tell Meri if Nikolas was happy, or if he asked about her. His dark eyes held no warmth toward her, and she had the feeling he would do whatever he could to keep Nikolas away.

Meri's frustration was almost beyond tolerance. She knew nothing of Nikolas's life now or of the women he filled it with. In her very darkest moments, she tortured herself, imagining him with Alique or any number of the women she had met at the ball that fateful night.

Eventually, she began to look fondly on her previous life as a mermaid, and that was when Meri knew she must act. She must move forward, either with Nikolas or without him, for this prison was slowly killing her.

* * *

Nik thought often of Meri; indeed, she was almost always on his mind, and it caused more than a few problems. He was so distracted at times that he made fundamental errors with the tasks he undertook, trying the patience of his estate manager. The poor man had told him more than once that he should snap out of his melancholy or get out of his hair. Most managers would have been spoken to severely for such words, but Nik liked his staff to treat him as a normal man, not a lord.

Besides, he was entirely correct; Nik was a liability. But what else could he do? Eventually he'd move beyond his obsession with Meri and life would return to normal. Except with each passing day, his longing for the woman he had helped create increased. The faintest whiff of the sea produced a yearning in him that had nothing to do with his past career as a sea captain.

The admiral's post was again in the offing. Adriana was preparing to make Nik the leader of her fleet but had been delayed by the sudden death of the king's brother, the recently married Prince Jiseve. The castle, and indeed the entire kingdom, was in mourning.

Nik groaned as he signed yet another request for estate funds. He had no desire to increase the amount of paperwork in his life and yet, as admiral, there would be a never-ending stream of papers to sign and meetings to attend. What had he been thinking? Running away, he supposed, just as Meri said he always did. And she was right. *There I go again, thinking of Meri.* She was always there, just one thought away.

He often wondered how she was coping, but from Kain he obtained slim pickings. Meri was keeping the place tidy and seemed happy enough, according to his friend, but it was obvious Kain disapproved of the arrangement. His steadfast refusal to talk about Meri made Nik grind his teeth.

So often in the three weeks since he had seen Meri, Nik had been gripped with the urge to saddle a horse and visit the cottage. He could easily have done so, but something prevented him each time - fear, or stubbornness, anger or uncertainty - Nik didn't know. What he did know was that this couldn't continue. He had to put Meri out of his life and his mind and get on with the job of running his estate, ensuring the safety of the kingdom, and creating a future for himself.

And each time he made that decision, bleakness swept over him, robbing his soul of all hope. *Damn it!* He was sick of himself. Something had to be done. He made the decision to approach the queen for a task that would take him far away, and give him the breathing space to see things as they really were. Perhaps then he could make choices about his future.

* * *

Another week passed, making it four weeks since the ball, and Meri was well into her plan. Kain had visited her twice this last week, making her impatient to escape this exile she had been banished to. For exile it was. Terrified of horses and on her own in this place, Meri was unable to leave unless by her own foot power, and that was not an option. Kain or someone else would catch up with her before long.

So, horsepower was the solution. At the beginning of the week, the very thought of Storm had terrified her, and certainly touching him had been beyond her. Now she stood at the fence to his paddock, her hand on his nose, battling the nerves that threatened to swamp her. Her hand trembled, but at least she had established contact with the fearsome beast. She kept hearing Nikolas's words in her head. *He's a gentle beast. He won't hurt you.* But every so often, he would snort, and she would almost fall over with fear. How would she ever be able to ride him all the way to Wildecoast, and then on to the Cosara estate?

Meri had learned that much from Kain Jazara. Nikolas remained on his estate, reconnecting with his people, and seeing to the running of his various enterprises - whatever they might be. However, Kain had hinted that he thought his friend might soon return to the sea.

The very thought sent panic through Meri for so many reasons. Number one was the fear that once gone, Nikolas would rarely return. She might never see him again, let alone resolve all the feelings between them. The second worry was her family, who would seek revenge on Nikolas, no matter what they had promised. Meri knew they would never leave him alone after he bested them. Lastly, Nikolas was only just returning to the world after suffering more loss and trauma than any man should have to endure. She knew he would require help and support and she wanted to be there to provide it. He needed her, and she freely admitted to craving his strong presence in her life. The past four weeks had been enough to show her that.

And so, she had embarked on a project to become used to Storm, for he was her only way out of this remote place.

Meri moved her hand from Storm's nose to his neck, running her fingers over the soft coat and concentrating on the feel of his hair, pushing the fear away each time it threatened to defeat her. She glanced at his head. The gray stallion had his eye closed as if enjoying the attention. Perhaps Nikolas was right, and Storm wasn't the monster he appeared? Meri slipped her hand further to the horse's shoulder and patted him. It brought her very close to him and she could feel the welcome heat radiating from his body. A few more days and she might be able to climb on his back and ride him out of this place - if she could remember how to tie the saddle to his back and place the bridle on his head!

Meri threw the bag of her belongings over her shoulder and pulled the cottage door closed. It was a miserable blustery day to set out on a trip, but it was now or never. Part of the process of overcoming her fear had been setting a deadline, or else Meri knew she would have gone on, day in and day out, telling herself she would be ready to leave in just a few more days. Kain had visited yesterday, and she was fairly certain it would be at least three days before he or anyone else came near the cottage, giving her plenty of time to get away.

She crossed to the fence and called Storm, who came trotting up and poked his head over the rail. She offered him a withered carrot which he accepted with a happy nicker. Meri smiled. She could do this. Storm really liked her. She patted him without even a tremor. She left her bag on the ground and went to retrieve the saddle and bridle from the stable. As she returned to the stallion, his ears pricked as he saw what she carried. He nickered again.

"That's right, Storm," she said, "we are going to Nikolas. I see you are happy that at last you might be free of this paddock. I know just how you are feeling." She patted his nose again and jumped as he snorted.

Stupid woman, he will not hurt you. He is just excited. Keeping up the reassuring thoughts, Meri placed the saddle on the top rail and climbed through. Storm turned to her and placed his forehead against her chest. Her heart melted. Nikolas was right. Storm was gentle. She stood with his head against her, allowing her heart and breathing to settle. All would be well.

When Meri had achieved calm, she patted Storm and reached for the bridle, placing the bit in his mouth and the leather straps over his ears and forehead. He accepted it readily and stood perfectly still as she buckled it at his throat. She took a deep breath and smiled, pleased with her progress. If only Nikolas could see her now, he would be proud. Well he would see her soon and welcome her with open arms. She ignored the voice that asked why he had not visited her if he wanted her in his life.

It had taken longer than expected but Meri was ready to take to the road. The saddle had been problematic and when she put it on back to front, Storm turned to look at her with what could only be called puzzlement. In the end she had worked it out, done up all the buckles, being careful not to pinch him. That had earned her another quizzical glance from the beast.

When all was ready and her bag tied to the back of the saddle, Meri led Storm over to the mounting post, put her foot in the stirrup and pushed off the block, only to have the saddle slide toward her. Her heart pounded against her ribs as she hastened to pull her foot from the stirrup. She stood with her forehead against Storm's shoulder, breathing deeply to bring her fright back under control. It was not his fault the saddle was too loose.

"Good boy, Storm," she whispered. "You did not take fright when the saddle slipped. You are a brave and loyal steed. Convey me to Nikolas safely and I will see you are properly rewarded."

That is going to get me a long way, talking to a horse! But Meri had heard Nikolas talk to Storm on many an occasion. She wondered if he understood the words or if it was merely the calm and confident way they were spoken. A large seed of doubt lodged in her heart. Could she really travel all the way on horseback to find Nikolas?

She pushed the question from her mind and tightened the saddle another three notches until Storm grunted. That should be tight enough.

Meri's second attempt at mounting was more successful, and after a moderate wobble she landed, quite ungracefully she thought, in the saddle. And froze. Her mind went blank as Storm fidgeted. Her palms were slick with sweat, her heart pounding against her ribs, and the rapid pace of her breathing made her dizzy. With an almighty effort, she brought her breathing back under control and waited for her heart to follow suit. She reminded herself she was here by choice and could change her mind at any point. One last deep breath and Meri had wrangled her fear back under control. *Until the next time!*

She gathered the reins and squeezed the horse's ribs, swallowing hard. *Your choice, you ninny!* Storm must have felt her indecision for he took a faltering step, stopped and turned around, as if to ask her if she were sure. Meri giggled at the look on his proud face.

She patted his neck, feeling braver. "Yes, Storm, let us go. Steady now, for I am unused to being on a horse's back." She thought for a moment. "I have ridden dolphins, of course. It might be very similar, though not so smooth." She laughed again as Storm plodded off up the road. His motion was odd, jerky, but Meri could balance quite well - at this pace. Anything faster would be another story. And thus, horse and woman left the cottage that had been refuge and prison and took the first steps on their journey to Wildecoast.

CHAPTER 21

NIK paced back and forth across the parlor outside the queen's reception hall. *Adriana enjoys keeping me waiting. She must, as it occurs every time I visit.* He loved his cousin, but she tried his patience to the limit. And keeping him waiting wasn't the only irritating habit she possessed. The last two weeks since he had asked for a task to occupy him, he had received no less than twenty invitations from the families of eligible ladies, seeking to entertain him at their estates.

He wouldn't be surprised if the orders he was to receive today would send him south, where he could take up many of those offers. If the locations were anything to go by, the king and queen were clearly endeavoring to cement relations with kingdoms far and wide. Very few were from within Thorius.

One of the few was from Alique Zorba's parents. Nik shook his head, imagining life with the delectable Lady Alique. She was clearly out to win the hand of a powerful man and he was in her sights.

The door to the Queen's Hall opened and the chamberlain ushered Nik in. He swept through the door and bowed before his cousin. Nik noticed dark smudges under her eyes that hadn't been there two weeks ago.

Adriana dismissed her chamberlain and when they were alone, she rose and kissed Nik on both cheeks. "How are you, Niki?" she asked.

"Sick of waiting, Your Majesty," he said, a residue of temper leaving his words sharp.

Her face hardened. "It is my prerogative to keep people waiting, dear cousin," she said, walking away to pour herself a cup of tea. "There has been much to do of late. I have shouldered many of Beniel's duties when all I wished to do was comfort him."

"How is he? I hear he returned recently."

She shook her head. "Beniel is distraught, though he hides it well. I just can't believe Jiseve is dead. There was a full enquiry, you know."

"And the findings?"

"Death by natural causes. He was taking medicines to aid virility, apparently they did not agree with him and his heart failed."

Nik grimaced. "An ugly business. Horrifying for the widow as well."

Adriana nodded, seeming lost in thought. "I can't imagine how Benae must be coping. She is pregnant, did you know? Beniel has appointed Ramón Zorba steward of Brightcastle to help Benae run the principality."

So, the rumored star-crossed lovers were still together. "There'll be changes."

Again, Adriana nodded. "My husband has not told me the full story, I think. Something troubles him, but he will not discuss it."

"Would you like me to talk with him?"

Adriana stepped close and laid a palm on his cheek. "You are sweet to offer, but no. Beniel will tell me in his own time." She smiled. "And now we must discuss your orders."

She gestured to a chair by the tea table and sat, waiting for Nik to do the same. "I am sending you south on a mission to gather intelligence from outside the kingdom. On your return, you will restock the ships and journey north to do the same and ferret out the depth of the dark elven menace. These are orders from Beniel himself."

"Shouldn't the king deliver the orders?"

Adriana tried to hide her concern for her husband, but Nik read fear in her eyes. "He is not well today but will be present to see you off on your voyage. Have no doubt, he has every faith in you, Niki, just as I have."

He couldn't help the flash of shame that gripped him. "I hope your faith isn't misplaced," he said. "Many would say it was."

"Then you will show them otherwise, cousin." She leaned closer to him. "You are happy about this task you will undertake?"

Nik frowned. "I'm resigned to resuming my place in Thorius. The voyage will give me thinking space and it'll be good to be back on the water. I just hope I don't let you down again."

Adriana squeezed his hand. "You always do your best." She considered him again. "Those invitations you have been receiving?"

Nik tensed. "Yes?"

"Feel free to visit with any from the south while you are on your voyage." She pulled a sheet of parchment from the table and her pen and ink. "Tell me the families you shall visit, and I will see the royal pigeons are dispatched to announce your arrival." She smiled. "We shall have a spring wedding in the family yet!"

As Nik left his audience with the queen, he reflected on the half dozen visits she had outlined for his southern tour. He didn't welcome them but at least he had cheered up his cousin and that eased his heart.

And the visits would distract him from thoughts of Meri which was, after all, what he wanted. Wasn't it?

* * *

Meri was not making good time on her journey, but considered it a bonus she had not yet fallen from the horse. Storm was an angel. She sensed the controlled tension in his muscles, as if he wanted to gallop until all the energy was released from his system. He had been cooped up for a long time. But after two hours of travel, the horse settled into a loping walk Meri almost enjoyed, and he appeared to relax underneath her. They were getting used to each other, she supposed.

At about the same time, she decided to leave the road and keep to the edge of the forest and fields. She wanted to be close to cover if someone came along. In her estimation, she would reach Wildecoast in another four hours and the road traffic might increase. She had no desire to meet anyone who might know her.

At least the cloak she wore, which belonged to Nikolas, disguised the brilliant red of her hair. Meri prayed it was enough to prevent her from being recognized before she reached Nikolas.

Meri was tiring fast when she arrived at the outer wall of Wildecoast city. Even late in the day it was bustling. After telling a soldier she was on a shopping expedition, she led Storm through the gates and into the lower streets of the city, relieved she had not drawn a second glance from the man.

The crowds took her breath away just as they had on her first trip. Markets flourished in this quarter, and sellers cried out, trying to interest her in fruit, ribbons, or even bolts of cloth. The fishmonger's wares made her mouth water, and she realized she was starving.

She had brought a few coins from the cottage but had no idea of their value. Would these sellers tell her? Frustration bubbled in her breast. She was so unprepared! No wonder Nikolas did not wish for a life with her. He must have thought she would never cope in this environment. Well, she would show him! Imagine how surprised he would be when she arrived at his estate, having made her way on her own.

Meri approached a kind-looking old woman who sold fruit.

"An apple or two for the pretty miss?" she offered, her watery blue eyes peering up at Meri. "They're a little withered but sweet."

"I am sure they are delicious, Goodwife, but I am unsure if I have enough to purchase one."

The old woman frowned. "Show me what you have, Miss."

Meri pulled the coins from her purse and laid them on her palm. One was a golden color and the others silvery.

The woman's eyes widened. "You must keep the gold coin hidden, Miss. No one will be able to change it, except the treasury or the jeweler. One of the silver coins would buy everything on this table."

Meri swallowed at the old woman's response. It seemed she was quite wealthy. "I will take six apples and you may give me whatever change you can afford to part with."

The woman took one of the silver coins, placed six apples in a bag along with many bronze coins and passed the bag to Meri.

"Can you tell me one other thing, Goodwife?" Meri asked. "How many of the bronze coins you gave me would buy one of those fish over there?"

"Ten of the coins would be enough. You be careful now. There's plenty of sellers in this street who would take your money. And if you show that gold coin, your life could be under threat. Keep it hidden. Lucky you asked me. Go in safety, Miss."

Meri nodded. "Thank you, Goodwife. Do you know where to find the estate of Lord Nikolas Cosara?"

"I've heard of him. His estate is reached by traveling south, but that's all I know. Perhaps if you ask around, someone else will give you directions."

"Thank you," Meri said. "You have been most kind."

The old woman nodded, and Meri moved off to the fishmonger. Soon she had a fresh fish and a smoked variety stashed in her bag. Her stomach grumbled but she lingered to ask the man about Nikolas.

"That cur! Back on his estate, is he?" he cried, spittle flying from his lips. "Heard he had exiled himself to the cliffs south of here. I suppose he's come crawling to the queen to ask for his old job back."

Meri's gut clenched at the words. Her Nikolas should not be spoken of like a criminal. He had suffered and still did. What did this man know of any of that? But Nikolas had said as much; that the families of all who died on the ill-fated voyage blamed him.

"I cannot say, Sir," she said stiffly. "I ask again, can you direct me to his estate?

The fishmonger looked her up and down then, his eyes narrowed. "Oh, I see now, Missy. Hoping to trap him with some game or other? Are you with child? Ha, I'd like to see *Lord* Cosara's face when you arrive on his doorstep. Give him back a little of his own medicine, eh?"

He nudged her and loomed closer, so Meri caught a whiff of his breath. Her stomach went from hungry to sickened, even though she was well used to the appalling breath of the killer whale. Meri swayed away from him and, just as she did, Storm stamped a hoof and pulled back his ears, sidling closer to the man.

"You keep that nasty beast away from me now, Missy. He's got a mean look to him." The man took a step backwards which flattened him up against the front of his stall. "What was it you asked?" he said, his eyes riveted to Storm. "Oh yes, Cosara's estate. It's to the south and west but that's all I know. Now take your beast and move along."

She scowled at his rudeness but left, pulling Storm after her. She patted the horse's head to calm him. "You are right, Storm. He was a most unpleasant man. Thank you for defending me and your master. I will be sure to tell Nikolas when I see him."

Meri asked at several more stalls and managed to piece together a vague picture of the locality of the estate. It was, as the fishmonger had thought, south and west of Wildecoast, perhaps half a day's ride from the city. She had been assured there would be locals she could ask for directions when she neared the Cosara estate.

Having obtained what she had come for, Meri led Storm back through the crowds and out of Wildecoast, then mounted and turned onto the southern inland road. After ten minutes, she dismounted and sat against a tree in the weak afternoon sun. She pulled the raw fish from her sack and polished it off in mere moments. While she did so, she kept a sharp look out along the road in both directions. It would not do for a passing traveler to see her chewing on a raw fish.

Disgusting the fishmonger might have been, but his produce was excellent. By the look of the eye, this fish had been caught only that morning. Meri was feeling satisfied for more reasons than just a full belly. She had come this far without falling off Storm, was getting to know him and forming a bond, and was well on the way to finding Nikolas. Surely all this would prove to him her determination to have a life with him, and that she could integrate herself into his world? Whether it would make a difference, she would soon find out.

Meri wiped her fingers on the grass, climbed back on Storm, and resumed her journey.

Night had fallen an hour ago and dread bubbled in Meri's stomach. Toward dusk, she had passed several small groups of travelers heading toward Wildecoast, consisting mainly of men. Many of them had eyed her with distrust or speculation but none stopped. The wind had dropped, and cold air cloaked her with its heavy arms. If she stopped to rest, she would be cold and vulnerable to attack. If she kept riding, she might ride too far in the dark and miss Nikolas's estate, not to mention the risk of bringing harm to Storm.

Now she was not feeling so confident or proud of herself. Nighttime in the ocean had meant increased danger, and mermaids congregated to improve their safety. Despite their superhuman capabilities, mermaid sight was no match for the huge sharks and killer whales of the deep.

Meri felt the dark on land could be equally perilous, when the senses were strained, and those up to no good could ambush an unsuspecting traveler. Would Storm know if someone was lurking in the dark? Perhaps, but would she be able to stay on his back should they be forced to run? She doubted it.

Good work, Meri! That has made you feel much better!

In the distance, she saw the glimmer of lights which grew brighter as she approached. Soon she heard a merry tune and people singing and clapping. Perhaps it was an inn? Nikolas had told her of the places where travelers stayed overnight. Should she stop? What if the other travelers harassed her or robbed her? But surely the proprietor would ensure the safety of his guests?

"There is only one way to find out, Storm," she said. "Besides, you need rest, my friend, and a bite to eat as well." She patted his neck and laughed as he nodded his head up and down. Perhaps he did understand her?

As they drew near the inn, the singing grew louder and Meri's courage dwindled. Crowds and scrutiny were nothing she craved, and both were to be found in ample quantities within the walls of this establishment. A huge man approached her as she dismounted at the front rail.

"Yes?" he said, looking her up and down, and studying Storm briefly.

She threw her shoulders back and looked up into a face that carried scars from past fights. His nose alone looked to have been broken several times. "I require a room for the night, and feed and a stall for my horse."

"You have coin?"

"I do."

"And your business?"

Meri frowned. "That is hardly any of yours. I am but a traveler seeking a safe place for the night, and in the morning, directions to the estate of Lord Nikolas Cosara."

"Ah," he said, nodding. "That makes more sense."

"Oh?"

"Word is Lord Nik is seeking a wife. Bound to be a few chits turning up at his estate. I wouldn't get my hopes up if I were you though, Miss."

Meri was tempted to ask what he meant by that but found it difficult to get past the news that Nikolas was looking for a woman to share his life. *Well, you knew he needed to settle down, woman!* It seemed she had come looking for Nikolas just in time. *Just let him try to replace me with some fancy lady!*

She must have looked fierce, for the man stepped back out of range. Meri nearly giggled. As if she could make an impression on that mountain of a man.

"If you go inside," he said, "I'll see to your horse and get him some feed. He's a fine beast, that he is."

"Thank you. Please take good care of him."

Meri watched as Storm was led away around the side of the building. Then she walked up the stairs and through the front doors of the inn. It was warm inside, and just as noisy as she had imagined. Several faces turned her way as she stepped inside, but she ignored all of them and ploughed her way through to the counter.

"What can I do for you, miss?" a scrawny man asked her. He was short, with a lean whiskery face and receding hair, and he wore a spotless white apron around his waist.

"I'd like a room and a meal, Sir," she said.

"I've two rooms left, one at the front and one at the back. Which would you prefer?"

Meri contemplated. At least at the back there was some hope she might see or hear if Storm was threatened. "The back room, please. And the meal?"

"A rich vegetable stew and fresh bread, my dear." He glanced around the common room and back at her. "I'll show you to your room."

Meri followed the scrawny man to the end of the bar and up the staircase to a room at the back. It appeared clean and tidy, with a wash basin and pitcher of water, two small beds and a chest against one wall. A window overlooked the back yard and a light shone from the stables. She could not see any horses from where she stood.

The bartender cleared his throat and Meri turned to face him. "You can eat in the kitchen, Miss. Quieter there. Use the back stairs when you're ready to come down." He nodded to her and left, closing the door behind him.

She frowned. Her host seemed nervous, or worried. It made her uneasy, and she started to wonder if this had been a good idea after all. But had she really had any choice?

She placed her sack on the bed and washed and dried her face and hands. There was a looking glass on the wall, so she wandered over to check her hair. She tucked a few strands back into her knot, straightened her skirt and left the room, taking the rear stairs which brought her to the kitchen.

Meri stood on the threshold, watching a large woman stir a pot over the fire. She knocked on the door frame and the woman turned.

"Take a seat, dear, and I'll dish you up a plate of my veggie stew. None like it anywhere in the kingdom."

I doubt that very much. "Thank you, Mistress." Meri took a seat at the kitchen table, thinking longingly of the smoked fish upstairs in her sack. But she might need it tomorrow, especially if she was late arriving at Nikolas's estate.

The plate was put before her and Meri's nose wrinkled at the scents wafting up from it. The lumps of vegetables looked hideous, but she had to be polite. At least the bread was fresh, warm and appetizing.

"Tea, my dear?"

"Oh yes please!" Meri broke off pieces of bread and dipped them in the stew before popping them into her mouth. She had learned it made the horrid, boring chunks more palatable especially slathered with lots of butter.

She passed an enjoyable meal with the cook who turned out to be the skinny barman's wife. They chatted about the weather and the recent royal wedding in Brightcastle, wherever that was - off to the west, it seemed - and the recent scandalous news of the death of the bridegroom. Meri revealed she was visiting with Lord Cosara and endured the woman's interrogation about her purpose. She muttered something about Nikolas having showed her a kindness and hoping to repay the debt. It sounded feasible enough and the cook didn't appear to think it out of the ordinary that a woman on her own would be traveling to meet the lord of the district.

"Would I be able to get directions to his lordship's estate, Mistress?" Meri asked, when she had finished her stew and was sipping her tea.

"Continue up the road about a half day's travel, and there's a lane which heads to the south. You'll see sheep in the front paddocks if I'm not mistaken, and there's a duck pond as well. Travel up the lane and his lordship's manor is at the end. Our daughter used to work in his household, but she left when the ship went down, killing all those sailors. Just couldn't deal with the thought that her employer abandoned his men and didn't want to wait until he did the same to her." The cook turned away and set about cleaning up the kitchen.

Meri sighed. There was still much anger at Nikolas regarding the shipwreck. He would struggle for years to put himself back in the good graces of his people, and many would never forgive him. *He needs me, I know he does.* Nikolas needed her to protect his back and defend him and tell him all would be well.

She thanked the cook and mounted the stairs to her room. Once she was inside, she leaned against the closed door, taking deep, calming breaths. This was all so strange. Being on her own in this foreign world was more difficult than she would have imagined. But tomorrow she and Nikolas would be together, defending each other against the world. She refused to countenance any other possibility.

She changed into her sleeping attire, let her hair down and combed it. Then she crossed to the basin to wash. She was drying her face on a towel, when someone grabbed her from behind, pinning her arms against her body and holding the towel against her face. She screamed but the cloth muffled the sound. Her heart felt like it had exploded, and she couldn't breathe. Fear gave her strength but even though she struggled violently, she couldn't get her arms free. Through the terror, a part of her brain stayed cool enough to remember what Nikolas had once told her - a man was vulnerable between his legs. If she could just...

She stepped sideways, clenched her hand into a fist and swung it backwards into her assailant's groin. Her attacker groaned and buckled over, releasing her. Meri slammed her foot against his shin, spun and landed two punches to the side of his head, bringing him to his knees, hands clutching groin and face. By now the man was shrieking fit to bring the roof down, but Meri was lost in a rage. Her only thought was to pound the man until she was safe. She kicked out with first one, then the other of her newly formed legs, hitting the hapless man on his back and sides until she had him writhing on the floor.

The door flew back on its hinges and slammed against the wall of the room, bringing her back to her senses. The cook and her husband stood in the doorway, wide-eyed.

"Step away from him, Miss," the cook said, her hands outstretched. "Now do as I say. Step away."

Meri's breath came in savage gusts as she looked down upon the unconscious man at her feet. When she looked back up at the man and woman, she read fear in their eyes. Clearly, they thought she might do the same to them.

"He attacked me," she gasped. "I was getting ready for bed and suddenly he grabbed me from behind. What else could I do?"

The cook placed a tentative hand on her shoulder. Meri's arm tensed involuntarily but she remained still.

"Gusta," the cook said to her husband. "Get him out of here, and then get Eugo to mount a guard on this room. If what the young lady says is true, we might expect more trouble."

That snapped Meri out of her trance. "What do you mean, if? Of course, what I say is true! Why else do you think that man was in my room? I did not invite him in. I do not attack people for no reason."

"So, you've done this before?" the cook asked, folding her arms across her ample bosom.

"I did not say that," Meri snapped. She watched Gusta drag the unconscious man into the hall and out of sight. "Will he recover?" Even though the man had entered her room with no good intention, Meri did not wish him to come to permanent harm. She had only been defending herself after all.

"I've broken up more than a few fights in my time," the woman said. "He'll live." She appeared as though she would like to say more but thought better of it.

All Meri wanted was to be left alone. Her legs and feet hurt, and so did her hands. "Thank you for stepping in when you did, Mistress."

"Go straight to bed, Miss. I'll have breakfast prepared for you at dawn, and then you must be on your way. There's already been enough trouble." She nodded as if she had solved another problem and left the room, pulling the door closed behind her.

Meri bathed her hands in the cold water and did the same for her feet. As she climbed into bed, she began to shake and soon her pillow was wet with tears. What had the man wanted to do to her? Was he just a robber, or had he thought to use her in some horrible way? Nikolas had warned her about men who took what was not offered, and she imagined her attacker might be one of those men. She shuddered, wondering how she would sleep that night.

When Meri opened her eyes, she could just make out her window as a lighter patch against the wall. It must be almost sunrise. Remembering the cook's parting words from last night, she pushed back the quilt and climbed from the bed. A knock sounded at the door.

"Who's there?"

A woman's voice answered. "I've brought you warm water for your wash."

Meri let the cook in, and the woman stomped over and replaced the dirty basin and empty pitcher with a clean basin and water. "Sleep well?"

"Yes, thank you," Meri said, surprised to find she had. No dreams, no lying awake thinking about what had transpired. No worrying about who else might disturb her, just deep, restful sleep.

"Breakfast is almost ready," the cook said, moving to the door. "Come down when you're packed." As she pulled the door closed, Meri saw Eugo on guard out in the hall.

She washed, dressed and piled her possessions back into the sack with the fish. She tramped down the back stairs to the kitchen, ignoring Eugo, who seemed happy to ignore her back.

After she had eaten her meal in silence, Meri pulled out her purse and removed a silver coin and several copper ones. "How much, Mistress? My horse was housed as well."

"That will do, Miss," the cook said, sweeping the coins into her apron. "You be on your way now and travel safe. Keep your head down though. People around here don't like what they can't understand, and I'm thinking they won't like you. Never seen a woman do that to a man. I'm not saying he didn't deserve it mind. Just…" Her voice drifted away, and Meri realized it was just as the woman had said. She didn't understand her, and therefore she wanted her gone.

Meri nodded. "Thank you for your help and hospitality. I hope I didn't bring trouble down on your roof." She stood, collected her sack and exited the kitchen and the inn. The rear door led to the yard and stables. Storm was already saddled, tethered to a ring near the stable door. He nickered when he saw her.

"I am happy to see you, too, Storm." She patted his silky neck, wrapped her arms around it and pressed her face into his heat. Comforted by his strong, warm presence, Meri was able to gather her spirits and tie her sack to the saddle. She mounted and rode to the front of the inn and then onto the road. Eugo followed her silently on an old nag that had seen better days, riding several paces behind her until she reached the top of the first hill. Then he turned back without a word.

"Looks like we are on our own, Storm, but I prefer it that way. Don't you?"

But Meri could have used some company when her thoughts began to crowd in on her. She just could not get the look of fear on the cook's face out of her head. The woman had been afraid. Of her. She had not realized what strength still resided within her body, even now she was human. Some residue of the mermaid lingered and had enabled her to defeat the coward who attacked her last night. She was not as vulnerable as she had thought. In fact, it might be those around her who had to beware.

Meri wondered what Nikolas's response might be to the incident. She had the power to kill a man and it would have to be contained if she wished to integrate into this society. Her head drooped as bleakness swept into her heart. She had run away from her home to escape the certainty of a life of ugliness and killing, and to fit in somewhere. Had she just succeeded in bringing her old problems with her into a new life?

No, she could not dwell on what had occurred. Nikolas would help her adjust. She had to believe he would not turn his back on her. But what had changed? What new arguments did she have when she finally confronted him? What if he really did not want to share a life with her?

He loves you. Just concentrate on that fact, for it is true. Meri took a deep breath and cast her eyes around the country she was riding through. As she ventured further inland, there were more farms. This was a landscape she had never been exposed to. Flocks of four-legged, woolly creatures roamed the paddocks under the care of young men and women, and sometimes children. Dogs barked at her as she passed. No one waved, but plenty stared as she and Storm ambled by.

Chickens scratched in the front yards and goodwives milked cows in the open barns. White washing flapped in the cold wind that swept down from the mountains. Storm took very little notice of any of it, but he did snort when flocks of fat birds started from the longer grass at the side of the road. The horse was too disciplined to do more than fling his head up, for which Meri was grateful. She might be learning to relax on Storm's back, but she knew any sudden movement could land her on the road.

Passers-by were unfriendly. They were mainly farming types with carts laden with produce for sale in Wildecoast, she assumed. Meri longed to stop them and see if they carried anything for her to eat, but she could not pluck up the courage. What if they tried to attack her and she lost her temper again like last night? She could not take the risk.

Images flooded her mind of herself, pursued by an angry mob, arriving at Nikolas's estate, begging for refuge; if she managed to stay on Storm's back in order to flee. She shuddered as she imagined her body, trampled under the boots of enraged farmers. Nikolas might never know her fate. She pulled herself up short. *Do not be silly!* She had always been prone to allowing her imagination to run away with her and now she must stay positive. Nikolas would help her with this latest problem - her savagery. They would work it out together.

The rest of the morning passed similarly, her mind flopping back and forth between optimism and fear. By early afternoon, she was exhausted. Her body trembled with the need to see Nikolas, to lay her hands on those broad shoulders and her head against his chest. Just the thought of him calmed her, made her smile, and heated a core she never realized she had until she became human.

They rounded a bend in the road and there was a lane leading off to the south. Woolly animals grazed in the meadow, and birds floated on a pond. Storm pricked his ears and nickered as if he remembered this place. She smiled. This must be Nikolas's home, surely?

"Not long now, Storm." She leaned over and patted his neck. "You and your master will be reunited. He will look after you as you should be cared for, not as a silly mermaid-cum-human has struggled to these last weeks."

Meri steered him into the lane. Storm's pace picked up as if he knew he was on the home stretch. The pace was easy to tolerate - just a fast walk - so Meri did not object. She was impatient to see Nikolas too.

Just as she was wondering how much further this lane could go on, they emerged from a grove of low trees into a clearing at the back of which was a two-story manor house. It was large, though nowhere near the size of the palace. The roof was red tiled, and the walls plastered and painted white. A fountain sat in the middle of the circular drive. Storm walked straight up and took a long drink while Meri continued to look around. Dogs barked from somewhere behind the house and a small furry ginger creature wandered over to rub itself on Storm's legs. She soaked up the tranquillity after her long hours on the road, and the trauma of last evening.

"Can I help you, Miss?" A craggy-faced man stood before her, frowning and scratching his beard. He had an air of wary politeness.

"Yes," she said, hesitantly. What should she say? Would Nikolas have told his staff about her? "I am looking for Lord Cosara. I am a friend of his."

The man's eyebrows lifted in surprise. "A friend you say?"

"Yes, I have been staying at his cottage on the cliffs and decided to pay him a visit. There are matters we must discuss."

"That wouldn't include a marriage proposal, would it?"

Meri started. Perhaps the man did know of her. "Did Nikolas confide in you?"

"No, Miss. Young women arriving here often have marriage on their mind."

She bristled. "I assure you I am not just another woman looking to ensnare his lordship. If you announce me, you will see Nikolas does know me."

"Ah, perhaps, but would his lordship wish to speak with you?"

Now Meri's anger threatened to get the better of her. She pulled it in with difficulty. The man was only trying to protect his master. "He will want to see me."

Would he really wish to see her? If that were true, would he not have visited her before now? She set her shoulders and looked the servant in the eye. "Would you please let him know I am here?"

"Even if I wished to, I couldn't, Miss. Lord Cosara is absent, and will be gone for some time, perhaps several months."

Meri's heart almost stopped. *Nikolas gone! He could not be gone. She needed him here, now.* "Where is he?"

The servant hesitated. "He's going to sea on a mission. We hope he'll return with news of an imminent marriage. We've waited long for a mistress on this estate."

Meri's eyes bulged. *No.* "He has already set sail? I heard nothing of that when I was in the city."

"The departure date is tomorrow."

She pulled Storm's head up. "Then I have time to catch him." She turned and began to ride back up the drive.

"Miss! Wait. You can't embark on a journey to Wildecoast at this late stage in the day. You wouldn't reach there until after dark, and that's if you galloped all the way. I can't allow you to take the risk."

It seemed the man did care after all. Meri stopped and considered. He was right. She could not gallop anyway, which would mean she would have to spend the night on the road, and that was out of the question after the events of last evening. She shuddered as she saw again the prone form of the man before her.

"You've reason to fear a night on the road," the whiskered servant said. His eyes softened. "Perhaps I was hasty in my judgement. I see you ride Storm, Lord Cosara's favored mount. Please come down and I'll see if I can help."

Meri scowled at the servant but then the fight went out of her. *Nikolas gone. It might already be too late.* The man walked to Storm's shoulder and helped Meri off the horse. She almost collapsed when her feet hit the ground.

"You're bone weary, lass." He led her to the front door of the manor. Before he could pull the rope to ring the bell, the door flew open and a rotund older woman with olive skin stood there.

"Ren! What are you doing?" Her sharp eyes took in Meri's condition and she reached out to take her hand. "Don't stand there, man," she said. "Fetch her belongings and see to the horse." She bustled Meri inside and closed the door in his face.

"Honestly, Miss, sometimes I despair of that man. Always bringing me problems. Not that you're a problem, mind, but you'd think he could see to these details without me giving him orders."

Meri was overwhelmed by the volume of words that came from the woman.

"I'm Ennay Aspey," she said, "and I keep house for Lord Cosara. I see you're in need of rest. Could you state the reason for your visit? I assume you're here to see Lord Nik?"

Meri's brain was trying to take in the grand hall of the manor, which was hung with tapestries of the sea, complete with sea monsters, ships and huge looming waves. A hallway ran off down a passage which seemed too long for the house.

"I'll have one of the guest rooms readied for you. Most of them are closed, but we keep two prepared in case of overnight guests. I suppose with Lord Cosara seeking a wife, I'll have to revise the number of rooms we have open. You never know when extra relatives of a proposed mistress will require housing."

Ennay stopped to examine her from head to foot, and suddenly Meri felt dirty and wrinkled, not to mention smelly.

"Who are you, my dear?"

"My name is Merielle, and I have been Lord Cosara's guest at his coastal cottage for several months. I was injured and he was kind enough to take me in. I must speak with him."

"Mmm," Ennay said, her eyes narrowing. "Kind, was he? Wouldn't be difficult with looks like yours. Wait a moment! Were you the lady who had the court aflap at the queen's ball last month? You made quite an impression, it seems. Lord Nik high-tailed it back here after the ball and hasn't said a word about it since. But I've other sources."

"I must speak with him," Meri murmured, mortified the whole countryside was gossiping about her, probably laughing at her, too.

"You're a day too late, my dear. He left yesterday for Wildecoast and even now will be preparing to sail with tomorrow's high tide."

Meri made a hasty calculation. "But that is midday!" she squeaked. "I must find him." She turned to rush back out the door but Ennay stopped her with a surprisingly firm hold.

"It's too late today to travel, my dear, and you're in no fit state to take to the road again."

"What am I to do, Mistress? I must speak with his lordship. I simply cannot leave matters as they are between us." Meri clamped on her words, unwilling to share more with the woman.

"Tell me what's so urgent that you must travel alone to find Lord Nik? It's not safe," Ennay said. "If I'm satisfied with what you say, I may help you tomorrow. If you take the coach, you could reach Wildecoast before his lordship sails. No guarantees, mind."

Meri hesitated. The coach would be quicker, but first she had to convince Ennay to trust her. In the meantime, the hours were ticking away as Nikolas prepared to escape once again. He had not learned a thing!

She nodded. "I thank you. Your help would be appreciated."

Ennay frowned. "Like I said, no guarantees. Now come this way and we'll get you settled and prepare a hot bath."

As Meri soaked in her bath, she found it difficult to appreciate the luxurious warmth. Disturbing thoughts simply would not leave her head. She was seized with an impatience she had never felt before. Nikolas was getting away from her and she was lying here getting warm and clean. It did not feel right. She should be pursuing him to the ends of the kingdom and beyond, falling at his feet and begging him to listen to her, to make her his, and to never run away again.

Common sense told her the Aspeys were right - she had learned Ennay and Ren were husband and wife - she would gain nothing by setting off this afternoon but put herself at risk. However, it did not help. Meri ached to do something, but there was nothing *to* do.

As the water started to cool, she stood, allowed the young chamber maid to wrap a towel around her, then stepped from the bath. The girl tried to dry her, but Meri gently pushed her away. "There is no need, child. Let me dry myself."

She turned to the dress laid out on the bed. It was a floral gown in red and purple with lace, flounces and layers that seemed completely unnecessary to Meri. Ennay had said it was the best she could do, but even Meri could tell it was quite out of date.

She squared her shoulders and allowed the maid to help her into the gown and do it up. The dress fitted which was the very best that could be said for it. Meri caught a glimpse of herself in the mirror and shuddered. *Hideous, absolutely hideous.*

Her chambermaid combed out her crimson locks, seeming riveted, and Meri forced herself to sit quietly while the girl styled her hair and applied rouge to her cheeks. After her efforts, Meri had to admit that, from the neck up, she did look almost her normal self.

"Thank you …" Meri waited for the girl to say her name.

"My name is Vinka, My Lady," she said. "You do have pretty hair."

"Thank you, Vinka. Now, if you would show me to the dining hall, I would be grateful."

Meri followed the girl back to the main part of the building and into a cozy dining room. A place was set for one and, seeing that, Meri nearly lost her courage. She simply must talk to someone or her worries would get the better of her. But Vinka bowed and left her alone. She tried to distract herself by examining the paintings adorning the walls and the miniatures that sat on the tabletops. One miniature was of an older couple. The man had a twinkle in his eyes and the woman smiled as if she held a secret. Both looked a little like Nikolas.

"Lord Nik's parents," Ennay said, bustling into the room with a bowl and a plate of bread and butter. "The poor love lost them when he was away on a mission. I don't think he's forgiven himself to this day for not being here."

"Did they live here?" Meri asked. Somehow, they did not look as if they inhabited a mansion.

"Oh no, my dear. They were simple folk and lived in a small village close to Wildecoast. Saniste was a healer and Vitavia his assistant. Lord Nik was given this estate by his cousin when she married the king. It was she who made him a lord. He has always been uncomfortable with the title."

Meri gave a small smile. Some things clicked into place with her words. Nikolas had the common touch and had never liked her calling him "lord". "The manor house is old though, is it not?"

"Yes, it belonged to a disgraced lord who treated the farmers poorly. He was stripped of his land and title, and it was given to Nikolas. He's a popular master."

"Even though he has been away for a whole year?" She knew Ennay's words were not strictly true. Nikolas was no longer so popular, but Meri admired his housekeeper's loyalty.

"We're used to Nikolas being absent. His duties always took him away for months at a time. But when he returns, he visits everyone and makes sure he sees to all the problems that crop up."

"You don't mind that he exiled himself?"

Ennay's face tightened. "He's had a difficult time."

Meri reached out and grasped the older woman's forearm. "All is well. I know of his losses."

"He told you?" Ennay snapped, her gaze suddenly probing. "He told *you?*"

Meri drew herself up to her full height. How dare the woman use that tone of voice? "Yes, he confided in me. Why would he not? Nikolas needed help and I was there to give it to him." She opened her mouth to add that he trusted her but then realized it would be going too far. Meri had kept too much from Nikolas to think he trusted her. But maybe one day...

"Can it be you truly care for Lord Nik?" Ennay whispered.

Meri's eyes brimmed with tears. "I care for him more than I have ever been able to express. That is why I must find him and explain myself. I cannot allow him to leave on that ship. I just cannot."

Ennay's face became determined. "Never you fear, My Lady. Seat yourself and eat this food. I'll summon Ren and see the coach is ready to leave at daybreak." She hastened from the room and Meri used a napkin to dry her eyes. Perhaps, finally, she had an ally.

CHAPTER 22

NIK stood with his hand on the foremast, watching the last-minute flurry of activity as his ship prepared to embark on its journey. Uneasiness lay in his gut and he didn't know why. Could it be he was running away again? But he wasn't. The queen had wanted this for months, the kingdom needed him. He was simply doing his duty.

Then why did this feel so wrong? Was he making the wrong decision to return to the sea? Nik let this thought settle within him and realized that being back on board felt right. The deck beneath his feet, the gentle rock of the ship, the shouting of the sailors - he had missed all of it. He had missed command.

So, it wasn't the return to his old career that unsettled him. Nik was a creature of instinct, something most sailors relied upon. The one time he had ignored his gut was the night of the shipwreck when he'd let himself be talked into taking a rest. That had ended in disaster, so he wasn't keen to ignore his feelings this time. But first he must discover why he felt this way. He couldn't cancel a whole voyage based on "a feeling".

He went for a stroll up the deck and stood looking out to sea as his sailors finished loading the supplies. It was midmorning, and they were due to cast off in two hours when the rest of the crew arrived.

Was it perhaps the trauma of his last voyage that had him feeling this way? He had always loved the ocean and Meri had helped him see the wreck had not been his fault. *Meri.* The thought of her made him edgy. How was she? She was still at his cottage, that much he knew. He received occasional reports from Kain on how his house guest was faring, but his friend never gave much away. Nik knew Kain was trying to get him to move on, but that had not been easy, especially after the night he and Meri shared after the ball. Sending her back to the cottage had been tough. Seeing her upset had been torture. Nik could well recall the hurt and bewilderment on her face.

He loved her, that much he accepted, and his love had changed her. They could have had a life together if only she hadn't lied to him. So close and yet so far. She would say he was running away again.

Was that the cause of his funk? Leaving unfinished business, leaving Meri, knowing he must move forward and make a life for himself without her? Did he even want that?

The answer was no. He didn't want to live without Meri, but he also didn't want to be thinking of the lies and Jon's death for the rest of his days. If he couldn't move beyond that, he had no right to make promises to her. *Damn!* This should be far behind him. Perhaps he must see Meri one more time, talk this through with her and make sure he was doing the right thing for them both.

There was a commotion on the docks and Nik looked up in time to see Adriana step from her carriage. He groaned. *Just what I don't need right now.*

He went to meet her on the dock, bowing low before her. "My Queen, it's wonderful to see you."

"Cut the act, Niki. I know I am the last person you wish to see this morning."

Nik widened his eyes in mock horror. "How could you say such a thing, Your Majesty? You know I'm always riveted by your company."

Adriana rolled her eyes. "I did not want to let you go without my blessing, and Beniel's. If something happened, I would never forgive myself." Her eyes did look a little misty. "Safe voyage, cousin. May this be a fruitful trip." She winked and Nik knew she was referring to his search for a wife. A search which had him grinding his teeth.

"Your Majesty, if you've manufactured this voyage just to get me out to the colonies so I may find a wife, I'll not be pleased."

"Don't be silly, Niki," she said, her eyes suddenly serious. "You know how dire the dark elven threat is. The king has decreed we must assess the menace and take steps to bring it under control. Your voyage is a very real part of that. I am not so flippant with the royal purse that I would send you off for no other reason than to find a wife."

"Mmm," Nik said, not entirely convinced. The getting of a wife was an important safeguard for the kingdom no matter what she said. It was just possible Nik's son might be heir to the throne one day, especially with Princess Alecia missing and her father dead. Goddess willing, the dead prince's unborn child might step into the breach, but that couldn't be counted on.

"I must get on with preparations, Your Majesty. These rogues need watching or they'll forget to load the food."

Adriana kissed Nik on both cheeks. He bowed and watched as the queen made her way back to her carriage. He was proud of her, not that he'd ever tell her that. Lately more weight had fallen on her shoulders, but she had never shirked her duties and the people respected her for the way she'd taken up the reins of power. Just as well, for the king was a changed man since his brother's death - withdrawn, morose, and sometimes not leaving his chambers for days at a time.

Nik shrugged off his concerns. Beniel would recover. Nik was living proof that the loss of a brother could be borne. He walked up the gangplank, casting his eyes over the sailors scurrying about. They appeared to be on schedule, but he still had the nagging worry this wasn't a voyage he should be taking.

* * *

Meri found it impossible to stay still as the carriage bounced along the road back to Wildecoast. They flew along behind two of Nikolas's fastest horses, and Ren himself was driving. Her companion in the carriage was the young maid, Vinka. The girl spoke hardly a word, for which Meri cursed her. She could have done with some distraction from the worries that drove her mad.

She had been up before dawn after a night where she tossed and turned; one dream had been of her fists pounding a hapless victim's head, the next of her on the water's edge watching Nikolas's ship sail over the horizon. They would be too late; she just knew it. And if they missed him, what then? How would she cope until he returned? She could not wait all that time to resolve what lay between them. *What if he returns with a bride?* The thought made her palms sweaty and her heart race.

The carriage slowed to a stop. *What now?* Meri stuck her head from the window and all she could see was those white, woolly creatures all over the road.

"Can't you make them move, Ren?" Meri asked, her head still out the window.

"They'll move, Miss, but if we spook them it'll be no quicker. Knowing sheep, we'll not break a gap through them. Have to wait for the whole flock to cross."

She pulled her head back in and released an unladylike groan of frustration. "I am getting out," she said, jumping from the carriage. She looked for the farmer, so she could ask him to move his charges at a faster pace.

There he was, strolling along behind his sheep, allowing them to dawdle across the road and into a paddock on the other side. Meri shooed some sheep as they passed her and created a gap in the road, but before she could usher Ren and the carriage through, more sheep skittered into the gap, desperate not to lose touch with their friends. She cursed under her breath and tried again, only to get the same result. She tried yet again, but all she succeeded in doing was providing entertainment for Ren.

"What is so amusing?" she asked, gritting her teeth.

"I told you there was no hope to break through 'em. Look, we're nearly there."

Sure enough, the farmer was just shooing the last of his flock onto the road.

"Morning, Miss," he said, lifting his hat. "Sorry about the delay. Just can't rush the sheep."

Meri did not respond. She just stood there, oozing frustration. Did he not know she had somewhere to be? These creatures were just as unpredictable as the masses of bait fish that swarmed through the oceans.

Meri looked at Ren, whose face suddenly sobered under her glare. She stalked back to the carriage, biting her tongue against harsh words. The carriage rolled on once she was seated, and Meri deliberately avoided looking at the maid for fear she would be smirking too. Damn these people. It was alright for them to be casual. They were not trying to catch the person they loved before he embarked on a three-month trip.

The sheep incident occurred halfway to Wildecoast and for the rest of the trip, Meri was certain they would be too late. Ren pushed the horses as much as possible; long bursts of galloping, interspersed with short rest periods when they continued at a brisk walk until the horses stopped blowing. She could not fault his devotion to getting her there on time. Regardless, time ticked by and the sun climbed to its zenith, the time when Nikolas's ship would set sail.

Arriving in Wildecoast, Ren showed papers to the sergeant at the gate and they were admitted, immediately turning left to follow the wall of the city down to the harbor. Meri craned her neck to get a better look at the docks. A magnificent ship was being untied from the central dock, sailors scrambling all over it. Watching from the bridge was a splendid man in black naval uniform. His silver buttons and bars flashed in the sunlight, and his tangled honeyed locks were tied in a black ribbon. *Nikolas.* Meri's gaze skimmed over him, searching for confirmation he was healthy and happy.

They pulled up near the central dock. It was then Meri noticed a large crowd gathered to farewell the ship. It seemed this voyage was something momentous. And here she was hoping to have a quiet word with the captain. Well, it had to be now and if the whole of Wildecoast heard her speak then so be it.

"Let me help you out, My Lady," Vinka said, preparing to exit the carriage first.

"There is no need to trouble yourself," Meri said, standing and reaching for the carriage door handle. It was jammed. No matter how she turned it, the stupid thing didn't open. She pushed hard and then placed her shoulder against the door.

"Please, my lady, we'll get Ren to help," Vinka said. "You will—."

The girl's words were cut short as the door gave way beneath Meri's determined shove. She tumbled from the carriage and landed in the mud and slop below. A collective gasp went up from the assembled crowd. Ren appeared at her side to help her up.

She stood, hands dripping mud, and stinky brown smudges all over her skirt. She could see, by Ren's expression, she looked much worse than she felt.

"My Lady," he moaned. "Are you hurt?"

She tried to smile but was less than successful. "Only my pride, Ren. Do you have anything I can clean up with?"

He pulled a handkerchief from his pocket and handed it to her. She dabbed at her face, gave it back, and squared her shoulders. "Wait here, please."

Meri made her way across the muddy ground to the foot of the gangplank. Nikolas had not noticed her arrival, but turned when she hailed him.

His eyes bulged. "Merielle!" His gaze swept from her muddy shoes to the top of her head. "Don't come up the plank, I'm coming down."

She folded her arms across her chest, trying to block out the amused faces of the sailors gathered along the ship's rail. Nikolas must have had some sharp words for them for they turned back to work reluctantly.

He arrived at her side and clutched her arms above the elbows. She almost swooned. He smelled good and his body warmed her like a fire on a chilly day. Why could she not be looking her best at this moment instead of wearing this muddy and hideous gown?

"I could not let you go without telling you how much you mean to me, Nikolas," she said, pushing her chagrin aside.

"How did you come to be here? I thought you were safe at the cottage."

"I could stay there no longer. It was a prison. I was compelled to take Storm and ride to find you, but you were not at your estate. So, I came here."

"You're unhurt?"

"I am well. Storm looked after me."

Nikolas shook his head. "I cannot believe you went to those lengths to track me down. You could have been injured. What if you'd fallen from Storm somewhere on the road?"

Something in her face must have warned him the trip had not been without incident. His grip on her arms tightened.

"What happened?"

"That is not important. What matters is our love. Have you learned nothing from our time together? You cannot run away from this."

Nikolas nodded. "I know that."

"You *what*?"

"I know that." He crushed her to him. "When I saw you just now at the foot of that gangplank, all muddy and determined, I suddenly knew why I had felt so unsettled. I saw you and the feeling dropped away. All I could think of was taking you in my arms and stopping you from falling off that plank into the water."

Meri looked up at him. "You truly want me?"

"I've always wanted you, Meri." He dipped his head and his lips met hers. She responded, allowing him access to her mouth, letting his hands wander over her back, her buttocks.

His hands stilled and she moaned. "Do not stop."

"We have an audience."

Meri gasped and stepped back but Nikolas did not let go of her hand, instead turning her to face the crowd of people who were clapping at the expression of their love.

He shouted some orders to his second-in-command, but Meri was too dazed by the kiss to register what they were. Before she knew what had occurred, she and Nikolas were in the coach with Vinka and the vehicle was moving.

"Where are we going?"

"I think we need some privacy, don't you?" He traced the outline of her mouth with a fingertip.

Even though this was all she had dreamed of, Meri could not quite accept that Nikolas had capitulated so readily, that he admitted his love and could get past all the hurt she had caused him.

They arrived at the castle in record time, or perhaps it was just that Meri had no concept of time when she was with him. He stood and opened the door, helping Meri out and then Vinka. He arranged for the girl to be housed for the night and hustled Meri into the castle then up to a suite of rooms he used when in Wildecoast.

Once they were inside, he drew her into his arms. "You feel good against me. I didn't know how much I'd missed this until I saw you."

"But Nikolas, you must be sure. We must talk."

"We *will* talk." He kissed the side of her neck until her legs were weak with longing. "First there is another thing we must do." His fingers were busy, quickly undoing the buttons down the back of her gown. He peeled off the bodice of the dress and his lips followed the line of her corset right down into the fold between her breasts. Meri arched her hips toward his, desperate to be one with him.

Nikolas pulled the dress off her hips and pressed his face against the fabric of her pantaloons where her womanhood nestled. She groaned. He was going to kill her with longing. All this was so new to Meri, so fresh, and the feelings still foreign, but welcome and exciting and overwhelming. Nikolas was a masterful lover and he was hers, at least for the moment.

Just when she thought she would melt with the desire to have more intimate contact, he stood and began unlacing her corset. He really was going to draw this out. "Nikolas, I need you now!"

"Patience, my love, we have all afternoon and night." He continued to unlace her while Meri's heart fell. He spoke only of today. Did that mean he would leave her then? Did it mean they didn't have a lifetime of love as she'd hoped?

"Meri," he murmured, "stop thinking and let me love you."

Her heart leapt. How did he know she was worrying about the future? She redoubled her efforts to put all thoughts out of her head; it was not difficult with his lips on her body, tracing the line of the fabric as it slipped from her curves.

"Close your eyes," he said.

She obeyed, soaking up the feelings, mindful this might be the last time they were together. It might have to last a lifetime. She pushed the thought away. The pantaloons slid from her hips and she stepped out of them. Her body burned with a blush at being naked before him; she wondered where his touch would next caress her.

After a few moments and the rustle of fabric, his arms encased her, and his lips brushed the sensitive skin between her breasts. She arched her hips, but his arms fell away and she again heard him remove a piece of his clothing. She burned to know which it was, but denied the urge to open her eyes. Again, her skin tingled with the press of his lips against her navel and his tongue moved down to the juncture of her legs. Meri could not suppress the moan that burst from her.

She grasped at Nikolas, determined to ensnare him; he slipped her clutches and she stood bereft, hearing more garments fall to the floor. Finally, his lips worshipped the back of her neck and his tongue licked molten fire all the way to her buttocks. She pushed against him and felt his hard length against her back. His arms enclosed her from behind, his fingers gently pinching her nipples until she cried out.

"Now, Nikolas, please."

"Hush, my love. I want to pleasure you as you've never been pleasured before."

That would not be hard, she thought. Nikolas was her only lover.

His hands spanned her abdomen and slipped lower to cup her moistened folds. He had no difficulty finding the hard nub of her pleasure center. His fingers slipped back and forth, bringing her to the shuddering edge of control before moving lower to enter her, two fingers testing her readiness for him. Meri toppled over the edge, her body quivering. His fingers returned to rub her hardness, bringing the quaking waves back again and again as she rose higher. It ended in a brilliant burst of pleasure and she was falling, falling back to earth.

Nikolas's arms cradled Meri as she returned to the present and reality, her breathing ragged and her legs so weak she knew she would collapse if he let go.

"I'm here for you, my love. Relax into me."

He scooped her up into his arms and walked to the bedroom, depositing her on his bed, face down. Meri was still reeling from the pleasure that had swept her, weak from sensations she did not know how to respond to. She barely noticed as Nikolas pulled her backside up, so she knelt on the bed, head down. Then his fingers were inside her from behind and she was climbing again, flying toward another climax.

She climbed higher and then he was inside her, pushing deeper until another sensation hit her; almost painful. Meri gasped and pushed back, urging him to take them over the edge together. He clasped her hips and pushed, hitting a trigger deep inside. This time her climax was longer and more consuming than the last but, no matter how fulfilling, she knew it could never last long enough for her.

He shuddered and cried out. "Meri."

She imagined his seed filling her innermost private place and felt incredibly connected to her sea captain. If only this could last forever.

He pulled them both to the side, still sheathed within her. "That was more than I could ever have imagined."

She placed a trembling finger on his lips. "Shhh. Words will only diminish what we have shared, my darling."

"I love you," he said. "Does that diminish it?"

Meri's heart leapt back to life again. "I know you love me. That is why we are here, joined like this."

"No, I mean I *really* love you. Not a love that changes, but a love that commits."

"What are you saying?" She could hardly bring herself to believe he might stay with her.

"I love you and I want you. I need you. I crave you more than food or water. You're my strength and you've brought me back to myself."

She stared at him. "You are all those things to me, and you saved me more than once, but I must know - can you forgive me my sins?"

He sighed and looked to the ceiling as if searching for the words. "I've been angry for a long time. I've been guilty for a long time. I expected the world to protect Jon when I couldn't. I was angry because that didn't happen. I blamed you and that was wrong. Now I realize you did all you could. You tried to save him and ensured his body could be found one day. You gave me that much, more than anyone else has. And you gave me hope, hope for the future. You helped me to free myself from the guilt I carried."

"Oh, Nikolas," she said, tears sliding down her cheeks. "I am so sorry for all the hurt I caused."

He cradled her against him, and she felt his heart beating with love for her. "I know you are, my love. It won't be easy but somehow, we'll make a life together. If you'll have me."

"Have you?" she said, her eyes suddenly dry.

"Marry me and stay with me forever, Meri."

She kissed him, reveling in the softness of his lips. "Yes, Nikolas. I will marry you, and I will devote the rest of my days to loving you."

THE END

THE LORD AND THE MERMAID

GLOSSARY

Places

Kingdom of Thorius (Thor- ee- us) -the kingdom of men which encompasses the King's seat of Wildecoast and the Prince's seat of Brightcastle, along with other smaller towns

Wildecoast (Will – dee – coast) -the capital city perched on the top of a cliff overlooking the sea on the east coast of Thorius; climate is mild but windy

Brightcastle - large inland town surrounded by forests and farms, three to four days ride west of Wildecoast

Amitania (Am – it – ay – nia) or *Elvandang* (Elle – van – dang) in elvish - the deserted city north of the Usetar Mountain Range in northern Thorius; once a thriving city; disputed ownership between elves and man

Usetar Range (You – set – ar) -the mountain range running across the northern parts of Thorius

People

Lenweri (Len – weir – ee) -the elven people who are tall and elegant with black skin and pointed ears and mainly dark hair; live in mountainous forests north and west of Thorius, in places encroaching onto Kingdom lands; also known as dark elves

Sis Lenweri - the faction of dark elves that wishes to take the kingdom of Thorius back from men

Defender - a race of shapeshifters who are created to defend those in danger; they sense those in need of their help; a Defender can shift into animal form and the ability is inherited through family lines

Mer – the race of people who live in the sea; consisting of mermaids and mermen; mermen are created from the souls of sailors who are killed by mermaids.

Characters

Merielle – mermaid who desires to be human; she has vibrant red hair and is not familiar with the ways of Thorian people; heroine of The Lord and the Mermaid

Lord Nikolas Cosara (Nikolas Cos-arra) – once captain in the King's Navy, now a recluse; he is cousin to Queen Adriana and the hero of The Lord and the Mermaid

General Kain Jazara (Cane Jazz-arra) – general of the King's Army and Nik's best friend

Lady Alique Zorba (Al-eek Zor-bah) – Ramón Zorba's younger sister and one of the queen's ladies-in-waiting

Princess Alecia Zialni (Al – ee – sha Zee – al – nee)) - the King's niece and daughter of Prince Jiseve Zialni who rules the principality of Brightcastle and is next in line to the throne. Alecia's story begins in Princess Avenger and continues in Princess in Exile.

Vard Anton - a shapeshifting Defender; army captain of Brightcastle in Princess Avenger; holder of many secrets; his story continues in Princess in Exile

Prince Jiseve Zialni (Jiss – eve Zee – al – nee) - next in line to the throne of Thorius, younger brother of the King, a widower; father of Alecia Zialni

Lady Benae Branasar (Ben-ay Bran-a-sar) – noble lady with an estate in Tylevia; heroine of The Lady's Choice; healer; now married to Ramón Zorba

Ramón Zorba (Rah – mon Zor – bah) - Lord of Wildecoast and squire to Prince Jiseve Zialni; his family have an estate south of Wildecoast; hero of The Lady's Choice; now joint Guardian of Brightcastle with Benae

King Beniel Zialni (Ben – ee – elle Zee – al – nee) - King of Thorius; lives in Wildecoast; older brother of Jiseve Zialni and uncle of Alecia Zialni; married to Adriana

Queen Adriana - wife of the King; lives in Wildecoast; Alecia's aunt; Nik's cousin

Doctor Achan Mosard (Uck - ahn Mow - sard) – court physician in Wildecoast

Jon Cosara – Nik's younger brother; disappeared at sea

Sergeant Grif Tyne – gate sergeant at Wildecoast and Nik's friend

Saniste and Vitavia Cosara – Nik's parents

Ren and Ennay Aspey – manager and housekeeper of Nik's estate, respectively

Nerissa - Merielle's mother

Pearl – Merielle's eldest sister

About the Author

Bernadette Rowley is a lover of epic fantasy who is a veterinarian by day and an author by night. She is currently published in the genre of high fantasy romance with eight books, all set in her fantasy world of Thorius.

When she was a young teenager, an aunt gave her a copy of The Sword of Shannara by Terry Brooks and Bernadette has lived in various fantasy worlds ever since. It's no surprise that her chosen genre when writing romance is fantasy.

"I can see these settings so vibrantly in my mind and hope my readers can too."

But Bernadette has no desire to spoon-feed her readers by laboriously describing her fantasy settings. She would rather the reader use their own imagination.

Along with sword and sorcery, dashing heroes and stunning heroines, this author includes strong healing themes in many of her books- an element central to her everyday job.

"When I started writing the Queenmakers Saga, I never imagined my day job would force its way into my stories as it has."

And of course, there are animals, especially Bernadette's beloved horses.

Bernadette lives in Brisbane, Australia, with the four heroes in her life- her husband Michael and three grown sons.

Connect with the Author

Website: www.bernadetterowley.com
Facebook: www.facebook.com/bernadetterowleyfantasy
Twitter: www.twitter.com/bt_rowley

Made in the USA
Las Vegas, NV
28 February 2021

18762041R00138